THIS MUCH HUXLEY KNOWS

A Story of Innocence, Misunderstandings, and Acceptance

GAIL ALDWIN

D1422236

Black Rose Writing | Texas

The author grants the final approval for this literary material.

First printing

This is a work of fiction. Names, characters, businesses, places, events, and incidents are either the products of the author's imagination or used in a fictitious manner. Any resemblance to actual persons, living or dead, or actual events is purely coincidental.

ISBN: 978-1-68433-731-6
PUBLISHED BY BLACK ROSE WRITING
www.blackrosewriting.com

Printed in the United States of America
Suggested Retail Price (SRP) $18.95

This Much Huxley Knows is printed in Sabon
For the purpose of consistency, *This Much Huxley Knows* is written in British English and uses British spelling and punctuation throughout.

*As a planet-friendly publisher, Black Rose Writing does its best to eliminate unnecessary waste to reduce paper usage and energy costs, while never compromising the reading experience. As a result, the final word count vs. page count may not meet common expectations.

Praise for

THIS MUCH
HUXLEY KNOWS

"This cleverly told story is funny and heart-warming while touching on sensitive, contemporary issues."
–Joanne Kukanza Easley, author of *Sweet Jane* and *Just One Look*

"I love this book and its characters. I'm hoping for a Huxley II, so I can see what happens next to Huxley and the lives he touches."
–Linda Benjamin, author of *Girls' Guide to Aging with Grit and Gusto*

"The talented Gail Aldwin has chosen to address some tough universal issues like political differences, racial prejudice and bullying, as seen by the delightfully aware and always entertaining seven-year-old Huxley."
–Jim Bates, author of *Resilience*

"*This Much Huxley Knows* is expertly crafted and I enjoyed being part of the microcosm of Huxley's life. By looking at things his way, I was able to get a glimpse of deeper truths that lie at the heart of human interaction."
–Madeleine F White, author of *Mother of Floods*

THIS MUCH HUXLEY KNOWS

The playground at St Michael's School is a car park tonight. Mum drives into a space and I wait for Dad to open my door. It's Saturday and this means my teacher won't be around. Mrs Ward says I'm a nuisance when I'm only trying to have a laugh. I think new-sense is clever, so it doesn't matter if she calls me that any more.

Families are getting together to make money for our school – there's never enough to go round. We're having an auction to sort this out. Grown-ups promise to do something, then it's sold to the person that gives the most money. My mum and Ben's mum did a lot of talking about the auction. With her new camera, Paula's going to take a photo of a family to go in a fancy frame. Mum is doing better by giving away two bottles of her homemade elderflower juice. Yippee! Now she'll have to buy the orange stuff from the supermarket that's much nicer. It comes in a bottle the shape of a telescope.

At last, Dad lets me out and I race over to Paula's car. It's called a Beetle but I've never seen insects that big. Ha-ha-ha. I press my nose against the window to look inside. My breath leaves a cloud.

'Come away, Huxley,' says Mum. 'You'll set off the alarm.'

I rub my sleeve over the glass to clear away the marks then rush to catch up. She holds my hand and I swing-swing-swing our arms high in the air.

'Steady on.' Mum's a jiggling skeleton. It's part of our game.

We don't usually walk through the main door because I'm meant to stand on the line in the playground ready for going into class. I always want to be at the front and I get there by pushing and shoving. If Mrs Ward sees, she sends me to the back and then the bigger children in the next class make fun of me. My teacher never watches when picking-on starts so I have to put up with it. It's not easy being in Year Two.

We dump our coats on a table in the hall and I spot Ben by the climbing bars that are pushed flat against the wall. As usual, he's wearing his Nevern Town football shirt. I hang around near Mum for a bit and watch what he's doing. With one foot on the bar nearest the floor, it looks as if Ben's going to leap to the top. Spider-Man can do it but not Ben. He gives up his chance and comes over to me.

'Let's go into our classroom,' whispers Ben.

'Why?'

'To mess around.'

This is not allowed although the idea is exciting. Mrs Ward has rules we've heard one hundred times before. I pinch my throat to turn my voice the same as hers. 'No touching the things on my table!'

'Or mucking up the books!' Ben joins in.

We sound exactly like Mrs Ward and I can't stop smiling.

'Let's poke about.' Ben's eyes go slanty as he whizzes them round the hall to check it's safe to sneak off. Mum and Paula are chatting – they won't see we're gone. This is our chance!

'You first,' I say.

Chairs are on the tables and it's creepy in the empty classroom. I head for the nature display to have a look at Zac's squashed toad. He said it was run over by a car and told everyone it was a great find. Mrs Ward didn't know what was in the bag until the paper split. Surprise made her jump out of her chair and the toad's leg fell off when it landed on the floor. After that, it wasn't such a great find but Mrs Ward still made space for it on a special stand. I pick up a felt pen that's lying about and dig it into the place where the toad's eye should be.

'Give me a go,' says Ben.

He presses in another pen to turn the toad into a Dalek from *Dr Who*. Me and Ben shout exterminate until we've got no breath left. Next minute, our school caretaker comes in. He shoos us back to the hall with the big crowd of parents. I barge through skirts and trousers and forget to say *excuse me* but Mum doesn't notice. She gives me a fifty-pence piece to spend at the children's table. I slip it in my pocket so I won't lose it.

On the stage, Zac's mum talks into a microphone that gives a horrible squeak. I stuff a finger in each ear to block out the noise. With the holes plugged up, voices go blah-blah-blah. I shake my head like I've gone bonkers. By yanking my hands free, Mum breaks the game. She drops down to bring us eyeball to eyeball. Listening to her serious voice, I stare at the powder on her eyelids that's smudged and golden. She paints it on with her mouth open same as a fish. I let a snigger slip out.

'If you can't behave nicely,' says Mum, 'I'll take you home.'

'I will be sent-a-ball.' Smiling stretches my cheeks.

'That's hard to believe when you don't even say the word properly.'

'But saying *sensible* is not a joke.'

Mum lets her eyes go up to the ceiling and back.

My dad is getting beer from the serving hatch. That's where we wait for our school meal but there's no sausage and mash tonight. I join the queue at the children's table. When I get to the front, I shoot my coin across and it nearly flies off the other side. A big girl slams her arm down to stop it. She slides a cup of orange towards me. I have a swig but it's not worth a whole fifty pence.

Ben's family and my family stand together when the charity auction starts. Everyone goes quiet. I can tell what's going to happen because I watch daytime TV with Mrs Vartan. She's our neighbour and looks after me sometimes. To bid at an auction you put your hand up and shout out a number. At school, we have to talk quietly although parents break the rule. The fun is only for grown-ups. It's boring being left out but I clap at the right time. I try to be the loudest clapper and it makes my hands sting.

'Thank you.' Zac's mum's voice is loud and strange when she uses the microphone. Her face is bright pink as if she's been under a heater. 'Next, we've a special lot from our very own Miss Lucy Choi.'

I don't understand why Zac's mum says Miss Choi belongs to her. Everyone knows she's the teaching assistant in my class. I'm allowed to call her Lucy because she's Mum's friend. Strange thing is, I forget and call her Lucy at school and Miss Choi at home! Sometimes the wrong name comes out by accident, sometimes I do it on purpose. Zac's mum reads out loud from the clipboard but I'm interested in watching Dad. He glugs back the last of his beer and then waves his arm in the air.

'This one's mine,' he shouts.

'Calm down.' Mum speaks in an extra loud whisper. 'It's only a birthday cake.'

Zac's mum beckons Miss Choi onto the stage. She shakes her head because she doesn't want to go but Zac's mum gives her a hand. One big step and Miss Choi's up there with the others. Her legs are pencils in her black jeans. Ben's Nanny Phil says everyone from Miss Choi's country looks the same. When she says stuff like that Paula tells Nanny Phil to shush or she'll get a reputation. To be funny, I say rip-you-station … although some people never get my jokes.

Dad and Ben's dad aren't always friends because Tony is a bit of an idiot. It's a little secret between me and Dad. One time, Dad called Tony a nutter and I got into trouble for spreading it around. It's not easy knowing what you can say and what you can't. Tony's name is odd. I can touch my toe and my knee at the same time but Ben never laughs when I do this. In my class, making friends and staying friends is hard. I suppose it's like that for grown-ups as well.

'Such enthusiasm for this fantastic offer of a homemade birthday cake in a Barbie or rocket shape,' says Zac's mum.

'Cracker of a lot, Lucy,' shouts Dad. 'I'll give you twenty quid.'

'What are you up to?' Mum is staring at Dad.

'Can't let you get away with that.' This time it's Tony talking. 'I'll top you to thirty.'

'Give it a rest,' says Paula.

Dad takes a new can of beer from his jacket pocket. Froth spurts as he opens it, so he licks away the mess.

'Excellent.' Zac's mum's voice bounces around the hall. 'Any more bids?'

'Forty pounds,' shouts Dad.

I can't understand why Dad wants a cake. My birthday was in September and I had a bouncy castle and a castle cake that came in a huge box. I don't think much of rocket cakes and Barbies are for girls. But Dad is having fun because he nudges Tony and says, 'Beat that'.

The dads are mucking around and I can't be bothered to wait for Tony's bid. I'm wondering about my next birthday. When I'm eight, I want a pirate party. Dad can wear an eye patch and Mum's hair is long enough to be Jack Sparrow. My hair goes over my ears to keep them warm.

All of a sudden, Dad's hand is up in the air again. 'Great stuff, Lucy,' he says. 'Make it sixty.'

Zac's mum's eyes are ping-pong balls. 'How generous.'

Miss Choi folds her arms and shuffles from side to side.

'Any further bids?' Zac's mum is staring at Tony.

'Why not,' he says. 'I'll go to seventy.'

Paula shakes her head, making her golden hair whip about her shoulders. Then she looks at the floor, like there's something very interesting on the wooden blocks.

'Eighty,' says Dad.

Mum is straight and stiff as a ladder.

'Marvellous,' says Zac's mum. 'Our highest bid of the evening. Any more takers?'

'I'm out.' Tony's smile turns his cheeks into folds. 'All yours, Jed.'

He gives a thumbs up to Dad and the clapping starts. I join in but I'm not sure what's really going on. After that, Mum finds our coats. She hangs them over her arm and pushes me towards the door. It's rush-rush-rush getting out of school and I don't have time to say goodbye to Ben. My booster seat gives an excellent view through the car window but there's nothing to watch in the dark. When we start moving there'll be street lamps and shop windows and headlights.

Mum's ring goes clink-clink-clink as she knocks it against the steering wheel. Soon as she's fed up with that, she presses a button on the radio and the voices change from talking to singing and back to talking again. I listen to the words but Mum can't be bothered. She switches the radio off and we wait in the quiet for Dad. I try to dream up something to say. Mum's the first one to make a noise – she blasts the breath of a dragon. This shows she's cross with Dad for doing a last-minute wee. Another word for wee is piss. I can't say that out loud or I'll be told off. It's better to keep it in my head. Piss rhymes with hiss and kiss! Playing with words keeps my mind busy until Dad arrives.

Mum starts the engine and we screech away. Dad isn't talking and Mum doesn't say anything either but it's not peace and quiet. I turn my face to the side and suck the two middle fingers on my right hand. It's a habit I got in to when I was a baby and at times like this, it's what I do. Dribble runs down my chin. Sometimes, sucking my fingers lets Mum and Dad think I'm asleep. They don't know I can hear very well, same as a bat.

'Poor Lucy!' says Mum. 'It was so embarrassing having you two squabble over her cake.'

'Come on, Kirsty. It's for a good cause.'

'Don't give me that.' Mum lets the car charge along the road. 'Why do you have to be competitive with Tony?'

'Got the better of him tonight.'

Mum snorts then slams on the brakes as the traffic lights turn red. My seatbelt does its job and holds me tight.

'Now we're down eighty quid and lumbered with a birthday cake we don't need. What the hell are you going to do with it, Jed?'

'I always wanted a rocket cake when I was a kid.'

'Unbelievable,' says Mum.

'What's wrong with that? Besides, I'm helping to raise funds for the school.'

'There won't be any money left for the half term holiday thanks to you.'

Sucking my fingers does not make me feel better now. I've got pins and needles in my head! No money means no fun. 'What about special treats?'

'Don't worry.' Mum's eyes stare at me from the mirror. Its full name is rear-view mirror and that's because she is looking back at me.

'You won't miss out.' Dad talks into space.

Behind us, there's a beep-beep-beep.

'Give me a break.' Mum jerks the car forward and we're on the move again. 'You and your bloody rocket cake. You might as well be living on another planet, the amount of use you are.'

'I want to go to Mars,' I say.

I think they hear, but no one replies.

2

Only me and Mum go to church on Sundays because Dad thinks it's a waste of time now I've got a place at St Michael's School. But this morning Mum doesn't want to go as she can't face seeing Lucy after the dee-bark-all that was last night. She says I can eat my toast sitting on the beanbag. This is my favourite place when all the little bits inside the bag scrunch around me. To be snug you have to dig your bottom in and wiggle about. Right after I'm comfy, Mum passes me a plate with squares of toast and honey. She knows triangles taste wrong.

'Don't make a mess,' says Mum.

'I won't.'

Mum's not listening. She's already going back to the kitchen. I want her to stay but it's too late to ask. I have to eat my breakfast on my own. The honey slips off the crusty end so that's the piece to fly like an aeroplane and land between my teeth. Crunch-crunch-crunch. A drip of honey slides down my chin. I stick my tongue out and manage to lick it off. I do my best to keep the crumbs on the plate. It's a hard job because my eyes are buzzing over to Mum and Dad in the kitchen. After I've finished eating, the plate shoots off my lap onto the floor. No one turns around. At the table, Mum sits reading a book while Dad opens and closes drawers with a slam. Even that noise doesn't stop Mum staring at the words. Dad begins to hum and I start to worry. Mum usually tells him to *shut up* if he makes silly noises. She doesn't say a thing today, just whips the pages over one after another.

I wish they would talk to send the quiet away. It's not nice when Mum and Dad don't speak. Sad feelings let my heart go sore and I give my chest a rub to feel better. My heart is kept safe under special bones called ribs. Lifting my top, I hold my breath to see them. Ribs are like wings in the wrong place. They should be on your back to help you fly. Pressing my tummy, I can hide my fingers under my ribs. I don't push them in too far or I might have a heart attack. Our old neighbour died from one of those, so I don't want to risk it.

Covering my tummy, I wriggle to get snuggly in the beanbag. At school, children break friends after there's been an argument. I suppose it's the same for Mum and Dad but they can't stay angry for long. I just have to wait for them to make up. Ages goes by and then Dad starts to walk about the room. He picks up the plate I left on the floor like a flying saucer had landed. With his other hand, he squiggles my hair.

'Let's go to the barbers, Huxley. It's time I took you for a proper job.'

Mum's eyes are marbles. 'He doesn't want to have his hair cut.'

This is true. I can tell when it's about to happen because Mum puts newspaper on the floor. It's a signal to hide under my bed. She always finds me and then I have to sit on the chair very still. Scissors are pointed but Mum is careful not to jab my eye out.

'What a surprise! You and your pudding basin technique.' Dad's face is screwed up – he's trying to be funny AND serious.

'Huxley needs a cut from a professional.'

'I don't!' I press my chin against my chest and watch a woodlouse crawl across the floor. It escapes into a crack.

'It's not the same as Mum doing it,' says Dad. 'At the shop they use special clippers that tickle your neck. After it's finished, maybe Tim will take a photo of us.'

'I'm not sure.' One sneaky look and I see Dad is smiling.

'Come on, Huxley. It's a dad and son thing.'

'He doesn't have to go,' says Mum.

'It'll be fun,' says Dad.

'Okay.' I hope Dad will also buy me a strawberry milkshake if I'm good. I'm excellent at slurping through a straw – it's my special skill.

'Happy are you, Jed?' says Mum. 'Sorting Huxley's hair can be your responsibility from now on.'

·   ·   ·   ·   ·

Dad says *hello Tim* to the man who points to a bench where we're to sit and wait our turn. There are big chairs for having your hair cut and Tim the barber is busy chopping hair. Beside him, there's someone else working. The man in Tim's chair has a big red cloth tied around his neck same as a giant bib. This makes me laugh because babies wear them. Ben's little sister Juno's got one as she's not great at aiming a spoonful of food in her mouth. I wish I had a sister or a brother but I'm an only. Mum says I have to get used to it.

In the barber's shop there's a special chair for very small children that's like a racing car. It's stuck up in the air to stop anyone from climbing in. I pop over to check it out. The headlights are painted on and the number plate isn't real. The one on our Focus has letters at the end that go LBH. These stand for Lovely Boy Huxley, that's how Mum remembers them.

'Over here, Huxley.' Dad flips the pages of a magazine. He's looking through *What Car?* but he isn't fooling me – I know he's not reading the words. If my teacher saw him doing that, she'd tell him to go back to the first page and slow down.

There are lots of mirrors in the shop. At home, I stand on the box where dirty clothes are put to look at my face. When I press my nose against the mirror, the tip goes cold. I can't do this in Tim's because there's a shelf in the way. Instead, I take a look at Tim. His hair sticks out in pins and there's a slug on his lip that's called a moustache. I wonder what it's like to have one of them. My dad shaves off the hair on his face with a razor. This is very sharp and it lives on top of the cabinet where I can't reach.

There's a clunking sound. Dad's magazine is now in the basket and he's reading a newspaper. The words on the front say BREXIT: BOOM OR BUST. Bust is another word for Mum's boobies but Breaks-it is boring. Mum and Dad are sick of it and I'm not happy everyone's falling out. On the floor are tiles stuck together in a diamond shape. My foot fits inside one nice and neat, so I try the others. Before I know it, I'm standing right beside the man in the barber's chair.

'Your turn next,' says Tim.

The man's hair is thin and silver. He's wearing goggle glasses and I wonder what it's like to look through them. I make my eyes spin around the place to check they're working. They ache if I do this for too long.

'Come back, Huxley.' Dad looks over the top of his newspaper and nods his head at the space beside him. This means I should be sitting there but then he disappears behind the pages again. I stay put because he's not watching any more.

'Right.' Tim whips off the red sheet and then spins the man around. The man doesn't take normal steps. Instead, he slides his slippers over the floor. When I do that at my house, I go extra fast but he is slow. He holds his jacket ready for going outside.

'Tim'll have you looking smart,' he says.

'I know.'

'Ask for a short back and sides.' He gives me a wink but I have no idea what he's talking about. He tucks his hand under my chin and I look up at him. There's a smiley face to go with his wonky teeth and bent body.

'Do you live in a crooked house same as the man in the rhyme?'

This makes him laugh in a great big ha-ha-ha.

'Huxley.' Dad folds the newspaper.

The man is putting on his jacket. 'It's important to zip in and button up before you go out in the cold.'

After his top button is fixed, the man sticks out his tongue. I don't want to sit with Dad because the man is being funny. He's sure to like one of my jokes. 'Zip in and button up to stop you catching new-moan-ear.'

He says my word in a mumble, then he gets it. 'Pneumonia! That's a big word for a little chap.'

'I'm not little,' I say, 'but I am funny.'

'I agree!' The man gives me a smile and a nod.

Next minute, Dad jumps up and stands beside me. 'Proper comedian.'

'Enjoy your haircut, Huxley,' says the man. 'Bye everyone.'

'Bye-bye.' It's just me speaking for a change.

Using two sticks, he hobbles outside. We watch him go to the special scooter parked by the door. Dad nearly walked straight into it when we arrived, but I am clever at getting out of the way. Lots of old people use them for going about town as they don't have much energy to walk. Scooters are powered by electricity that comes in a special box called a battery. I bet his scooter goes extra fast because the paint is green and shiny.

'Has he been here before?' Dad asks Tim.

'Once a week since the start of the month,' says Tim. 'He's got a new flat at the top of town. Don't get me wrong, I have every sympathy for the disabled. It's just I can't help thinking those types bring it on themselves.'

'Disabled is a strange word,' I say. 'If you diss someone it means you don't like them but when you're able it means you can do stuff.'

Tim and Dad look at me, then Dad shakes his head. 'Why don't you go and find that newspaper I was reading, Huxley.'

'Okay.' I grab the newspaper from the basket but the corner tears. This isn't great. In my hand is a ripped triangle. Oh dear. Tim is still talking to Dad, so I better wait. He goes on and on about the homeless. I know it's true that some people don't have a house to live in but Tim doesn't sound sad, he sounds cross.

'My daughter's been on the council waiting list for years but she's never offered a thing. There's too much pandering to his sort. We'll have the whole dross of society in our midst before long.'

'Daaad!' I can't keep my words in a minute more.

He turns and looks at the scrap of paper as I wave it in the air.

'Drop that in the bin and then come here, Huxley. Tim's ready for us.'

Double quick, I'm over by the chair where the man had been sitting and Tim puts a spongey block on it. Dad helps me up. Next thing I know, Dad's sitting beside me and we're both wearing bibs! He acts silly with his eyes dodging around the space. I copy him and we're being crazy. We have to stop when Tim asks about our style. Sons and dads get the same sort of cut on trips to see the barbers, but with us it can't really happen. My hair covers my forehead and Dad's doesn't. The second Tim finishes with the clippers me and Dad have bridges going over the top of our ears! I'm okay until we're outside. Then, there's a problem with short hair. It lets cold air go around my neck and my ears and it hurts. Dad buys me a takeaway strawberry milkshake from the café next door to stop me crying. I don't want my hair short and it's hard to drink and walk all at once.

Back at home, Mum makes beans on toast. I'm very happy about this although Dad sniffs to show he's not pleased. I think it's great getting the bread soaked in sauce and squashing the beans. Mum usually tells me it's not good manners to play with my food but she doesn't bother today. I turn the whole plateful into mush and slosh the lot down my throat. It's fun when you don't need to chew.

'I bet the man at the barber's shop would like this food,' I say.

'Why?' says Dad.

'It would save him gnashing his wonky teeth.'

'What are you two going on about?' asks Mum.

'That's for us to know and you to find out.' Dad gives me a wink. I smile back because it's a dad and son thing.

'You're incredible, Jed.'

I know from the way Mum talks, she doesn't mean it. I want to stand up for Dad. 'You're being star-cast-stick.'

Pointing my finger to turn it into a wand, I hope sparks will fly out. There isn't a flash of light but there is magic. Mum and Dad start laughing.

At the end of school, me and Mum dash off on our bicycles to meet Miss Choi at the park. There I go again – I don't have to say Miss Choi when I see her out of school! Mondays are not great because she doesn't work with us and Mrs Ward has a bad mood from doing everything. She is a wolf that huffs and puffs. It would be great if Mrs Ward blew the classroom down, but she never does.

We pedal to the tunnel where the notice says CYCLISTS DISMOUNT. This means we're meant to get off our bikes and push them to the end of the secret passage going under the main road. We're in a hurry and there's no one checking, so Mum says we don't have to bother. Squeezing both my brakes, I move a bit at a time and I won't fall off with my toes touching the ground. After I've gone past the tricky bend, it's go-go-go and I race along. I can almost ride straight up the ramp at the other end but we twist loopy-loopy round the bars that block the way.

The next part of cycling is on a muddy track that goes along the edge of the golf course. I aim for the bumpy lumps of earth and pretend we're riding through a forest. This is exciting because there might be wild animals out there. I haven't seen one but you never know. At the post that stops cars driving in, it's safe to breathe again. After that, there's no more taking it easy. I pedal on the pavement and Mum rides in the road beside me. We're in a race and I'm panting. My knees go up and down like mad. At the high street, we turn up the road to Waverley Park. There are loads of cars and Mum has to be careful. I shoot ahead where the path is clear.

'Hello, Lucy!' I'm happy saying her first name. It's a change from being in class.

She takes her headphones off. 'Hello Huxley. Good time at school?'

'You know how it is.' I kick the pavement.

'Like that, eh?'

I don't have a chance to reply because Mum's brakes squeak. She stops next to us but I'm not hanging around. I cycle through the gates and along the path to the tree with branches near to the ground. It's excellent for climbing. I lay my bike down and the wheels spin. Pinging the strap on my helmet, I dump it on the saddle. When Lucy and Mum get close, I hear them talking about what happened at the charity auction and how Dad and Tony were a right pair. Boring! I pick up the prickly case of a conker that has rolled onto the grass. It's bendy and the conker won't come out so I throw it back. Now, they're sitting on a bench and Mum says the words *idiot* and *sorry*. This kind of talk is interesting. I come a bit closer to let my bat ears start working really well.

'It doesn't have to be a child's cake,' says Lucy. 'I can bake any sort of cake with all that money going to the school fund.'

'Eighty quid! I don't know what got in to Jed.'

'That's easy,' I shout. 'It was beer.'

'Shush, Huxley.'

Her voice is sharp. The smile drops off my face and my eyes sink to the path. Next thing I hear is the bench creaking. I look over to see Mum rocking backwards and forwards. Cool! She's getting ready to race. My heart goes bam-bam-bam and I rub my hands together. I'm not sure when she's going to begin.

'First one to the tree!' says Mum.

She has a good start but I dash ahead and touch the trunk before her. Puffing her head off, Mum gives a salute. Yippee! I am the winner and Mum staggers back to sit with Lucy. It's time to climb the tree that's tall as Mount Everest. By reaching and pulling, I make it some of the way although it's mission impossible to triumph to the top. The branches are far away and my legs are too short. I think about going down but I can't put my feet in the right places. If I try hard I might do it. Yikes! It isn't fun coming to the park and having to play by myself. There's only one thing for it.

'Help!' It usually takes a few shouts for Mum to come over. I think she knows that being stuck is one of my special skills. Hanging on to the branch, I wave with my free hand. 'I want to get off!'

Mum goes on chattering. She's ignoring me but I know Lucy hears as she keeps turning her head. I need to make a lot of noise to stop them talking.

'I can't move!' I use my extra loud voice and before I know it, Lucy is on one of the low branches.

'Hang on,' she says. 'I'm coming.'

Lucy is a very useful person. She tells me where to put my feet and I get nearer and nearer the ground. At the bottom, she reaches out and swings me back to earth.

'Are you alright?' asks Lucy.

'I'm okay.'

'Champion.' Lucy slaps my back.

We turn around and watch Mum tapping a text. Then, she tucks her phone into a pocket and comes to join us. 'That's handy,' she says. 'I've got time for a coffee before Jed's home. Let me buy you one, Lucy. It's the least I can do.'

'Oh yes,' I say. 'I'm ready for a strawberry milkshake.'

We lock our bikes to the stand next to the café and then go inside. Me and Mum wait at the counter while they crunch coffee beans for cap-on-chin-nose and they whizz up my strawberry milkshake. Lucy is on the sofa to stop anyone else sitting there. I lick my lips as I carry my drink over. I'm good at doing two things at the same time.

'Careful.' Lucy helps me land the glass on the table and we don't spill a drop. To make her job easy, Mum arrives holding a tray with two coffee cups on it. While she gets comfortable, I'm busy with the stripy straw, slurping the froth from the top of the milkshake. It's a noisy business but I can still hear Mum and Lucy. I like talking to grown-ups, so I try to think of something interesting to say. Lucy goes to the same church as us and each Wednesday, she is the adult leader of Light Club. Children go there in the evening to play games and make stuff.

'When am I going to start Light Club?'

She hears my question and smiles. 'Now you're seven you're at the top of my waiting list. Why don't you come next week to see if you enjoy it? We're doing potato printing. You'll have fun.'

'What's potato printing?' I ask.

'You cut a shape on a potato and use it to stamp a pretty paint pattern on some cloth.'

'Potatoes are for eating,' I say. 'Chips are best, then mash and jacket potatoes are last because the skin is yuk.'

'Perhaps we can cook with potatoes another time,' says Lucy.

'Not after they're painted.'

'Of course not, Huxley.' Mum finds her phone and passes it. 'Have a play on this.'

I take the mobile to keep busy. The game collecting coins is fun and I can't help shouting *hurray* one or two times. I wave the screen in front of Mum to show her my score but that's when she sees the red bar. This means the phone is running out of charge and I have to give it back to her in case there's an important call from work. Now I don't have anything to do. Mum points to the basket next to the till where there are a few toys. I have a look but the things are meant for little kids. Over by the toilet, there's the man from the barber's shop. He's reading a book. One day when I grow up, I will read thick books. At school, I choose my reading book from the green box. These have words and pictures on each page, and the writing is small. Some children in my class take home books with only a few words, and I don't count that as reading. Zac and the others on diamond table have nearly finished all the blue books – they'll be on green next. I'm going to race through my reading to stay in front.

Taking pigeon steps, I am closer to the man. There are flakes of white on his navy-blue jumper. The bits must have dropped off his head. He can't help being disabled but having a head that's coming apart is funny! I can't help laughing so much I nearly fall over. The man looks at me. I gulp big breaths to calm down.

'What's going on?' he asks.

I have to think fast. My teacher says it's against the law to make fun of people who are different. I don't want to be in trouble with the police! I think really hard to come up with a joke. 'Laughing is good exit-size.'

The man stares into space while he works out what I've said then he smiles. He gets me.

'Exercise!' he says. 'I used to be fit. Never needed a mobility scooter until a few years ago. My poor old legs.'

'I can't see them under your trousers.'

'Shall I turn up the hems to let you have a look?'

I wonder what's so interesting. 'Okay.'

Dad is speedy when he rolls up the sleeves on his shirt but this man is slow. I go on my hands and knees to help. Quick as a flash, I see above his socks where it's rubbery and hairy.

'Not very pretty,' he says.

'No!'

'I'd show you my whole leg if there weren't all these people in the café.' He jerks his head to one side and smiles.

I'm not sure I want to see more. 'Don't bother.'

'Please yourself.'

Oh dear. Did I say the wrong thing? Now, I am bothered and I'm sorry for wanting to make a joke about him. I don't know what to do, so I turn to his scooter. He drove it right into the shop! It's parked next to the man and it looks very interesting. There are yellow pads on each end of the handlebars. I wonder if they help with turning. It must be the same as riding a bike. I bet I could do it, no problem. I reach out to give the nearest handle a squeeze. The pad is springy and fits nicely in my hand.

'They're made from foam called Neoprene,' says the man.

I give another squeeze.

'Can you say Neoprene, Huxley?'

Yes, of course. But I'm not going to speak in case I get something wrong.

'Can you say Leonard? That's my name.'

'I say the things I want to say.'

'Naturally,' says Leonard.

'Where did you buy them?' I stroke the springy ends. 'They're yellow like the sun.'

'I bought them off the internet.'

Moving a bit closer to the scooter, I put my trainer on the flat piece for his feet when he's riding around. 'I've got a computer at my house.'

'I bet you have. I suppose you've got lots of games.'

I step even nearer. 'Dad plays chess but my best game is finding treasure.'

'I don't play on my computer although I've got loads of Disney DVDs. Would you like to come round to my house and watch one? I've got *Dumbo* and *Bambi*.'

Waggling my foot, I make it go tap-tap-tap on the scooter. 'They're old ones.'

'Well, I've also got *Ice Age*. Is that more your thing?'

My foot's now in the right place for driving the scooter. 'We're going to get Netflix.'

'You'll have loads to choose from.'

I grip both handlebars – I'm ready to drive away.

'My flat's above a sweet shop. I suppose you like chocolate.'

'Cadbury Dairy Milk is best.' I nod my head because I know what I'm talking about. As I do this, I see Mum rushing over. Hopping away from the scooter, I pretend I haven't been on it. One big smile and she's never going to guess.

'Come over here, Huxley.' Mum grabs my arm and yanks me away. 'You mustn't go bothering people.'

'Don't!' She's always pulling me.

'You're being annoying.' Mum makes me stand beside her.

'He hasn't been any trouble.' The man looks in my eyes. 'Remember, Huxley, you must always do as your mum says.'

'Afternoon, Leonard.' Now Lucy's here. 'Have you met Kirsty and Huxley? They belong to our church.'

'I saw Huxley at the barber's shop,' says Leonard. 'But I'm pleased to be introduced to you, Kirsty.'

Leonard holds out his hand. He has white skin with brown splodges on his fingers.

Lucy stares at Mum. Mum is staring at Leonard. In the quiet, I wonder what's going to happen next.

'Leonard's recently moved into one of those new flats, Kirsty. The church did a leaflet drop for the residents and thankfully Leonard decided to join us.'

Leonard flaps his arm – he's ready for a handshake. I think Mum is in a trance.

'This is an opportunity to welcome one of our new members.' Lucy's voice is getting loud.

'Of course!' Mum comes back to her senses and gives her hand to Leonard. They shake but it's not what I call a good one because Mum pops her hand in her pocket straight after.

'I see you got a smart haircut, Huxley. Nice and neat.'

'We didn't manage church this week,' says Mum.

'My mum and dad fell out.'

'Be quiet, Huxley.'

'Then they weren't talking.'

'Don't exaggerate!'

'It happens to the best of us,' says Leonard.

'This will have to be a quick hello and goodbye,' says Mum. 'We need to get to the station.'

'Give me a minute and I'll walk with you,' says Lucy.

'Nice to meet you, Kirsty,' says Leonard. 'See you next time in church.'

For some reason, I'm bundled out of the café. While Mum unlocks the bikes, I throw myself around to feel warm. Checking my handgrips, I give them a squeeze. They aren't springy like Leonard's ones. Lucy joins us as we push our bikes along. When we get to the station, I will hide beside the ticket machine and jump out to give Dad a special surprise. It'll be extra funny if he falls over from shock! Dad is always pleased we're there for him. With my plan finished, I listen to Mum and Lucy talking. It's add-hop-shine again. This means Lucy can get a baby all on her own without actually having one in her tummy. It's a good word because having a baby makes you happy. Adding hop and shine together is also a happy-making thing. I spring from one foot to the other just to check. I know I'm right because I can't stop smiling.

'Surely, being a teaching assistant shows you're experienced with children,' says Mum.

'Working with children is only one hoop to jump through.'

This gives me an idea. 'Are there hoops to play with at Light Club?'

'We've all sorts of things,' says Lucy. 'You'll meet lots of new friends, too. In fact, Leonard was asking about being a volunteer helper.'

'You're not serious,' says Mum. 'He looks dodgy.'

Lucy tuts and shakes her head. 'You can't judge a book by its cover. Anyway, I need more people to help run the club. It's not as if many parents are willing to help.'

'Well, you know I'm far too busy.'

'Exactly! That's why I'm pleased Leonard's offered.'

'Can me and Leonard start Light Club on the same day?'

'Sorry, Huxley. Leonard won't be joining for ages. There are lots of forms and checks to complete before he can begin.'

'That's a shame,' I say.

'That's a relief,' says Mum.

Every now and then me and Ben go to a play session after school at the swimming pool. Nanny Phil looks after Juno whenever we go on a boys together treat. Ben is lucky to have Juno. I keep asking Mum if I can have a brother or sister but she's not interested. A towel rolled into a cylinder sticks up from the top of my backpack. (Mrs Ward said she was glad I used the word *cylinder* in class. It's good to make people feel gladly.) Mum's bag is stuffed as well. The second the knocker bangs, we know Paula and Ben are there, so me and Mum pile outside. I walk in front with Ben and we start a game of bumpety-bump. Crossing our arms, we try to knock each other over. We're ten pins at the bowling alley! Mum laughs and I think she might want to join in but Paula's too busy chatting for this to happen.

Dad says he will put Mum's laughter into a jar and seal the top. That way if we need cheering up there's always her laughter to listen to. Dad never really does it but we're the same, me and Dad, with our excellent ideas.

'I'm just like Dad,' I say.

'Tell me about it,' says Mum.

'I'm like my dad, too,' says Ben.

'Not quite as bad,' says Paula.

Then the mums are whispering but with my bat ears turned on, I can hear everything. They say *bugger* and *pillock* and this makes them laugh.

These are rude words, I think. My brain whizzes into gear and turns the words to bug-ear and pill-cock. I have a little ha-ha-ha to myself and keep the ideas in my memory.

My mum once called Dad a dipstick when she was cross with him. It's a word I sort of understand. Well, I know what chopsticks are and that using them to eat food is very hard. The mums are still laughing and I'm not sure if I should join in. I think it's okay because Dad says Mum has a strange sense of humour. I give a blast that's loud as a ship's horn. Mum chuckles even more.

At the leisure centre, me and Ben climb onto the high stools where there's a shelf to put drinks and a huge window to see right over the swimming pool. I spot a man strapped into a special swimming chair and a lady is swinging him right out of the water. The man's wearing glasses – no need for goggles! Taking hold of two walking sticks, he stands up and his long trunks are dripping. I have a good stare to make sure I'm right. Soon as I know it's Leonard, I nudge Ben.

'That's Leonard,' I say. 'He uses the special chair because he's disabled.'

'I know the boy in blue arm bands.' Ben points to the row of little kids sitting on the edge of the small pool near us. There is a boy kicking his legs in the water to make a splash while the others are sitting still and being sent-a-ball. Ben starts waving his arm like a mad thing and the boy waves back. In the muddle, the boy slips into the pool. Me and Ben laugh as we watch his head bob up and down. Just in time, the teacher grabs him and rescues the boy. It's not clever to laugh at someone drowning but we can't help it.

I turn around to check where Mum and Paula are in the queue. They're not at the front. This means we can mess about a bit longer. It also means we have to wait. I do some watching through the window to use up the time until we go in. All of a sudden, I see a crowd of people busy at the poolside.

'They're blowing up The Giant In-flat-a-ball,' I shout.

'It's not a ball.' Ben's face is scrunched. 'It's inflatable.'

'I know.' I slap my forehead. Ben never gets my jokes. 'It's a triangular cylinder.'

'You're showing off,' says Ben. 'It's the same as a roof on a house.'

I know this, but it's not worth arguing with Ben. Bit by bit, I watch it get bigger. When it's blown up, they send it from the edge to the middle of the pool.

'Come on, boys.' Mum beckons us over and we race to the changing rooms.

I can swim widths and lengths without wearing goggles but The Giant In-flat-a-ball is best. It's hard work climbing to the top. I stretch my arms to reach the knobbles then dash my legs into place. I'm faster than Ben at scrambling up, he's better at balancing on the top. We're great at being kings on the rooftop. I have a wonderful view and I can see right into the café where Leonard is sitting by himself. It's sad he's not having fun in the water with us. He had a go in the disabled swinging chair so it's not too bad. I give Leonard a wave and wait to see if he waves back. I don't think he sees me as he's staring at the back of the pool. There's a window onto the park at one side and a load of showers going the other way. Some swimmers are having a soaking that makes their hair go flat against their heads. Beside them, a mum gives two little children a proper lathering with shampoo and I can see a bare bottom! I don't like having a shower at the swimming pool and anyway, we've got a bath at home.

'Wakey, wakey.' Ben jiggles my shoulder.

Why does he think I've been asleep? I'll show him! Turning my hands into fists I shake them in the air. I'm a champion. Oh dear, next minute I'm sliding down and crashing into the pool. My mouth is full of water but in the pool it's okay to spit.

When I reach the top again, I find Ben still sitting there.

'Let's play our special game,' I say.

He knows how it goes and closes one eye. I do the same because we have to look straight in the water. Seeing a shadow, I shout at the top of my voice, 'Shark!'

'Shark!' Ben waves an arm and points about the place. 'Shark, shark!'

We're so busy shouting and pointing, I nearly slip off the top. I grab Ben's shoulder and he keeps me steady. Just then, the lifeguard blows his whistle and tells us to get off. We've been making too much noise. I go quiet and try to ignore him. It doesn't work because the lifeguard is down the ladder and giving sharp bursts that hurt my ears. There's no more hogging the top for us. We bounce along the side and into the water.

Mum and Paula stay in the shallow end where it's warmer. I can do handstands and go underwater but Mum doesn't want to have wet hair. She swims across the pool like she's a giraffe with her head out of the water. When the lady on the loudspeaker says anyone with a red band has to leave the pool, I dash for The Giant In-flat-a-ball. Mum catches my arm and pulls me back. She chucks me up in the air and I make a big splash as we queue for the steps. There are loads of people getting out and most of the changing places are taken.

'Go in the family cubicle,' says Paula. 'It's usually free.'

Mum wraps a towel around her body, making her into a sausage roll. She flings another towel over my head. It's one way to dry my hair.

'Your eyes are a bit pink,' says Mum.

I give them a rub-a-dub-dub.

'Leave them alone, Huxley,' she says. 'Try blinking instead.'

I open and close my eyelids blink-blonk-blank. The itching stops a bit. I am truly tired after my adventures. My tummy is empty and I think a mouse is nibbling away at my insides. I'm happy Paula's brought a packet of raisins for me and one for Ben. It's fiddly to get at them because they're all pressed together. We sit in our snuggly clothes munching away. By the time the packet is half empty, the raisins are loose and it's easy to pick them out.

Mum wiggles into her knickers and whips on her jumper. I flick a raisin in my mouth and while I'm chewing Paula stands. She's wearing black joggers and a bra. (That's a sling to stop boobies from swinging around.) It's while I'm thinking about bras and boobies that I notice the red lines going across Paula's tummy. They look really strange, like she's been scratched by a wild animal. Watch out for sharp claws! I know I shouldn't stare but I can't help it. Paula turns her back to me so she can talk to Mum.

'I can't get rid of them,' says Paula. 'I've tried olive oil, Bio oil, you name it.'

'Don't worry too much. Stretch marks turn silvery in time,' says Mum.

'You would think.' Paula tips up a bottle then presses something shiny on her hand. 'I'm trying a new product I bought over the internet. Can you do the ones behind my hips?'

There's a squirting noise like a fart. Me and Ben giggle then Paula's stroking her tummy and Mum's doing her back. After one second, disaster happens. Ben drops his packet and raisins scatter over the floor. I dive to pick them up and find one that's a tiny head with a beard.

'They're for the bin.' Mum takes them from me. 'Be helpful and share yours with Ben.'

As I'm a good boy, that's what I do.

I want to start a new box of Krispies to get another Sillybones for my collection. I've got loads of blue and red ones but I'm hoping for a golden magic bone. Mum spots me on my knees – I'm a dog digging to the back of the cupboard.

'You've got to finish the open packet first.' She grabs the belt on my trousers and yanks me away. I slump onto my chair and scrunch up my face to show I'm cross. Pouring a pile of flakes into my bowl, Mum doesn't say anything else. Before I've time to speak, she's slopping milk over.

'Not too much.' I hate it when Mum makes my Krispies go soggy. 'You know I don't like milk.'

'You like strawberry milkshake.'

'That's because it's red.'

'Milk's good for you,' says Mum.

'There's lots of it in a bar of Cadbury. That's why it's called dairy milk chocolate.'

'More sugar than milk I think you'll find.'

'There's a picture with a glass of milk on the wrapping.' You have to tear where the foil is stiff to open the packet. Two squares on my tongue gives a mouthful of goo. 'I want some chocolate in my packed lunch.'

'School rules say no.'

'Ben takes homemade chocolate brownies to school.'

Mum mumbles something – I can hear the words *bloody* and *Paula*.

'You shouldn't say bloody,' I tell her. 'That's rude.'

Mum looks at the ceiling and takes a breath. 'Thank you for reminding me, Huxley. What would I do without you?'

This sort of question doesn't need an answer so I eat my first spoonful of breakfast. By turning my arm into a digger, I let the bucket swing to collect a load. Dribbles of milk run over my chin and they go drip-drip-drip. When I've finished, I float my empty bowl on the water in the sink. One big wave capsizes it and this morning my jumper isn't soaked for a change.

Dad is taking me into school today as Mum has to be at the office early. She needs to find out how much a house costs and then sell it. When she's good at her job, Mum gets a bonus. This makes Dad very happy and sometimes he splashes out on a bottle of bubbles. Last time it happened, I tried a sip and it made me sneeze.

As I'm all set to leave for school, I wait for Dad on the porch. I've got my book bag but Dad's still looking for his briefcase. Barley our neighbour's cat comes to say hello. He's a ginger cat and he thinks our mat is excellent for rolling on. He waves his paws in the air like he wants me to tickle him. I need to be careful of his claws that scratch. How Paula got marks on her tummy I just don't know.

'Away with you.' Dad slams the front door. This makes Barley whizz down the path and squeeze under the gate. 'Cats should keep to their own gardens.'

'But Barley is a friendly cat.'

Dad walks beside me and I swing my book bag high. He doesn't get the message about playing a game. I think he's grumpy because of Barley and I'm grumpy because he doesn't like cats.

'Paula's got scratches on her tummy,' I say. 'I saw them after we went swimming.'

'Yeah, yeah.'

Dad looks at his watch and starts taking extra long strides. I run to stay up with him. He keeps going until we're through the tunnel and almost at school. Standing beside the last road we need to cross, Dad takes my hand. The traffic is busy.

'Mum stroked Paula's back and that made her go squishy,' I say.

'What?' Dad looks for a gap in the line of cars.

'It's true.'

'Not now, Huxley.'

We dash across the road then Dad's walking fast on the pavement.

'Me and Ben ate raisins and Mum was wearing knickers.'

'Really?' Dad stands still and looks into the distance. 'Mum in her knickers … what was Paula doing? Don't tell me they were shopping for clothes again.'

'We were at the swimming pool!' I get very cross when Dad doesn't listen. 'Paula has scratches round her middle and Mum gave them a rub!'

'That can't have happened. You must have got it wrong.'

'I didn't.' I stamp my foot to stop Dad from doing more walking. We're near the school gate and loads of people are rushing past us. Me and Dad are an island. I listen for the bell and hope it won't go off before I've made it to the playground. I can't stand still any longer, so I hop about waiting for Dad to say something. Right then, Zac's mum walks over and Dad steps away like he's all surprised. I think he isn't pleased to see her but it serves him right for not talking to me.

'Morning,' she says.

'Morning,' replies Dad.

'That's copying,' I say.

'No, it isn't,' snaps Dad. Then he takes a big breath and smiles at Zac's mum. 'It's simply being polite.'

'Quite right,' says Zac's mum.

'Good week?'

'Absolutely,' says Zac's mum. 'Especially after your generosity at the charity auction. Such a large donation to the school funds. Thank you very much.'

'No problem,' says Dad. 'I wasn't going to let Tony be a cheapskate.'

'That's one way of looking at it.'

'Well, we need to support the school.'

'Precisely.' Zac's mum's smile shows lipstick on her teeth. 'Must press on.'

When she's well ahead of us, Dad turns his finger into a pretend toothbrush. I have to laugh and this reminds me of the time I had a ha-ha-ha to myself. 'Is bug-ear a rude word?'

Dad changes his eyes to slits while he's thinking.

'Is it a mini beast that makes a home in your ear?' I ask.

Dad shakes his head, 'Bug-ear?'

'Yes. Bug-ear, bug-ear, bug-ear. Do you have to take medicine to fix a bug-ear?' I love being funny and then Dad doesn't know what to say.

'Oh, bugger.' Dad puts a hand over his mouth to stop more words falling out. 'That's not very nice.'

'It's only a joke.'

'Never mind the joke. Where did you hear it?'

'From Mum and Paula.'

'Well don't go repeating it.'

In the playground, I swing my book bag extra high and it nearly clonks Dad on the nose. 'Steady on, Huxley. Hold that bag sensibly. You mustn't let Mrs Ward see you behave like that.'

I stand up straight and think about marching. I can kick my legs high-high-high.

'Listen.' He bends over so that he can whisper to me. 'There's no need to say anything about Mum and Paula.'

'Do you mean about bug-ears?'

'Yes.' Dad's forehead shows train track lines. 'Don't talk about stroking skin or scratches either.'

'Ha! You believe me now!'

'Not entirely.' Dad lands his hand on my head as if a massive spider is crawling over my spiky hair. I want to run away but Dad holds me.

'Say goodbye before you rush off,' says Dad.

'Bye-bye bug-ear.'

I take a chance and dash to the line where my class waits. As I turn around to watch Dad leave, I hear one of the other dads shouting *good on you, mate* and *you saved me a few quid*. I think they're talking about the charity auction and I'm happy they're slapping Dad's back like he's a hero.

6

My gran lives in Spain and that's far away. At the end of October, I have a whole week off school for the half term holiday but I won't see her. This is sad making. The good news is she's sent money to buy a new piece of train track. I want a special turntable that makes Thomas the Tank Engine go in different ways. It means I won't need to take him off the line. Me and Mum pop into Skinners after school. It's a big shop that sells clothes and beds and handbags. The toys are next to where you walk in – we don't use the ask-all-laters – the electric stairs that go up a floor.

There are boxes and boxes of games. Some are piled into towers and Mum's scared I'll knock them over. It's like walking round a maze! I want to find the track but it's not in the same place as last time. I need a bit of help and stand next to Mum. She's talking on her mobile and swipes her hand to stop me bothering her. I get out of the way just in time. She's going on and on about a house. That means she's talking to Vijay at her office. I can't wait any more and I stamp my foot to make a loud bang. I do it so hard my leg hurts. Now I want to cry and my mum doesn't care. I blink my eyes and try to squeeze out a tear. Nothing happens. I might as well look around again but jigsaws and colouring books are not my thing.

'Can't you deal with it?' Mum's voice is loud. 'It's my afternoon off and I'm supposed to be shopping with Huxley. Have you tried asking Tony?'

I'm a bit interested because I hear Tony's name. He's Ben's dad and Mum doesn't think it's fair Tony got the big job she was after.

'Well, if you definitely can't manage … okay … okay … if it's an emergency.'

Mum puts the phone in her pocket. Hurray! We can look for my track at last. But Mum isn't smiling and she isn't wearing a helpful face. She is doing up the buttons on her coat.

'Come on, Huxley. We've got to drop over to the office.'

Oh no! I'm not having this. Her staring eyes are going straight into mine. I turn my head so I don't look at her and it's just then I spot some boxes hanging from a rack near the way out. I make my eyes close up tight. This helps me to look really hard and I see through the plastic on the boxes. Inside each one is a train engine or a carriage. Over there must be where they've moved the track. I'm keen to dart across, but Mum is in my way.

'The sooner we get there,' Mum ties her belt, 'the sooner we can come back.'

'I don't want to go.'

'I know.' Mum sticks out her hand like she wants me to hold it. I'm not falling for that trick. I tuck my arms behind my back. 'Let's leave now and I'll let you play on my chair. Vijay will spin you round in a circle.'

'I need my track.'

'We'll buy it later. Come with me and be a good boy.'

I know what she's up to … trying to make me say yes to something I don't want to do. In a flash, I have an idea. I crash my bottom onto the floor and sit cross legged. This is called a sit-down strike. 'Not going.'

'Don't be silly, Huxley. You know I've got important work.'

I fold my arms by putting one arm on top of the other – I'm building a fence.

'It'll only take ten minutes then we'll come back and I'll help you find the track.'

I think hard to be sure I don't speak. Keeping my lips glued together, my forehead goes heavy because I squish my brain.

'Huxley. Not now.' Mum grips my arm and tries to make me stand up. Instead, I slide along the floor. When I use my energy, I'm too strong for Mum. She stops pulling and I scoot back to where I started my strike.

'Oh, no!' Mum's face is pink and she turns her head from side to side. Then, she puts her hand on her forehead. She does this to me if I say I'm not feeling well but she always works out I'm okay really. She's waiting there and not saying anything. I don't mind sitting on the floor as I do it all the time at school.

'Okay, Huxley. If you're not going to shift, I'll leave you here.'

She thinks I'll give in and go with her. That won't work because I'm not a baby. I know what I'm doing. I've been on my own in here before. Mum once popped into the ladies' toilet and I didn't even miss her. 'I'm staying.'

'It's not a good idea, Huxley. What if they shut the shop and you're locked inside?'

'A sleepover with the toys, yippee!'

'Get up, Huxley. I don't want to be angry with you.'

I'm not moving. Mum closes her eyes until she speaks again. 'Let's not fight over this.' She turns her lips to make a smile but it's a pretend one. 'We'll come back another day when we've plenty of time. I'll buy you a strawberry milkshake from the café as well.'

That's more like it but I stay put. 'Nope. I've got a lot of searching to do. It has to be the right track.'

'Quickly! I'll help you look and then we can go to the office.'

I stay sat. 'I don't want to hurry.'

'For heaven's sake.' Mum turns in a circle then stares into my eyes again. The black bits in the middle of her eyeballs are the ends of a liquorice stick. I won't try one of them again – the taste is horrible. 'You have to come with me. I can't leave you here.'

'Why not?' I'm thinking fast and come up with a genius idea. Mum's office is in front of Skinners. It's got big windows without any brick walls. 'I'll stand at that rack by the door.' I point my arm to show her where I mean and she looks over. 'You'll be able to see me from your office. I'll find my track and then everything will be okay.'

'Staff don't let children stay in the shop on their own.'

'They won't know I'm here.'

Mum grunts. 'Well, that's true. There's never anyone around when you need them.'

'They can't leave the till over there.' I point to the other side of the shop. I seem to know more about Skinners than she does.

Mum looks over at the rack and takes a couple of steps. I shuffle along on my bottom. Even I can see her office from sitting on the floor by stretching my neck.

'Vijay's at his desk.' I wave my arm to show her.

Mum turns to check. 'I suppose … but I'm not sure.'

'I won't move a muscle. I'll stay by the rack to find my new track. When you've finished at the office, I'll be ready.'

'If you absolutely promise to stay put and don't go anywhere else.' Mum lets breath whoosh out of her mouth. 'You wait there and I'll be back in a few minutes. Remember, I'll have my eyes on you all the time.'

'Okay.' I hop up and walk straight to the rack by the window.

Mum follows me. 'Remember, Huxley. I'm trusting you.'

'I promise to be good.'

Before she goes out, Mum switches back and says in her serious voice. 'Don't let me down.'

Mum's office is so close I'm not bothered about her going. She'll be back soon, anyway.

There are lots of boxes with engines. I haven't got Edward. He's a blue engine. He's another sort of blue to Thomas, not as bright. They've both got puffy cheeks and I want puffy cheeks as well but mine only go like that if I do an extra big smile. I asked for Edward for my birthday although I got a carriage instead. That's okay because when they're joined together it makes a very long line. There are lots of different kinds of track. Looking at them is fun. I've got pieces with joining bits that stick out at both ends. These are very useful for track that wiggle-waggles. I've also got a humped-back bridge and a station.

There are long pieces of track that are piled high but the turntable is in a special package. I've seen it before, that's how I know. Hanging at the bottom of the rack is a square box. It's the right shape, it's the right size, it's just what I want! I press it against my heart as I'm happy. It is the last turntable. I am lucky no one snuck ahead of me to grab it. Now I've got it in my hands, I take a look through the plastic side. There's a clever turning knob that's extra cool but I'm not allowed to take the turntable out of the box. Bad luck! I am thinking very hard, working out which engine should go on it first, but that doesn't stop me from hearing a knock-knock-knocking. I look over to see Leonard on the other side of the glass door. He's smiling and beckons me over. Crouching down, I pretend I haven't heard. When the knocking comes again, I need to say hello because I am a polite boy.

I look over to check what Mum's doing in her office but she has her back to me. She's not going to see me open the door. I jam my shoe in the crack. 'I'm looking at trains and track.'

Leonard smiles. 'I used to be a railway enthusiast and I went train spotting. You write the numbers of engines you see in a special notebook. I've got it somewhere.'

I'm not sure what he's going on about so I give Leonard's scooter a good stare. How does a mobility scooter get on a train? Even for me it's hard jumping on the carriage because there's a big gap from the platform. I need to be careful or I might fall and be killed!

'I haven't always used a mobility scooter,' says Leonard. 'I was young and fit once upon a time. I took a train up to Scotland for a holiday one year.'

'We go on a plane to Spain in the summer. That rhymes – plane and Spain! My gran lives there and when she puts washing on the line it dries in seconds.'

'Is that right?'

Leonard looks around the place as if he doesn't want to talk any more.

'Bye bye, Leonard.'

'Hold on, Huxley,' he says. 'I want you to do me a favour. Ask your mum if you can come with me for a little while.'

The battery on Leonard's scooter hums. This is very interesting. I want to squeeze the lemon handles again to check they're still springy. I wonder what it's like to ride on a scooter that goes with electricity. Holding out the box with my turntable inside, I show it to Leonard.

'Why are you jiggling?'

I stand still. 'Because I've found my special track.'

He leans closer. 'Great stuff.'

'Yes, it is.'

'Where's your mum?'

'She's at her office,' I say. 'I have to stay in the shop.'

'As she's not around, I'm sure she won't mind you helping. I'd like you to come along the road with me.'

I want to go but I'm not allowed to move. My eyes dash over to Mum's office and she's at the computer with Vijay. There are two heads, bumpy-bumpy behind the screen.

'I tell you what,' Leonard continues, 'I'll give you a ride on my scooter. We won't be long and your mum will be proud of you for being helpful.'

This is true. Mum tells me so when I push post through Mrs Vartan's letter box after the postman does a mistake. She's our neighbour over the road, not the one that died. Turning the handlebar, Leonard brings the scooter close to me. I tuck the track under my arm and stretch my free hand for a quick squeeze. I remember it's made of knee-on-prene but I don't know how to make the last silly-ball funny.

'Come on,' he says. 'I'd like you to help get money from the cashpoint. My fingers don't work as well as they used to.'

'Just a minute.' I dash off to hide my turntable. I want to help Leonard but I don't want anyone grabbing my track. I can't take it out of the shop without paying for it. That's stealing! In the end, it's easy. There's a little shelf where the rack goes all the way to the floor and I hide it underneath where no one will see. Back at the door again, I only open it a slice because I'm good at getting through small spaces. Then I hop about while Leonard swings his legs to make room for me on the scooter.

'Jump on board. You can squeeze onto the platform.'

I think he means the standing bit. 'Like at a station?'

'Oh yes,' says Leonard.

This is exciting! I slide next to Leonard and then he moves his legs back. His knees press against my bottom.

'It's splendid having you as my special helper.' Leonard drives the scooter.

We go over the lines on the pavement no trouble. 'Ya-hoo.'

I don't understand why the scooter starts going slow. 'Can't we go faster?'

'I want to be sure you can press the buttons on the cash machine. Show me your hands.'

I swizzle around and wave my fingers in the air. It's daring to ride without holding tight but I don't fall off. Leonard's got one of his legs on each side of me. 'I use Dad's card all the time to take money out.' This isn't true although I am excellent at taking notes from the slot and passing them to him.

Leonard lets the scooter jump forward so I turn back and grip the handlebar again. I wish I could do the steering. Leonard lets me put my fingers on top of his and that's nearly as good. This is fun! I am facing front and watching where we're heading. It takes another minute to reach the cash machine. Leonard tells me the numbers to press and I'm very careful. I get everything right first time. He smiles and tucks the notes into his wallet. It's a shame he doesn't need more money because I want another go.

'I'd best return you to the shop now. I'll sort out the scooter.'

It goes beep-beep-beep as Leonard steers backwards then he goes straight.

'The next time I see your mum, I'll tell her you've been a big help.'

It's only then I remember that I'm not supposed to leave the shop. My heart begins to rat-tat-tat. 'Oh no! Don't tell Mum! Please don't say anything!'

'Why ever not?'

Worry makes me hot because Mum will be cross. I don't want any trouble. She won't buy my track if I've done something wrong. I need to go in the shop and wait next to the rack. I really want my turntable. I've wanted one for ages and ages. I have to get back fast. 'Stop the scooter!'

Leonard puts on the brakes and I bump against him. Breath comes out of his mouth in a huge puff. I scramble over his leg and off. I'm thinking fast. 'You mustn't tell Mum.'

'Shall this be our little secret?' he asks.

I nod my head up and down a few times so he gets the message.

'I promise not to say a word.' Leonard's face squishes into a smile but I don't stay to talk. I run along the road and when I'm almost at the shop, I hear Leonard call my name. Looking back, I see he's waving a huge bar of Cadbury Dairy Milk in the air.

'I'll keep this for you,' he shouts.

I can't think about chocolate because I have to dash. I give Leonard a wave and then race inside. My heart is going boing-boing-boing like a tune on a bongo drum. I flick the turntable from its hiding place and hold it against my tummy. Sitting on the floor, I stare at the shiny white tiles. After a bit, my heart stops beating fast and by the time Mum's shoes are click-clacking towards me, I'm back to normal. I don't look up in case she's cross but her voice is cheerful.

'You've made yourself at home, I see.'

I'm not sure what she means.

'Jump up, Huxley.'

My legs are springs and I leap in the air. Mum puts her hand on my shoulder to stop me bouncing. Her lips are straight and flat and I can't guess what she's thinking. I decide to check if she knows the truth. 'When I looked at your office, your head was bobbing about.'

'Told you I'd be watching.'

'I only saw your hair.'

'I've got eyes in the back of my head.'

Oh bother! She might have seen me with Leonard.

'Don't look so worried, Huxley. I'm here now.'

If I am in trouble it's not BIG trouble.

'Let's pay for the track and I'll buy you a strawberry milkshake to drink on the way home.'

Slurping through the straw as we walk, I let the froth slide down my throat but my mind buzzes. Did Mum see me or not?

Ben likes playing football and scoring goals at playtime but I don't. It's okay watching a match on TV because me and Dad shout at the players. It's not real football at school as they're only allowed to kick a tennis ball. Jumpers mark the goal and Ben keeps moving them around. Walking at the edge of the pitch, I pretend to be a linesman. I don't have a flag but that doesn't stop me waving my arm in the air. 'You're offside.'

Zac ignores me and runs to the corner of the playground, kicking the ball in front of him. That's called dribbling. When I think of Zac with spit running down his chin, I have a chuckle.

'What's so funny?' shouts Zac.

I can't tell him the truth. 'You're not sticking to the rules!'

'That's rubbish.' He picks up the ball and starts walking over to me. He doesn't seem to know about handball either. Before I have a chance to say anything, he's right in front of me – I can feel his breath on my face. 'Get lost, Huxley.'

Puffing out my chest makes me tall but two of Zac's mates are closing in. I see Ben over the other side messing with the goalie. He can't help me and I'm a little bit scared. All I can think to do is stare at Zac's chin. Juno dribbles because she's only little and she has a muslin cloth to mop up the wet. I imagine Zac with one around his neck. I can't help spluttering.

'Yuk,' Zac takes a step back. 'Keep your lurgy to yourself.'

'Let's get on with the game,' says one of the boys.

'Okay.' Zac rolls the ball and straight away the three of them chase across the playground. That was a lucky escape. I thought picking-on was going to start.

I go over to the climbing frame but only the little kids play on it today. My class has it on Thursdays and that's a long time to wait. Some playtimes I hang around with girls. Samira thinks up special games like she's a doctor and she can mend my broken leg. Samira is friendly and helpful. I mean, if I really did break my leg, I'd go to hospital. With Samira's dad working there, she knows about it. Her family comes from another country but I don't mind. I watch Samira as she twirls, trying to be a dancer on TV. I'm not keen on joining in, so I move away. On days like this, I sneak off to my cubbyhole behind the bicycle stand. School rules say I'm not allowed to go there but I don't care. It's best to hide when no one wants to be friends. I crouch and start putting leaves in a neat pile. There's a brown one just right for crunching in my fist. After I open my fingers one by one, little bits of dead leaf fly away in the wind. I find a bigger leaf but before I can crush it to bits, I hear footsteps coming. I forget about leaves and squidge down to stop anyone seeing me. I'm as good as a hedgehog for curling up tight.

'Huxley's dad paid eighty quid for a Barbie cake!' I stretch my neck and take a peek. There's Zac and his two mates in a huddle. They're talking extra loud because they know I'm hiding. I duck out of sight.

'You shouldn't be here,' I shout.

They start whispering and I have to think fast. My brain whirrs and my heart goes bang-bang-bang. Leaping from my hiding place, I search through the leaves for a stick. I need to defend myself but there are only twigs.

'What you looking for, Huxley?' says Zac. 'A feather to go on your Barbie cake?'

The two boys fall about – they think it's the funniest joke in the world.

'Your dad's an idiot,' says Zac. 'And you like Barbie.'

That does it. Putting my head down, I rush towards him. I'm a bull ready to gouge out his insides. The other two catch my shoulders, spin me around and ram me against a tree. My arm hurts a lot. All I can hear is their laughter. I take my chance and fly at Zac but he's too quick. He gets me in a headlock. I struggle but he's holding me so tight I can't breathe. Blood roars in my ears and everything goes blurry. There's only one thing to do. My mouth is stiff as I sink my teeth into his hand. He yowls like a dog and I break loose but I'm not free for long. The teacher on duty is marching towards me.

•　　•　　•　　•　　•

I am sent to work outside the office. I have to write a letter to Zac but my words are muddled. It is not fair! The rest of my class are doing PE and the climbing bars are out and doing PE is my best thing about school. I have a little cry because I'm missing out and tears drop onto the page. My writing goes smudgy where the paper is wet. I flap it around to dry, then I use my sleeve to give it a pat but I make a hole. I try pressing the edges together to mend it. There's a mess same as a giant's fingerprint. My eyes dart around to see if I can find a clean sheet but I mustn't leave my seat or I'll be in more trouble.

The children from my class finish in the hall and wait in a line ready to walk back to the classroom. They need to be quiet before the leader opens the door. Mrs Ward stands beside me and watches them pass. I put my work on my knees and hope she won't ask to see it. Sadness makes my head heavy and I lean on the table. I close my eyes and pretend to be somewhere else.

'Stop flopping around,' says Mrs Ward. 'Sit up!'

I do this carefully to keep the paper hidden.

'You've got a few minutes to finish writing about how sorry you are.'

So that's what I'm supposed to be doing.

'Where's your work?'

I shrug my shoulders. As I do this, the paper slips from my lap.

'What's that?'

I scramble to grab the page but Mrs Ward is there first.

'This is a mess.' Mrs Ward's eyebrows join in the middle. 'You'll have to start again.'

'I'm too sad for writing.'

'Well, if you hadn't bitten Zac you wouldn't need to.'

'He did picking-on me first.'

'That's no excuse,' says Mrs Ward. 'Only animals bite. You should be ashamed.'

Mrs Ward goes over to the shelf and finds a new piece of paper. 'Do the writing then you can draw a picture. You must be quick – your mother is on her way to collect you. I can't believe a boy in my class would behave this badly.'

Now I am VERY sad and sniffing doesn't stop my tears.

'Blow your nose!' says Mrs Ward.

I get my sleeve ready but she shoves a tissue in my face.

'You really should have a handkerchief in your pocket. That's another thing I'll mention to your mother.'

Mrs Ward goes in the office and then my Head Teacher walks towards my classroom. They're doing a swap! A bit later Mum arrives and she gives a little smile but she can't talk to me because Mrs Ward is waiting. She disappears behind a closed door. My mind is full of worries about what Mrs Ward is saying to Mum. I can't hear through the bricks and I can't think of anything to write to Zac. Why should I say sorry when I'm not? He started the picking-on and he told lies. It's not fair – no one listens to my side! I hold the pencil tight in my hand and push it across the page. The letters are big and black. I remember to put a finger space between the words so I won't be told off. Next, I start a picture of a rainbow and I hope it will be okay.

Mum and Mrs Ward come out of the office. Mum's not smiling just staring. She is unhappy. Mrs Ward's face is red and that means she's still cross. I wonder if my letter will make her feel better. She reads the words then folds the picture in half. My heart is cut in two like the rainbow. I swallow hard to stop my tears.

'We'll see you in the morning, Huxley. Come back to school ready to be friendly with everyone,' says Mrs Ward.

I don't want to be friends with Zac. Staring at the ground, I choose not to talk. There are bits of glitter twinkling between cracks in the floor.

'Come on, Huxley,' says Mum. 'Tell Mrs Ward you're going to be good.'

I'm not sure how the glitter got there.

'Mrs Griffiths, you should know that the children in my class are taught to be obedient.'

Oh-bee-die-ant. The silver sparks are in a pattern of dots and dashes but there are no bees or ants.

'Huxley does as he's asked at home.'

'In school, he has to behave well and be friendly,' says Mrs Ward.

The glitter is winking at me.

'You can do it, Huxley,' says Mum.

I press my foot over the crack on the floor. I bet the glitter will stick to my shoe. 'Okay. I'll be good.'

'Fine,' says Mrs Ward.

Mum takes my hand and we walk outside but going home early isn't fun. When I check my shoes, none of the glitter has stuck. Even our car isn't happy. The hubs are turning black because it's ages since we've been to the car wash. Last time we went through the machine, jets of water smashed against the windows to swish the dirt away. It happened in minutes so getting the Focus clean is a miracle.

'Can we go to the car wash?' I ask.

'Not now.'

'If we go today, the machine will wash away all the bad things I've done.'

'If only, Huxley.'

•   •   •   •   •

After we're home, Mum starts cleaning the oven. This is a job she usually hates. She wears bright yellow gloves to stop the squirty white foam from burning. The stuff's called Mister Makegood and I think this is a bit silly. I'm not allowed to help because she wants to do the job quickly. I try on a spare pair of gloves but they're too big and go nearly up to my armpits. I wonder if Mister Makegood has a wife and if she is white foam as well. Although I'm talking out loud Mum doesn't bother to say anything. She takes a long knife from the drawer and stabs the black splodges inside the oven. No wonder she says it's a dangerous job and I'm to stay well back. She isn't in the mood for talking so I take off the gloves and go in the lounge. There's always something to do in there, but I don't feel like playing this afternoon. I lie on the sofa and stare at the ceiling. In the corner there's a brown patch where the bath overflowed and water came drop-drop-dropping. I'm not bothered although Mum says she can't live it down, the fact that she was too busy on her laptop to notice a flood! It happened ages ago. Dad's still waiting for the ceiling to dry out before he attacks it with paint.

Soon as the knocker goes, I rush to answer the door and Mum follows. Ben trips up the step, tumbles towards me and then we do a fist bump. This means me and Ben are friends. Mum helps Paula lift Juno's buggy inside and there's lots of chattering. Mum is happy to see Paula and I'm happy to see Ben. While they're taking off their coats, I check on Juno but I mustn't wake her. She's snuggling Daft Dog so I know she's happy, too.

'When can I have a little sister?' I ask.

'What have I told you?' says Mum.

This means I must stop pestering. I don't like the word because I am not a pest. Mum and Paula go in the kitchen and there are lots of mutters. I think they are talking about me biting Zac but I am not interested in listening. Me and Ben find the train track and take over the lounge. I show him my wonderful new turntable but he wants to use cushions from the sofa to make bridges and hills. It's hard for the engines to go all the way around. Actually, crashing is the best bit. Thomas the Tank rams against Ben's engine. I'm an excellent pusher but Ben is good at pushing back. We can only play rough if no one gets hurt.

'You got into trouble for fighting today,' says Ben.

'It wasn't my fault. Zac did picking-on.'

'You should have told the teacher,' says Ben.

'Why are you friends with Zac?'

'He's great at scoring goals.'

'I hate playing football.'

'That's why he's not friends with you and he is friends with me.'

This is true but it doesn't mean Zac's better. 'I'm clever at making up games about Thomas the Tank Engine.'

'Yes,' says Ben. 'That means I'm friends with you at home and friends with Zac at school.'

We take a break from our game to have a drink of juice and a Healthy Snack Paula has made with seeds and honey. It's sticky and we wash our hands before we can start work on the trains again. Just then, the knocker goes and this time it's Lucy. She pops her head around the lounge door to say hello then she goes in the kitchen with the mums. Ben is busy stacking the engines, so I go and take a sneaky look into the kitchen. Lucy is giving Mum a hug and tells her not to worry. All of a sudden, Juno starts crying and I dash back to where we're playing. I pretend I've been there all along. Paula carries Juno back to the others in the kitchen. It's like they're altogether and they're leaving us out. I don't care because Ben and me are on a mission to save Thomas from getting stuck on the mountain. There's loads of snow and ice making him slip and slide. Hurray for James the red engine who gives Thomas a push. After they reach the top, both engines fall down the other side and the track breaks up.

While me and Ben are building, there are voices coming from the kitchen. When I listen to Mum's talk, some of the words jump out. Today, they keep saying *ex* this, *ex* that, then I realise it's not ex at all. They're talking SEX. This is a word I'm not allowed to say at school. Sneaking over to the doorway, I see Lucy laughing so much she has to hold her tummy. Mum talks quietly but I can still hear what she says even though she bangs her hand on the table with each silly-ball. It's a word I don't understand but I try to make it sound funny: lip-bee-dough. Perhaps it's to do with kissing because you use your lips for that. Or maybe it's about making playdough. It is very hard to understand some words. Next thing, Mum pipes up about having a good snog and this means I'm right. Snogging is another word for kissing! They start laughing again and I get why it's a joke. Ben wanders right into the kitchen to find out what's going on. They go silent and gulp breath. There is a perfect answer to this problem. I become a roaring lion and rush over to give them a fright. Mum puts on a serious face but she can't help smiling.

Everyone leaves before Dad comes home. I know from the squiggles on his forehead that there are worries in his head. He strips his tie from the collar of his shirt and turns it round his hand like a bandage. Mum opens a bottle of beer for Dad and pours a glass of wine. I have cranberry juice that's almost the same colour as Mum's drink. We sit at the kitchen table and I wait for Mum to dish out lasagne. This is one of my favourite dinners although I'm not sure how it will taste when Mum and Dad are serious. I dip my carrot stick in the cheesy topping where there's a big dollop of the melting bit. I give a good blow to cool it down before popping it in my mouth.

'Watch how I use my knife and fork,' says Mum.

She does a bit of cutting then spears a chunk.

'Or you can scoop.' Dad shovels a parcel onto his fork.

I hold my fork and copy him. There are only chewing and swallowing noises then Dad leans forward and we're eyeball to eyeball. 'Why did you bite Zac?'

I drop my fork and it clatters on the plate. At last! Now I can say what really happened. Mum always takes sides with Mrs Ward and then gets in a bad mood and doesn't want to hear one more thing. But Dad's around so I can tell the truth. 'He was doing picking-on with two other boys. Zac was the leader. He said you were an idiot and I like Barbie.'

Mum turns her eyebrows into arches and stares at Dad. 'It sounds as if it's bullying. Why did Zac call Dad an idiot?'

I want to say something. It's telling-on but I don't care. 'Because he paid eighty pounds for a Barbie cake.'

'Little bug…' Dad puts his hand over his mouth.

'Bug-ear?' I say.

'Shush,' says Dad.

'I can't believe it,' says Mum.

'You wait till I see Zac's mother,' says Dad.

I think that means Dad's on my side.

'Not if I see her first,' says Mum.

I think now Mum's on my side, too.

Next there is a long silence. Mum's eyes keep swishing around, Dad stares at his beer then takes a sip. Finally, Mum speaks. 'Did you tell Mrs Ward what Zac said? When boys say nasty things, it's called provocation.'

'I tried to find a stick but I didn't prod, I didn't prod-o-station him.'

'It's a good job you didn't,' says Dad. 'Biting Zac was bad enough.'

'That's not the worst of it,' says Mum. 'Lucy tells me Mrs Ward thinks Huxley's got anger management problems.'

'Lucy says?' Dad goes a bit pink in the face.

'Yes, *Lucy* does!' says Mum.

Dad unbuttons the collar on his shirt.

'I can't believe you're getting soppy over Lucy again! You do realise she could flirt for England. She doesn't actually mean anything.'

'Of course,' says Dad. 'I've seen her chat up a carrot stick before now.'

I look at the last bit of carrot on my plate. 'Do you want this, Dad?'

He jams it in his mouth and gives a crunch. 'I know Mrs Ward won't agree but I think it's normal for a child to bite if they're cornered: primeval instincts of survival. Anger management, what rubbish. She might as well call Huxley a criminal.'

'That's right! Have a rant to cover up your little infatuation with Lucy,' says Mum.

'What's in-fat-your-station?'

Mum's face is puffed as a balloon and she lets her eyes zigzag from me to Dad. I think she might choke so I jump off my chair and give her a proper pat on the back.

'You're funny, Huxley!' she hoots.

Then Dad's laughing as well and I am, too. This is much better than having them cross with me.

8

After school, me and Ben are taken to the park. He hides behind a tree and it's my job to find him. I shout *gotcha, gotcha* but the wind takes away my words and blows them over to the other side of the world. I do the hiding next and he does the shouting. Mum and Paula follow us down the long path that leads to the playground. We're quick with our game and always stay in front. When we're through the gate, Paula takes Juno to the baby swings. She's too little to go on the roundabout with bright yellow poles. Ben jumps on first with me coming up behind.

'Keep to the centre of the roundabout and hold on tight,' says Mum.

I squidge down and sit with my back against the red middle stump. The metal is cold and goes right through my clothes and into my skeleton. It reminds me about being alive. Ben copies and we link arms to stop us flying off the roundabout.

'Are you ready?' Mum does a heave-ho on the pole to start us moving.

'Go faster,' I say because it's part of the game.

'Are you steady?' She starts to trot.

'Faster!' My trousers are sliding away from me and I can't stay sat up straight.

'Let's go-go-go.' Mum runs around in a circle and pushes the pole and we're spinning very fast. I'm nearly lying on my back and Ben has turned onto his tummy and we're looking at each other. He's smiling at me and I'm smiling too. This is a happy scare-making time. We're holding tight to the poles and I pull myself to sit up again. Mum isn't pushing any more, she just belts the poles as they fly by. We're not going as fast as when she was running but this is okay. I like watching the trees, and the fence and the grass go blurry. Bit by bit we come to a stop, and then it's time to get off the roundabout. It's hard to walk straight if your head is a planet twirling in the sky.

'Want another turn?' Mum slaps her gloves together. The wind nips my ears but Mum is snuggly in her scarf. She wears lots of clothes as she feels the cold but I am hot-hot-hot. I unzip my jacket. Taking it off isn't easy because I'm floppy. I stumble back onto the roundabout.

'Let's do it again,' I say.

This time me and Ben are standing up. I lean against the stump and hold a yellow pole tight.

'Ready or not, here we go.' Mum starts pushing again, running around and around. I let my jacket fall off my shoulders and then it's easy to whip out my arms. I hold the sleeve to make my jacket blow in the wind like a flag.

'I can't do it any longer.' She gives up pushing and we come to a stop. Picking up my jacket, Mum dumps it on the bench.

'Let's have a slide,' says Ben. 'I'll race you.'

He's there first and I chase him up the ladder. From the top I can see over to the tennis courts and I am as high as the rooftops on Park Row. Mum shouts and gives a wave. She stands by the swings with Paula. They laugh when Juno shakes her legs and one of her wellington boots flies off. It lands upright and Mum pretends to try it on.

'Cinderella, you shall not go to the ball!' shouts Paula.

Mum makes a job of cramming her foot into Juno's boot. This is funny! I put my elbows on the railing at the top of the slide and hold my hands around my mouth to help my voice be extra shouty, 'Oh yes, you will go to the ball!'

Mum throws her head back and her laughter is the same as bells tinkling. It's fun watching the mums messing with Juno. Paula picks up the boot and puts it back on Juno's foot. She rocks from side to side on the swing and it looks like another game of shaky-booty is about to start.

Ben is on his hands and knees for shooting down the slide headfirst, 'Three, two, one!'

He rocks forward and back.

'Ready or not, here I come!' He flies from the top and speeds along with his arms stretched. He doesn't go to the end and instead lies there blocking the way.

'Shove over,' I say. 'It's my turn.'

Ben won't budge so I swoop and give his feet a bump that sends him falling over the edge. He's not hurt because he races round to the ladder and the chase begins again. After we've done this a few times, I'm puffed out and thirsty. 'Let's get our drinks.'

Ben doesn't bother to answer but dashes to the bench where the mums sit. He dives under Juno's buggy to grab his sports bottle from the tray. Mum opens her bag into the shape of a frog's mouth and I dig inside to find my box of juice. Using the sharp bit of straw, I pop the silver foil and take a gulp.

'Single use plastic,' says Paula.

'There's only a few left in the cupboard,' says Mum.

'Just saying.' Paula's eyebrows go bounce-bounce.

My juice tastes better than Ben's water and that's why he usually wants a sip. Today, he's not interested and instead swings his bottle around by biting the cap and turning his head. I don't care what he's doing. My juice is nice and he's stuck with water. One time he tried making me drink from his bottle to save the planet. I don't think he was right. Anyway, who wants to drink from a chewed cap? Too many germs!

I pass my empty juice box to Mum and Ben drops his back under the buggy. Paula jigs Juno on her lap and says a rhyme about marching to the top of the hill. When it's time to go back down again, Paula pretends she's dropping Juno and this makes her laugh and laugh. I hold Juno's hand for a second before Paula starts the marching song again. Ben grabs the neck of my jumper and pulls me away. One minute later, we're beside the gate that lets us into the rest of the park. Ben looks at me and I look at him. The bolt keeps the gate shut. I give it a try and it slides along easy-peasy. I take a sneaky look at Mum and Paula. They're busy chattering so they don't see us. Ben gives me a smile and jerks his head towards the trees. I know what this means even though he doesn't say any words. He wants us to explore outside the playground. There's Mount Everest the climbing tree or we can play hide and seek around the bushes. The gate is open and I am only going to take a few steps. I don't think Mum can call it wandering off.

Scratching noises have me turn around. I watch squirrels dash up a tree trunk. I think they're having a game of king of the castle. We get a bit closer for a better look. They are really quick but once they've scrambled to a safe place they stop very still and do a bit of staring. It's the same for me when I've been running and need my breath back but I don't stare like squirrels. It's a rude sort of stare if you can't take your eyes off something. One of the squirrels dashes along a branch where the leaves are curled and crunchy. The other one chases. They leap from branch to branch and then they rush up and down the next tree. Ben smiles at me and I get what this means. We're going to follow them.

We move on a bit and watch out for grey blobs and toilet brush tails. The squirrels are hiding! Ben lifts an armful of leaves and chucks them in the air. I watch them twirl and drop. I think about copying Ben by making a leaf storm. Just as I duck to collect a pile, I see there's a man riding an electric scooter and he's coming our way. I squint my eyes but already I know it's Leonard. I pretend I'm telling traffic where to go by swinging my arms in the air. Leonard steers the handlebars to make him zigzag. It's a joke because he'll find us in the end. I practise a few star jumps while I wait for him to come close.

'What are you doing, Huxley?' he says.

He must know because he's been watching. 'Exit-size.'

'Oh yes, I remember,' he says. 'Exercise!'

'And watching squirrels.'

'They're rats with fluffy tails. Gone are the days when native red squirrels used to live here.'

'Red same as my jumper?' I ask.

'No.' Leonard shakes his head as if he's bonkers. Me and Ben laugh.

'More a kind of ginger,' says Leonard. 'I bet you like ginger beer.'

'Me and my dad only drink proper beer,' says Ben.

'What's your name, son?'

'I'm Ben.'

'That's a good name. I'm Leonard, by the way. Tell you what, I brew ginger tea at my house. Want to come round and see how it's done?'

I'm not happy about Ben chatting to Leonard. He's my friend first. 'My neighbour's cat is called Barley and he's ginger. He likes having his tummy tickled.'

'Don't we all?' Leonard sticks his hand into the basket at the front of his scooter. He gives a flash of purple wrapping. Straight away I know he's got chocolate. Quick as anything, he breaks off some pieces and me and Ben get two each. 'Better eat up before anyone sees. I don't want to be blamed for spoiling your tea.'

With a chew and a swallow, we stuff our chocolate. Leonard covers the end of the bar and returns it to the basket.

'Don't you want any?' I ask.

'Not me. I've got a health condition that means I have to watch how much sugar I eat.'

'That's too bad.'

Leonard puts his hand over his eyes and stares into the distance. 'There's your mum over in the playground, Huxley.'

I look where Leonard's looking and Mum's coming out of the gate.

'I'd love to tell her how helpful you were the other day but I'll keep it hush-hush.'

I wonder what he's talking about. A second later, I remember the cash machine. This makes my brain fill up with worry. 'You promised to stay quiet.'

'Okay,' says Leonard. 'I won't say anything...'

'What happened?' asks Ben.

Suddenly, Ben's very interested. He looks at Leonard for a moment and then back to me. I am pleased and proud that me and Leonard have a secret. Ben's got Zac in school but it's not as good as having a proper grown-up man for a friend. My chest is full of air and I am tall and special.

'Tell me,' says Ben. 'It's not fair, leaving me out.'

I know about being left out, and Ben's right, it's not nice. I see Mum jogging over. She's too far away to hear and I can't help boasting. 'I took money out of the cash machine for Leonard.'

'Cool,' says Ben.

'But you wanted to keep it secret,' says Leonard.

'Ben won't say anything.' My eyes whizz over to Ben and he's smiling.

'I take cash out of the machine all the time,' says Ben.

Mum's puffed out when she arrives. She stays on the path and shouts over. 'Come here right now! You'll catch a cold without your jacket on.'

Her arm is stiff as a stick and my coat hangs from her fingers. I try to think of something funny to say and soon as I'm close enough to push my hand into the sleeve, I have it! 'I am oh-bee-die-ant.'

Mum rolls her eyes to the sky and back. 'Call that obedient? You know you're not allowed to wander off on your own.'

'I'm not on my own.'

'You must always listen to your mum,' Leonard talks in an extra loud voice. 'It's important to do as she says.'

'I'll thank you not to … distract the children.' Mum answers Leonard in her sharp voice.

'I've been explaining about red squirrels. Long before I was stuck in this chair, I used to be quite an expert.'

'It's not a chair, it's a scooter,' I say.

'We have to go home. Do up your coat, Huxley.'

'That's right,' shouts Leonard. 'Zip in and button up.'

It's hard to make the metal bit slide into the slot for zipping but I catch it at last. I'm snug in my jacket and Mum does up the flap around my neck.

Leonard drives the scooter a bit closer so he can talk in a normal voice. 'I thought you might be worried. I kept the boys talking to stop them going further.'

Mum doesn't say anything although she gives Leonard a look.

'I know what boys are like,' says Leonard. 'Always asking for trouble.'

'Not these boys, Leonard. Besides, you shouldn't encourage them.'

Now it's Leonard's turn to give a look.

Next thing, Paula staggers to join our group. She's tired out from pushing Juno in the buggy. There's a football scarf hanging out of her pocket and she pulls the end to wrap it around Ben's neck. 'You're not to go outside the playground without me. That's the rule. Hold on to Juno's buggy and we'll walk back double quick.'

Paula strides along the path and Ben has to skip to keep pace. Mum's catching up with her and overtaking. She has my hand and I'm being dragged. I can't even say goodbye to Leonard because she's in such a hurry. She doesn't slow down until we're walking up the path to our house. Once we're inside, me and Ben are made to stand beside each other in the hall. We haven't even taken our coats off! I lean against the front door and wait to find out what's going on. Ben does the same and we bump together like we're dancing. I am cheerful but Mum isn't pleased.

'Listen boys,' she starts. 'It is sometimes difficult to know whether people are being genuinely friendly or when they might want to do something bad.'

Mum nods to Paula who gulps and then speaks. 'Kirsty's right. It's our job to keep you safe and make sure no one takes advantage of you.'

'Why would anyone add-van-stage?' I ask.

'Stop being silly,' says Mum.

I think she's the one being silly. 'You can't do maths on a van and a stage!'

Ben laughs. 'Course you can't.'

'Right, stand up straight,' says Mum. 'You have to concentrate and listen carefully. If someone takes advantage it means they're not thinking what's best for you, they're only thinking of themselves.'

'Like picking-on,' I say.

'Picking-on?' asks Paula.

'He means bullying,' says Mum.

'It's different to bullying,' says Paula. 'It's to do with adults not treating children properly.'

'And, it's about not going off on your own,' says Mum.

'I get it,' says Ben. 'Don't wander off and don't talk to strangers.'

'Exactly,' says Paula.

'I didn't talk to a stranger,' I say. 'It was only Leonard.'

'We don't know him,' says Mum.

'He goes to the barber's shop and he goes to the café and he goes…'

'A stranger is someone who's never been inside our house,' says Mum.

'Strangers look strange,' says Ben.

Mum nods at Paula and then Paula nods at Mum. The bumpy outline of a face is called a profile. I've never noticed before but Paula's nose is a small triangle. Mum has a lump in hers and that's not a straight line.

'That's everything covered,' says Paula.

'Huxley, I don't want you talking to Leonard again,' says Mum.

Oh! That's what this is about. 'Leonard talked to me first.'

'That's as maybe,' says Mum. 'You can only talk to him when I'm around. Promise me you won't talk to him on your own again.'

'Ben was with me.'

'Huxley, you know what I mean.'

'Okay, okay! I do.' But I don't say the words *I promise* so that means it doesn't count. I can talk to Leonard again if I want.

We follow Mum to the kitchen. She searches in the cupboard and I guess we're going to have a snack. Mum passes a pack of fig rolls to Paula who reads the words on the side.

'Almost healthy,' says Paula. 'But only one each.'

I take the roll I'm given and when Ben's got his, we go into the lounge. Instead of making a tower with the cushions from the sofa, Ben lifts the giant jigsaw from the shelf. He drops the pieces plink-plonk onto the floor. I'm not really interested in helping. I sit next to the radiator and let the bars warm my back. Nibbling at the roll, I eat the soft figgy bit in the middle last. I suppose Leonard does look a bit strange with his goggle glasses, but his scooter is cool.

9

Light Club is finished and I am waiting for Dad to pick me up on his way back from work. Sitting on a bench, I watch Lucy brush the floor to clear up bits of playdough and chunks of potato that spun off the table. The older children walk home by themselves but I'm not allowed to do that yet. It's a stupid rule because I know the way home and I'm sent-a-ball. I find a dustpan and brush under the table and try to help by sweeping up a few sweet wrappers that missed the bin. Next minute, Dad rushes in with his coat undone and his scarf flapping. He must have run from the station.

'Sorry I'm late.' He slumps to catch his breath, then he stands up straight. I can't understand why he does a silly wave at Lucy – she's right beside him! Lucy stops brushing the floor and holds the broom handle tight, making her knuckles show.

'Hello, Dad.' I stop cleaning up and move so that I stand between the two of them. Lucy sinks her chin onto the top of the broom handle and becomes much shorter than Dad but still taller than me. My dad is big as anything and he's got shiny skin on the front of his head. When I grow up, I want a big forehead same as Dad.

'Have you had a good time, Huxley?'

'Yes.'

'Huxley's very well behaved,' says Lucy. 'His first night at Light Club and he's joined in with everything. He always says *please* and *thank you*.'

'That's my boy.' Dad smiles like he is really chuffed and I am proud. I show my happy face to Dad but he's staring at Lucy. I grab hold of his jacket and shaking it, the coins in his pocket jangle. I think Dad is ignoring me.

'I didn't wash my hands after I went for a wee.'

Lucy jerks her head. 'You didn't what?'

'I had a wee and didn't wash my hands.'

'Is that all?' Dad laughs. 'There are worse things.'

Lucy and Dad are smiling at each other.

'Mum doesn't think so.'

'Let's not worry about it.' Dad starts patting me like I'm a shaggy dog but I don't mind.

'Are you going to come along next week, Huxley?'

'Yes.' I'm happy in the middle. It takes a whole minute of standing there to remember. 'Please.'

'I'll look forward to it.' Lucy brushes the floor again.

'We'd best be off, Huxley.' Dad holds my hand. We only walk two steps before he stops and turns around. 'Isn't there anyone to help you tidy up?'

'It's no problem,' says Lucy. 'We're going to recruit more helpers. You'd better be off home to Kirsty.'

'Okay.' Dad's on the move.

Yikes! I have to scramble out of the way. Somehow, he still manages to stumble over me.

'Sorry, mate.'

I'm not hurt and Dad didn't mean it. 'You can't help being butter feet.'

I am trying to be funny but Dad doesn't notice. He just gives me a little push and we head for the door. I don't understand what's happened to his sense of humour. Perhaps he doesn't know Mrs Ward calls everyone butter fingers.

We rush along the pavement to stop us from being cold. The problem is, I can't walk fast and talk at the same time. I scrape my trainers to be on a go-slow. It doesn't matter if they get marked – it's what they're for. I quite like being outside in the dark. The sky is a wizard's cloak with stars that blink on and off. It would be cool to have one like that … even better than Harry Potter's!

'Pick up the pace,' says Dad. 'We'll never get home with you dawdling.'

'I want to talk.'

'Okay.' Dad squeezes my hand. 'Tell me what you did at Light Club.'

'A sweet tin was passed around and we got to choose. I took one that was wrapped in green paper and it was chewy and chocolatey. I think I got the best sweet because a girl groaned soon as I pulled it out.'

'You have to keep sweets in your mouth, Huxley. Think of your manners.'

I wonder what he's going on about. 'I didn't pull it out of my mouth! She wasn't happy when I grabbed it from the tin.'

'That's okay, then,' says Dad. 'What else happened?'

'We sat in a circle and I had to share my good news and my bad news.'

'What did you say?'

'I said trains are good.'

'Not if there are leaves on the track. Whichever train I catch, it's always late.'

'I play with Thomas the Tank Engine and he's on time.' I smile at Dad and he smiles back. I'm clever at playing trains with Ben. We think up exciting games. 'I wish Ben was at Light Club.'

'This is your chance to find some new friends.'

'Making friends isn't easy.' I kick the paving where there's a broken bit. Dad pulls my arm so I don't have a chance to stop and have a proper look. 'Ben only likes me because Mum and Paula are best friends.'

'Tell me about it.'

Dad is looking straight ahead. I don't think he's listening properly. I'm not going to say it over again just because he asks me to. 'Wash your ears out.'

'Cheeky monkey.'

I run ahead to hide behind a tree. Soon as I hear footsteps coming close, I jump out but my dad is never scared.

'What was Lucy doing while you were at Light Club?'

'She helped on the potato-printing table. We had to take turns. It was hard to cut the potato into a shape. I made a diamond and used black paint to stamp around the edge of a big sheet of material. Lucy said I was making a great border pattern but I didn't finish it as the others needed a go.'

I swing my free hand through the air. This one is cold but the other is warm with Dad holding it. I blow breath on my fingers to heat them up.

'What did the cloth look like when everyone finished?'

'It was a bit messy. Some people can't keep their hands to themselves. It's going to be a Light Club banner but there were fingerprints everywhere. That's because the older ones barged until they fell over and Lucy told them off.'

'Good for Lucy.'

'The other table had playdough on it. We were supposed to make a plate of food using different colours. I made a banana and a pear, but one of the others put together a fried egg that looked really cool.'

'We had Play-doh when I was a kid,' says Dad. 'I loved the smell of it coming straight from the pot.'

I wonder what Dad's talking about. Lucy's playdough is made in a saucepan. She puts in drops of colour then adds loads of salt so no one will want to eat it. 'While I was rolling my playdough into a banana shape the boy next to me kept saying it's a doo-dah, it's a doo-dah.'

'He was being silly,' says Dad. 'Doo-dahs aren't normally yellow.'

'My willy's pink at the end where the skin's loose.'

Dad chuckles. 'Thank you for sharing.'

I have a laugh as well but I didn't even know I was being funny. Afterwards, we both go quiet. I'm not talking because I'm thinking about playdough. It's a good word and so is doo-dah. They both have two silly-balls and they make a happy tune. I skip along the pavement as I say the words in my head. Just then I remember the one Mum used and it rhymes with playdough.

'I know a word with three silly-balls that Mum thinks is very funny.'

'Three syllables, huh? That's quite long.'

'It rhymes with playdough. Can you guess what it is?'

'I'll have a think.' Dad stops walking and turns his head to watch the stars. A puff of breath comes from his mouth when he speaks. 'I've got it – rodeo.'

'Row-day-oh. It's got three silly-balls and it ends in oh, but it's not a word, is it?' I actually think Dad's cheating.

'You find rodeos in America. They have competitions for riding on bulls.'

'How am I supposed to know that?'

'True. Anyway, you've set me quite a challenge. Let's walk on a bit and I'll try to think of something better.'

There is a line of parked cars on my side of the road and also along the other one. Some houses have their lights on upstairs and downstairs. This means everyone is home for the night. I ate my tea before Light Club and I'll have a bath soon as I get in. It's going to be late to bed for me!

'I've got it,' says Dad. 'Libretto.'

Dad's word is quite close but I think he made it up. I practise my word in my head: lip-bee-dough. 'Yours sounds the same at the beginning and the end but the middle's wrong.'

'Suppose you tell me your word.'

Dad's not very good at guessing. 'Okay. It's lip-bee-dough.'

'That's not a word,' says Dad. 'Who's cheating?'

'It is a word,' I shout and my breath comes out like smoke. 'I heard Mum say it. Mum and Paula and Lucy were laughing and talking about sex and snogging.'

'Lip-bee-dough.' Dad stops walking again. 'Libido.'

'That's right.'

Dad's face is squished up to show he's confused. Now's a good time to remind him of the other news I just can't keep in. 'Mum rubbed Paula's back.'

'Hold on a minute.' Dad puts up his hand to stop me walking. 'What exactly happened?'

Doesn't he ever listen? 'Mum rubbed Paula's back when we got changed after swimming ... and then another time Mum and Paula and Lucy were saying the words sex and snogging and lip-bee-dough.'

'You were at the swimming baths, and the other stuff, all the talking was at home?'

He's finally got it. 'Correct!'

'And what were you doing?'

'We were watching *The Incredibles* ... most of the time.'

'Were you spying on Mum?'

I tip my chin up to make my head fall back. It's easy to count the stars in the sky like this.

'Admit it, Huxley.'

As I reach number five, my neck hurts so much I have to straighten up. Dad's wearing his serious face. I know I must tell the truth. 'It was just a game.'

'I'll have to get to the bottom of this.'

I'm happy because ha-ha-ha, it's not my bottom he needs to get to! This is funny but I don't want to share this very clever joke with Dad. His forehead has turned into lots of lines and that's a bad sign. There is also the fact he doesn't talk any more. We turn the corner to our house without saying another word.

10

I'm still hot from my bath so I jig in my pyjamas to let the air cool me. Mum searches the shelves for a book she hasn't read one hundred times before. She chooses Captain Underpants because Mum knows I enjoy these stories best. Swishing back the duvet, she lets me jump into bed then she squishes beside me. Captain Underpants comes in books with chapters so Mum has to start at the beginning. I know some of the words from the first page and I say them out loud as she reads. Our voices are happy. Mum smiles and strokes my hair. One good thing about my trip to the barber's shop is that Mum's nails don't catch. The story gets better and better. Mum is near the end of the chapter and I grab my pillow to squeeze it tight. A really funny bit is coming and I have to be ready. I don't want my laughter spilling out before the time is right. My skin stretches across my nose when I can't stop smiling. Mum makes me wait by dragging out each word. After she finishes, Mum snaps the book shut. I make my arms into the nose cone of a rocket and pretend I'm heading for Uranus like in one of the Captain Underpants adventures. My foot is tangled with the duvet and I splat onto the bed.

'No more messing.' Mum straightens the sleeves on my pyjamas that have rolled up in the rumpus. 'Time for sleep.'

'I can't help going crazy! The story is great.'

'I know.' Mum folds the corner of the page and packs the book away again. 'Under the covers and I'll give you a tuck in.'

'Okay.'

Mum pulls up the duvet, squashing it under my chin.

'Night-night,' she says.

I scrunch up my lips and Mum plonks her face next to mine. She makes a loud kissing sound but I am even noisier. I cling to her neck but she's too strong and pulls away.

'Love you lots.' She walks to the door. I'm not ready for her to go.

'I love you this much.' I hold my arms out wide-wide-wide.

She turns and smiles, 'You're not too old for that game?'

'No,' I say.

'I love you this much.' She stretches her arms, rushes towards me and scoops me up in one of her huge hugs. Her hair tickles my neck and I have to laugh. Next thing, she's kissing my face so that I'm squidgy and warm.

'Definitely time for sleep now.' She pats the duvet then switches off the light.

I hear her footsteps on the stairs so I shout after her, 'Love you more'.

She doesn't call back, so the game is over. Mum never shuts the door but leaves a gap to keep the darkness away. It's cosy in bed with my engines lined up next to me. I turn onto my side and whisper to them but having a chat is the last thing I remember until the engines roll off the bed. They're being naughty because they must stay in bed to have a good night's sleep. As I stretch to reach them, I tumble to the floor.

Whenever I fall out of bed, my mum and dad race to help me. I lie on the carpet rubbing my elbow but no one comes. Perhaps the bump wasn't loud enough. I think about ways to perfect my falling out of bed act. It's then the voices start. I don't need to have my bat ears working – I can hear most of the words! It sounds like a friendship has broken. I hope it's not the one between Mum and Dad. Straight after, the talk turns to shouting. Oh dear, oh dear. I want to find out what's happening. If I get a bit closer, I might be able to work everything out. Just then, I come up with a brilliant idea and it's not an excuse. I really want to do a poo. Well, I will squeeze my muscles to push something out. The toilet in the little room is better than the one in the bathroom.

It's got a wooden seat I can sit on for ages because I need to think hard for doing a number two.

Creeping down, I'm pleased the stairs don't make a noise. From the cloakroom, I hear the words Mum and Dad say. I don't shut the door as that makes it go clunk but I pull it so a finger of light slips in.

Mum says, 'Calm down, Jed.'

It goes quiet then Dad is half laughing and half shouting. 'What's everyone going to think? You know what the gossip's like around here.'

'Who's going to say anything? It's only Huxley's chatter.'

Hearing my name sends my ears hot and tingly.

'If he tells other people what he said to me, there'll be all sorts of questions.'

'Like what?'

'Like you're having an affair with Paula.'

'Don't be ridiculous.' There's a clank-clank-clank and I guess Mum is cleaning the pans that are too big for the dishwasher. 'No one would believe it!'

'People always get the wrong end of the stick. You do spend a lot of time with Paula.'

'What else are we supposed to do? Hours and hours in the company of little kids is not exactly stimulating.'

Stink-you-baking? I snigger then slap my hand over my mouth. I wonder how a stinky cake tastes. Not very nice!

'Acting like sensible adults might help,' shouts Dad over the pan noises.

'You've got room to criticise? Don't forget about Lucy and the rocket cake fiasco.'

'That's nothing compared with you and Paula canoodling,' booms Dad.

Now Mum is crash-crash-crashing the pans and it's so loud my bat ears ache. 'We were in the changing room at the swimming baths! Trust Huxley to misunderstand.'

'Give me that tea towel and I'll dry up if you stop making such a racket.'

'What about your shouting?'

Quiet happens all of a sudden. My thoughts are floaty as a feather soon as there's nothing to hear. I sway around because listening really hard gets me dizzy. I jump off the toilet but there's no need to flush as I didn't do anything. I pull up my pyjama bottoms and by accident, I crash against the door. It bangs open and hits the wall with a clonk. I hide beside the toilet. In the dark Mum and Dad will never see me. When the light switch goes on, I am a cricket bat, stiff and straight. I have to blink back the shine.

'What are you doing in here?' asks Dad.

His face is a moon and there's Mum's face next to his. She is the sun. I know the sun goes round the moon and that's why we can see it each evening.

'Have you got a tummy ache?' asks Mum.

I nod and give my tummy a rub.

'Of course, he hasn't. He's been earwigging our conversation. Let's be having you.' Dad reaches over, grips me under my arms and lifts me up.

I scrunch my eyelids together as I don't want to answer any questions.

'Give him here.' I'm passed from Dad to Mum like a package. Mum can't hold me for long now I'm big, so we drop into a huddle on the stairs.

'Stop your messing, Huxley,' says Dad. 'You should be in bed.'

'I only came down because you were shouting.' I tuck my head under Mum's chin.

'We're not shouting now.' Mum pats my back and jigs me around. 'Shush-shush-shush.'

'Don't go all soft on him,' says Dad.

My dad isn't being kind so I try to get him back. 'Dad was gooey over Lucy at Light Club.'

'Tell me something new,' says Mum.

'This time Lucy was gooey back.'

Mum turns my face to make me look straight at her, 'What was she doing?'

'I can't believe this,' says Dad.

'She was smiling at him with dog eyes.'

'As if,' says Dad.

'Like this.' I open and close my eyes very quickly then I put my hands around my chin. Mum stops jiggling me on her knees so I snuggle against her.

'Christ, Jed. You should know better!'

Dad screws up his face. 'You believe Huxley over me?'

'I'll be speaking to Lucy. This is beyond a joke.'

'You're not serious,' says Dad. 'I mean, look at him.'

'Face of an angel,' says Mum.

The way they're talking about me is nice but Dad's eyebrows are flat. There are lines on his forehead, too.

'Take him off to bed before he causes more trouble.'

Dad doesn't give me a goodnight kiss because he goes to put the kettle on. It's Mum who chases me up the stairs and into my room. She presses the pillow around my shoulders and flattens the duvet. When she leaves, I listen for the creak from the corner step as she goes down. Bubbles of words reach me from the kitchen. I am safe and happy in my house with my mum and dad.

11

'I've already accepted the invitation.' Mum's voice catapults into my bedroom.

'You could've asked me first,' says Dad.

'Didn't have a chance,' says Mum. 'Besides it's only supper and we can always say Huxley needs an early night if you want to escape early.'

My ears prick up. What are they talking about? It's Saturday and things are different at weekends. I fill my chest with breath and shout, 'I can stay up late – it's the Saturday rule'.

Everything goes quiet and I think I'm being ignored, then Mum shows up in her fluffy dressing gown.

'You're right, darling.'

'Then why did you say it?'

'Never mind, let's start the day. Later, we'll have a lovely evening round at Ben's house.'

'Oh good!' I am filled with excitement. 'Saturday means I can stay in my pyjamas until lunchtime.'

'Okay, there's no rush. Have a little play.'

There's lots to do in my bedroom when my engines want to go on an adventure. They go trundle-trundle-trundle and that's the sign Thomas and James are ready to race. I turn my duvet into Mount Everest to see if they're better at getting to the top than me. James has enough steam to race right up in a straight line, but Thomas goes round and round like a can in the opening machine. Next thing I hear is splattering water coming from the bathroom. Someone is in the shower. This gives me an idea! James can't reach the top because there's an avalanche that squelches him back to the start. Thomas is the champion. Hurray! He always wins because he's clever. My game is like the story Mrs Ward told in class. The one about the tortoise and the hare. It means slow and steady is okay.

My mum says the shower is temper-and-mental and it'll be the next bloody thing to go wrong. I have a bath most nights so I don't care but Mum finds it hard to wash her hair without a hose. Sometimes the shower drips on me when I'm in the bath, a fat cold plop on my head always makes me jump. I go into the bathroom to see what's happening. There's a traffic jam! Mum's foot sticks out from behind the shower curtain and then the rest of her appears. She's wrapped up in a towel and today she is the filling in a fig roll. Soon as she moves away, Dad drops his pyjamas and shows his hairy bottom. He forgets to put the end of the shower curtain inside the bath and Mum is grumpy. We don't want another flood! I get busy doing a wee and jiggle around so a yellow river slides down the water hole. Mum tells me to be quick. I do a final spurt and then put the seat down.

Dad spends the day messing around with the breadmaker. Tony's not getting the better of Dad with his homemade beer and organ-sick vegetables. Mum says he's fussing but Dad means to show off with his wholemeal bread. She says it's not much of a gift so she puts a few twigs into a bowl and stuffs a candle in the middle. I don't understand why they're going on and on. Me and Mum are always dropping by at Paula's, although having the dads along is a special oak-station. I am so funny! Special oak-station means special occasion! I'm laughing so much my tummy wobbles. I have to be calm as Mum is giving me a strange look. It's not fair that she doesn't like my jokes and I have to keep them in my head. Mum tries again with the candle display. After hours of work, she dumps it in the bin. I am not surprised – it wasn't very good.

We set off. Mum's bag has two bottles of wine in it and they clink together as she walks. I want to hold Dad's loaf but he says it's still warm and he doesn't want it ruined. He carries the loaf wrapped in tissue and it looks like he's got a baby in his arms.

'I want a sister or brother.' I don't mind which but I'm fed up with being an only.

'Not now.' Mum's heard it all before.

Because no one talks, I decide to dawdle. This means walking very slowly. I hang back long enough to take Thomas the Tank Engine from my pocket. Outside the corner house, I show him where goldfish live in the pond. I expect he'd want to go on an underwater search for treasure, but I can't throw him in and risk drowning.

'Come on, Huxley,' says Mum. 'It's cold.'

I have to hurry up because they're waiting for me. With my gloves and scarf and hat I'm warm. Mum isn't wearing anything on her head as it mucks up her hair. Too bad she has to wear a helmet when we cycle – that's the law! I run along the road to catch up. They're waiting for me to ring the bell as it's my job. It's a big surprise to see Nanny Phil open the door. I laugh because I know what's going to happen and there's a great rumpus with her dig and poke routine. Mum and Dad watch until Dad pushes past us, and Nanny Phil shoves over to let Mum inside.

After we've got our coats and shoes off (we're allowed to keep our socks on), Dad takes the wine and bread into the kitchen where Tony is cooking. Everyone else bundles into the front room. Mum and Paula start chattering so I watch Ben play with his finger-football boots. These live in a tin with a goal and a mini football. He lets me have a go but as he's defending, I don't stand a chance. I leave him to play while I find out what Juno's reading. Sitting with her blanket on the sofa, she's staring at the pages of her book so hard, she doesn't see me. I expect it's her best book, the one about fairies, and she won't want to share. Mum and Paula are also on the sofa and this means Nanny Phil has to sit by herself in the armchair.

'Come here.' She squiggles her bottom to free a tiny triangle of space for me. 'Park your bum.'

Paula looks over but doesn't say anything so I cram onto the chair. It's very tight and not easy to breathe with Nanny Phil's arm wrapped around me. I give her a quick poke to make her budge over.

'Are you enjoying school with your new teacher?'

I've been in Mrs Ward's class forever. 'It's okay.'

'I bet you're the same as Ben and playtime is your favourite.'

That's when Ben's busy with football and I'm left out. 'Going home is best.'

Nanny Phil laughs. 'Don't you have a favourite lesson?'

'Not really.' PE is good when the climbing bars are set out but I can't be bothered talking about it.

'There must be something good,' she says.

I have a long think. 'Samira plays fun games.'

'Samira, eh?' says Nanny Phil.

Paula's eyes are half closed. I'm surprised she can see. Nanny Phil holds up her hands as if she's had enough.

'There's no need to pull a face, Paula,' says Nanny Phil. 'I've no intention of saying it again.'

'It's not just me who believes you're wrong,' says Paula.

'Saying what?' I ask.

'Words,' says Nanny Phil.

I think I know what they're on about. 'Like four-in-ear?'

Nanny Phil's eyebrows hunch together. She usually gets my jokes and this one's easy because she says this word all the time.

'Foreigner?'

Finally, she's got it! But Paula hisses and Mum shakes her head.

Nanny Phil chuckles. 'The sooner Brexit's done the better.'

'But Samira was born here!' says Paula.

'And her family's not from Europe,' says Mum.

Nanny Phil shrugs. 'Can't help what I believe.'

Paula opens her eyes so wide, her eyeballs might pop out. 'You can't go around saying that. Get with the times, Mum.'

Nanny Phil doesn't say anything, just starts to hum. It's a tune I don't know although it seems to make her happy. Paula and Mum begin to chat and they're not including Nanny Phil in their talk. I really don't understand but it's to do with Samira and what Nanny Phil says. I think Paula and Mum are leaving Nanny Phil out and that's not kind. If Nanny Phil is saying not nice things about Samira that isn't kind either. Oh dear, oh dear! Nanny Phil digs me in the ribs and everything flies from my brain. I have to laugh.

The mums cook most of the time but for a special oak-station, Dad and Tony do their bit. Dad is on waiting duty and comes in to find out what we want to drink. He says a G and T will please the ladies. Me, Ben and Juno have juice. At Paula's house this comes straight from the fridge so it's nice and cold. I gulp mine back like it's a race. Strange thing is, soon as my beaker's empty, no one offers me more.

In the dining room, Dad's bread is on the table. It's the shape of a bell landed on its side and takes up a lot of room. We squeeze in to let everyone sit and then Tony brings in a big, hot bowl of chicken something or other. A spoonful lands on my plate. There are pasta shapes and this means it will taste okay. Paula gives me some cherry tomatoes and sticks of cucumber in a little bowl. With a long knife in his hand, Dad starts carving up the loaf he's made. It's hard to saw through but when the end falls away, the bread is brown on the outside and a cave in the middle.

'I can't imagine what's gone wrong.' Dad picks off a bit of crust. 'It tastes okay.'

'Not any good for making a sandwich,' says Mum.

'Use it to mop up the sauce,' says Dad.

'Ta-dah.' Tony appears again and this time he's showing off a proper-shaped loaf on a special board.

'Impressive,' says Dad. 'But making white bread is a whole lot easier. It's to do with the yeast.'

'This isn't just any old loaf. This is tiger bread. See the way the glaze is evenly striped.'

'Grrr.' Paula growls like a tiger.

'Grrr, grrr,' Ben joins in.

Tony holds the blade against the bread and bits flake off as he cuts. The slice is white and holey. What a shame! I thought the stripes would go right the way through. All of a sudden, I remember the marks on Paula's tummy and words blurt out, 'Tiger bread and tiger tummy!'

Nobody is interested in what I'm saying, so I try again in a very big voice, 'Paula's got lines on her tummy like a tiger!'

'Shush, Huxley,' says Mum.

The whole table goes quiet. Mum looks at Dad and then at Paula.

'What's that?' Tony's face is all confused.

Paula shakes her head. 'There's no need to discuss my stretch marks at the table.'

Dad bursts out laughing. 'You've got to hand it to Huxley, he always sees the funny side.'

'Not now!' says Mum.

'Oops. Let's call this an example of foot in mouth syndrome, Huxley,' says Dad. 'You know, saying the wrong thing. At least we're in it together, mate.'

The mums are cross with us for getting our feet in the way but I like being mates with Dad.

By the time pudding is brought out, everyone is happy again. This pudding is called fool which I think is silly. Me and Ben shout *fool* with each spoonful Paula dishes up. Everyone joins in and even Dad and Tony are now in a good mood. When I take a close look, there are specks of red in the pink colour. 'Looks a bit like sick.'

'Shush,' says Mum. 'That's not a kind thing to say.'

'It's pink like ham,' says Nanny Phil. 'Don't suppose I'm allowed to talk about ham either.'

'Stop being silly, Mum,' says Paula. 'It's raspberry so everyone should be pleased.'

The pudding tastes of custard and it goes in my mouth and down my throat without the need for chewing. Glug-glug-glug and it's all gone.

'We've survived dinner,' says Dad. 'Shall I make some coffee?'

'You stay put,' says Tony. 'I'll do the drinks in my own house.'

'Not if I give you a hand.'

'Stop your squabbling,' says Nanny Phil. 'I'll do it.'

Me and Ben leave our parents sitting at the table. It's best to escape because we're full of dinner and there aren't any more treats. In the front room, we start piling cushions from the sofa to make a tower. Watching from her own special chair, Juno sucks her thumb. She doesn't join our game and this means we can be extra rough. Taking it in turns, we ram into the pile like we are strong enough to knock over a block of flats. This reminds me of Leonard.

'Do you want to go to Leonard's place one day? He lives at the top of town.'

'We're not allowed.' Ben thumps a cushion, trying to change its shape.

'He's got chocolate and DVDs.'

Just as Ben is ready to answer, he charges at me and gives a huge cry. 'Aargh!'

Coming in to see what's going on, Nanny Phil doesn't tell us off but picks up Juno.

'I'd best be taking you off to bed.' Nanny Phil cuddles Juno and carries her out.

It's only now we're being quiet again that we hear voices. They keep saying Brexit this, Brexit that and then Paula's saying Brexit-ear. Me and Ben sit with our backs against the wall and stretch out our legs.

'What does Brexit mean?' asks Ben.

I know the answer because my dad told me. 'There's a place called Europe and there's our country and Brexit means breaking it off.'

'No, it's about bread and eggs it.'

He's got it wrong but his words make a puzzle in my head. Ben smiles, 'It's a joke!'

I nod my head and put my arm around his shoulder. We're good at being funny! Voices from the other room keep coming – they can't stop.

'Do your mum and dad fall out much?' I ask.

'Sometimes,' says Ben. 'Mum gets more cross with Nanny Phil for saying stuff.'

'Like four-in-ear?'

'Yeah. And other things.'

Just then, Nanny Phil comes back. 'Your sister's out like a light, Ben. I might as well be off home now.'

Ben's shoulders jump up and down. It's a strange way to say goodbye.

'I'll see you soon.' Nanny Phil kisses Ben's cheek then plonks her lips on the top of my head. Ben wipes away the wet but I don't mind. She waves and walks backwards to the door. 'I'll see myself out. Ben, let Mum know I've gone when she surfaces. There's absolutely no point in me joining the discussion.'

We have another game of towers. This time we try standing on top of the cushions like we're statues. It's hard to stay straight and Ben cheats. He barges against me until I can't balance. I pretend I'm leaving the room to tell Mum but Ben drags me back and calls me a baby. That's the signal for wrestling to start. First, he jumps on top of me and spreads his arms and legs same as a spider. Then I slip through a gap and pounce on Ben. He's too quick and flips me over so that he's on top again. I can't move and Ben has squashed me into a pancake. I have to cry out in case this is the last breath I'm ever going to take.

'Off you get.' Tony grabs Ben's arm and pulls him away.

Mum helps me up. 'Where's Nanny Phil?'

'Putting Juno to bed,' says Paula.

'Juno's asleep and Nanny Phil's gone home,' says Ben.

'Without saying goodbye?' Paula turns to Mum. 'Do you think she heard us talking?'

Mum's lips are a flat line and her eyebrows turn into semicircles. 'Bloody Brexit is making us all loopy.'

'Well, it can't be an excuse for saying things that upset people.'

Oh dear, I hope I didn't upset Paula about the tiger tummy. I don't want to be left out like Nanny Phil. Grabbing Mum's arm, I pull her close. 'Is Paula cross with me and Dad?'

'You'd better not talk about Paula's tummy to anyone else,' says Mum. 'But, I think she's got other things to worry about.'

'What?' asks Paula.

'Who will babysit if Philippa's gone off in a huff?'

'Christ,' says Paula. 'I hadn't thought of that.'

Me and Mum go to church on Sunday. She's on the rota for serving coffee after the service and it's too late to swap. We get there early to set out the cups and saucers. It's great shouting *good morning* to people as they go past the coffee bar and into church. Mum isn't keen on me doing all the talking and she sets me some work. My job means putting cups on top of the circles pressed into the saucers. I am being helpful and it's fun building a tower. I bet it's like the block of flats where Leonard lives. I wonder if he's coming to church.

'Oh Huxley.' Mum takes the top storey off. 'They'll be knocked over.'

'They won't,' I say. 'I've done it properly.'

'Here.' She gives me a fistful of spoons. 'Put these out.'

Spoons go onto saucers next to the cups. They make a chinking noise as I drop them. Sometimes they slip-slide around. I am busy and being careful so I don't have a chance to look for Leonard. After we've finished, we sneak into the church through a side door. We are the last ones to arrive and everybody is already standing to sing. We can't go to the front row easy-peasy as there's a mobility scooter in the way. I think it must be Leonard's! So, he is here and I've been too busy to say hello. I turn sideways and move like a crab to go around the scooter. I watch Mum do the same and then it's hurry-hurry-hurry.

I slump on a chair beside Lucy on the front row and Mum sits behind. Lucy shows me a happy smile, but I'm in a bad mood because Mum has tricked me into not seeing Leonard. I fold my arms and press my lips out. If I had a pencil, I could hold it there and use my nose to keep it in place. Everyone on my table at school laughed when I had a pencil moustache! I can't act funny in church so it's another reason for being in a bad mood.

'Sit up straight,' whispers Lucy. 'After five more minutes, we can have some fun.'

I don't want to listen to the man with the microphone. There are clouds filling my head. These are humpy and bumpy same as the way I'm feeling. Lucy nods and gives me staring-eye messages. This means I have to look where she's looking – at the man. He's boring and he's not wearing the black dress I think is funny. I don't like the colour of his tie, either. It's brown and I don't like brown because it's the colour of poo. Then, I remember it's also the colour of chocolate. I wonder if Leonard has any Cadbury chocolate in the basket of his scooter. I turn around to look but it's no good trying to see with a forest of heads in the way. The music starts – I'm not joining in singing because I'm grumpy. Next minute, my fingers are twitching because they know they're needed. I am the loudest clapper in church and I don't want anyone to be better than me. Clapping makes my hands hot and this sends all the rubbish thoughts flying out of my head.

Lucy leads the line and I am at the front of the children. We leave the grown-ups in church to do praying. Being first into the church hall is another reason for starting to feel better. I race for a chair and plonk down. You have to be quick or you're left to sit on a bit of old carpet they roll out each week. There's a lot of blah-blah-blahing from the leader of Junior Church. Afterwards, we go to the tables to play games. The oldest children choose what we play and I'm not happy that my table is stuck with Ludo. I let out a groan as I've played it one hundred times before. I'm given the blue counter and that makes everything start to get nicer. This colour is lucky for me but the game takes ages. I'm not winning and I want it to stop. I wish and wish to go running around. Suddenly, my wishing comes true! The door to the courtyard is open and we are allowed out. I spin around in a circle looking at the sky. The clouds are thick as a duvet. Just as I'm thinking this, someone lands a hand on my shoulder. I turn but I can't work out who got me. It might be Zac but there are lots of smiling faces. They all know the thing I don't (the person that made me *it*). I have to rush and get someone back, but everyone scatters soon as I'm close. Then, they're standing in a circle around me. I stamp my foot as if I'm ready to chase and they dash away. This is a good joke because I'm only kidding. The ones that were tricked come piling back to the group. In a bit, I really do start running and I get the boy trapped in the corner. I tap his arm and rush off so he can't catch me.

It starts drizzling and we go inside to stay out of the wet. There's only story time and then Junior Church is over. We have to sit and wait and listen for a bit longer. At the end, the mums and dads collect the little children. I am sent-a-ball and can walk to the coffee bar on my own. The second I set off, I hear Lucy say, 'Hang on, Huxley'.

I have to stop.

'Are you going to find your mum?'

'Yes.'

'Let me hold the door open for you.' She gives it a push and then stands in the way to stop it closing. 'I'll wait here and watch while you find Kirsty.'

I make my eyes spin around as this is a very silly thing to say. 'She's only in the coffee bar.'

'I know,' says Lucy. 'I just want you to get there in one piece.'

One what? Lucy said piss instead of piece! Ha-ha-ha. I don't need the toilet! I start walking through the church very fast. I'm so funny I might explode! Half way along, I stop to lean against the wall because laughing blows all the breath out of me. I turn to see Lucy still standing there, watching me.

'Get a move on, Huxley,' she calls.

I set off again and it takes one second to reach the coffee bar. I hide next to the counter.

'I see you, Huxley!' says Mum.

Bum! Now Mum's found me and all I want to do is look for Leonard.

'Give me a hand with loading the dishwasher.'

'Okay.' But, I don't really feel like helping.

Mum grabs my hand and wraps my fingers around a bundle of dirty spoons. They have to stand with their faces poking up in the basket. After I'm finished, I take a sneaky look around the end of the counter. Leonard is sitting beside a table on his electric scooter. Next thing, he's zipping in and buttoning up his coat. Oh blast! That means he's going home. I have to do something now or I won't be able to talk to him. Only, I think Mum can read my mind. She comes over and grips my shoulders, turning me back behind the counter. Leonard is on the other side of the coffee bar but it's too high for me to see him. I will talk to him anyway.

'Hello, Leonard,' I call.

'Morning, Leonard.' Mum talks louder than me and my words get covered by her voice.

'Wonderful service!' Leonard's scooter is humming. 'Although I must be off.'

'Good idea,' says Mum.

One of the helpers bangs another tray of dirty cups on the counter.

'We'd better sort these.' Mum sloshes leftover drink into the sink and starts putting cups on the dishwasher rack. It's then I see the purple wrapping of a bar of Cadbury dancing in the air. (Not by itself, it's in Leonard's hand!)

'I'll save this for another time,' comes a wizard's voice and the bar of chocolate disappears.

I have to laugh. Mum's lining up saucers in the bottom tray and doesn't notice. It's mine and Leonard's little secret.

Mum finds more dirty spoons and it's my job to load them in the basket. As I poke them in place, I wonder why Mum doesn't like Leonard. It's too bad for me because he's the only grown-up that gets my jokes. When I've finished with the spoons, I kick the wall where there's a crack and little bits of dust crumble to the floor. Crouching, I swipe the dirt into a hole by the cupboard so that I won't be told off, but this makes my hands messy.

'What are you doing now, Huxley?'

I don't want to tell her why I'm on the floor.

'Look at your mucky hands.'

I can't rub off the dirt onto my trousers with Mum watching.

'Nip to the ladies loo,' says Mum. 'You can wash off the bits in there.'

'I'll go to the proper toilet in the church hall.'

'That'll take forever. I'll stand outside and I'll explain if anyone needs it.'

The light in the ladies goes on by itself. I run some water and reach the container of soap easy-peasy. Sticking my hands under the dryer, it's so noisy Mum will know I've done a good job. She decides to hop in after me – now it's my turn to be on guard. Zac and his mum are standing with a man I've seen in church but I've never talked to him. I watch Zac's mum's shiny lips move then she takes Zac's hand and starts rolling back his sleeve ... oh no! I hope she's not going to ... I squeeze my eyes shut. I don't want to watch and then I'm all hot because I can guess what's happening. I open my eyes for a moment and the man is shaking his head. I bet the bruise has nearly gone. Zac's mum catches me watching and says in a loud voice, 'There's been a reconciliation since Huxley apologised'. I want to shout out, *Mrs Ward made me!* Although this is true, I don't say anything.

Mum comes out of the toilet and sees what's going on with Zac and his mum and the man. She yanks me back to the coffee bar by tugging my top. When we get there, I have to pull my clothes straight. Mum is standing beside the pole that keeps the ceiling up and she's holding her hand in front of her mouth. She can't stop staring and I think her eyes are getting water in them. Just then, Lucy comes over. I squash against the wall to make room for her to pass.

'Hey,' she says to Mum. 'What's up?'

Mum wipes her eyes. 'See who's spreading gossip.'

Lucy turns to watch the three of them in a huddle. 'What's she going on about this time?'

'Remember the letter that came home from school?' says Mum.

'She's not still talking about the B.I.T.E.' Lucy spells the word. This is because she doesn't want me to understand. But I can work out what letters mean.

'Everything's such a mess.' Mum takes a tissue from her sleeve and snuffles.

'Don't worry,' says Lucy. 'It'll blow over.'

Zac and his mum wave goodbye to the man. They step through the doorway and onto the pavement. Mum crumples the tissue and sticks it in her sleeve.

'It's typical of you to down play everything!' Mum's face is pink and her eyes have gone to specks. 'Reminds me of your flirting with Jed. *It doesn't mean anything!*'

'Hold on,' says Lucy. 'That's not the same.'

'It's one thing after another at the moment. The bloody flirting … the bloody…'

Mum looks at me and gulps. I have a gulp, too. I think I know what's in her mind. It doesn't take a genius to guess when she's just seen Zac.

'Bloody biting?' I say.

Mum's eyes go round in a circle like juggling balls. 'I was going to say bloody cake.'

'We're not back to that again.' Lucy crosses her arms and her shoulders are nearly up to her ears. 'It wasn't my fault Jed got overexcited about a rocket cake.'

'As we're talking cakes,' says Mum, 'you can stuff it.'

'Stuff it with what?' Lucy laughs. It's the sort of ha-ha-ha that flies away. No one joins in. I knock my trainers together and watch to see if I leave marks on the white toe caps.

'Let's not fall out,' says Lucy. 'Nothing's going on.'

'How do I know?' Mum's voice is sharp – I think she's angry. When I turn my head to look at her, I am right. She's stiff with no bend in her bones. I press my back against the wall. I want to be so flat they don't notice me.

'Come on, Kirsty. We shouldn't be talking about this here.'

'Why ever not? Seems to me you should take the Christian teachings seriously. Flirting with my husband isn't very amusing.'

Lucy's mouth falls open like she can't believe what she's heard. 'It's only a bit of fun!'

I am a poster stuck to the wall. I need peeling off.

'Come on, Huxley.' Mum grabs my wrist and tugs me away from the coffee bar.

'Best you think on, Lucy.' Mum shouts this over her shoulder as we head outside. The coast is clear for going home as Zac and his mum are away. Sometimes, I just don't understand Mum. I know I should be ash-aimed about what I did to Zac, but I think Mum should be ash-aimed about the way she's been to Lucy.

13

Ben is catching up. His birthday is soon and he'll be seven like me. Paula is round our house talking about his party. This means me and Ben and Juno can watch a DVD. *Pirates of the Caribbean* is too scary for Juno so we have *The Incredibles* again. I've seen it one hundred times before, but it doesn't matter because I'm with Ben and Juno.

Sitting still isn't easy when my bottom is itchy. It's not the same as getting flea bites from Barley the cat – they make me want to scratch and scratch. An itchy bottom means I've got to move around. First, I roll sideways alongside Juno and she puts her hand over my face. Her fingers are baby carrots and I give one a nibble. She pushes me away and I squiggle next to Ben. He lets me stay there for a minute, then he gives me a shove that has me slip-sliding to the floor. I wish for him to copy me or start a play fight. It's a shame he's staring at the TV. On the carpet, I pretend I'm a soldier crawling over mud but even this doesn't interest Ben. It's no good. I decide to go and see what Mum and Paula are doing. I peep around the doorway to the kitchen and find them sitting on the floor. There are hoops, tins and trays for making cakes dropped around the place. These things are usually in the cupboard and grown-ups prefer to sit on chairs. I am confused by this so I squat down ready for a watch and listen.

Paula gives a puff that sends her fringe flapping. 'This is hopeless! I'll have to find something else. Ben insists on 3D.'

'You could try going to Skinners. They might have what you need in the kitchen department. Or at least a bowl that could go into the oven.'

Paula holds her head between her hands. 'I should never have promised him a football cake.'

So that's what it's about. I go back to the lounge. Juno laughs at the TV and when she gets excited the bunch of hair on top of her head flicks around. Ben lies back taking up my place on the sofa. I squeeze beside him and he budges over. 'I know what sort of cake you're going to have.'

He doesn't answer because he's staring at the TV.

'You're having a special birthday cake.'

He's smiling at the cartoons.

'It will be a football cake.'

'Yeah!' He sits up all excited. 'I'm having a football cake and it's a spear.'

'A spear?'

'Yes. It's got to look like a real football. You know, round as a spear.'

'You mean sphere.'

I'm happy that I say the word properly. Ben screws up his face because he's wrong. Folding his arms, Ben shows me he's fed up so I give him a nudge but he moves away. He doesn't want me around. I creep out of the room and go back to my spying place. The cake tins are packed away and Mum and Paula are at the table.

'How about mini-footballs?' says Mum. 'You can roll a chocolate truffle mixture into shape. One for each child. I heard cupcakes are very popular at girls' parties.'

'He's set his heart on a real-sized football. Anything else and he'll be disappointed.'

'We can't have that now, can we?'

'Shut up,' says Paula.

'If Tony had won that bloody auction lot instead of Jed you could've had a rocket cake.'

'That's not good enough, unfortunately. Maybe I could ask Lucy to help. Or could you put in a word for me?'

'I've fallen out with her,' says Mum. 'It was a stupid argument.'

'What happened?'

I guess Mum is going to tell Paula about it. I don't want to hang around because I've heard it before. Boring. Back in the lounge *The Incredibles* are boring, too. I do a little dance so that Ben will play with me. Juno thinks it's funny and scrambles over to join in. At last! Ben isn't going to be left out and we have a game of monkeys jumping on the bed. We're not on the bed but that doesn't matter. The sofa is nearly as bouncy. When we've had a proper jump, we tumble together and land in a heap. Ben crawls out from underneath me and Juno. He's not squashed like a toothpaste tube, thank goodness.

'Juno and Ben.' It's Paula calling. Me and Ben know this means it's time for him to go home. He darts behind the chair and I squeeze between the wall and the sofa. Juno begins to blub because she's left out and Paula starts cooing to cheer her up. Next thing I know, the TV is switched off and the whole room goes quiet. I can't make a sound or I'll get caught.

'I know you boys are hiding.'

I swallow. Huxley Griffiths is my name, still and squashy is my game.

'Come on boys. I'm going to count backwards from five and then you can both jump out and give me a scare.'

'Five, four, three, two...' Paula treads around. 'Where are you?'

There's a swishing noise and that means she's pulling back the curtains. A little squeal leaves my lips.

'That's two, now number one.'

Ben growls. He's a giveaway.

'Keep quiet,' I shout. Now I'm a giveaway.

'Out you come,' Paula drags the sofa away from the wall and it's like she's shining a light on me. Bother. 'Found you, Huxley. Now where's Ben?'

'I am good at keeping secrets,' I say.

Ben's head pops up from behind the chair. 'No, you're not. You told me about Leonard.'

'What about Leonard?' Paula's face is scrunched up and then Mum is right beside her.

'Yes, what about Leonard?' Mum stands with her hands on her hips.

'Your arms are making triangles,' I say.

Mum's face turns from me to Ben and back. 'One of you has to tell the truth.'

'He took money out of Leonard's bank.' Ben creeps from his hiding hole.

'I am disc-gust-ted.' I try to make a joke because Ben is such a teller-on. I want to get busy and forget everything, so I push the sofa back to its place.

'Disgusted? What do you mean?' A slit appears on Mum's forehead. I don't know what to say.

'Ha-ha-ha!' Ben's laughing at me.

I know how to get him back. 'Leonard gave Ben two squares of Cadbury chocolate when we were at the park.'

'What?' says Paula.

'And he ate it all up!' I say.

'Oh my God!' says Paula. 'Leonard's giving sweets to children. He could be a paedophile!'

'Hold on a minute!' says Mum. 'He might be weird but he goes to church every week.'

'Exactly!'

'You wouldn't be worried if he was handing out Green & Black's seventy per cent cocoa.'

'Not funny,' says Paula.

'This business with the bank is far more worrying.'

'Come over here, Ben,' says Paula.

He trudges next to her just as my mum drops onto one knee and looks into my eyes.

'It's okay,' I say. 'I think you might be proud. I pressed the numbers for Leonard to get his money.'

'When was this?'

She holds my arms in her pincer-crab fingers. The back of my neck stretches as I look at the bits of brown in the carpet. The specks are small as stars in the sky.

'Tell me, Huxley.'

'You know when I promised to stay by the train track in Skinners?'

'Yes.'

'Well, Leonard knocked on the door and I was being polite.'

I don't say any more in case that's enough.

'And then?'

She doesn't sound too angry.

'I went out of Skinners to help him take money from the cash machine.'

'No!' says Mum. 'You were supposed to stay put!'

I can't see what Mum's doing. I'm looking down again and staring hard and wishing the specks on the carpet really were stars. Then her cheek is warm next to my face. Paula and Ben are around us like a rubber ring.

Mum says, 'I only left him in Skinners for a few minutes. It was an emergency at the office … and Tony wasn't there to sort it.'

'What were you thinking of?' says Paula. 'Don't try blaming Tony.'

'Let's get to the point,' says Mum. 'What the hell was Leonard thinking?'

Mum puts her hand under my chin and squeezes my cheeks. We're eyeball to eyeball. 'I need to know everything, Huxley. Tell me exactly what happened.'

It's the half term holiday but I don't get to watch TV in my pyjamas. Mum has to be in the office so she drops me at Ben's house. His bedroom is at the front and it's called a box room. Barley sleeps in the recycling box that lives on our porch. I think this makes Barley and Ben the same but Ben says it's not a proper joke. I won't say it again. Underneath Ben's bed there are drawers and a cupboard and he's got a rug and curtains that are the colour of broccoli. Juno's room is bigger with a cot and a bed. She'll sleep in the bed soon as she's old enough. For now, Paula uses it in the middle of the night to stop Tony's snoring driving her nuts.

My house has a very big kitchen with a table and some of my toys. There are more things to play with in the lounge. At Ben's house, the kitchen isn't big enough to swing a cat but that's not a kind thing to do. I'm sure Barley wouldn't like it. When I get there, I find Ben and Juno sitting at the table in the dining room. They have their own special chairs and Juno is almost as big as Ben. I have to sit on an ordinary chair so I am small. Paula's in her dressing gown and her hair's tied on top of her head.

'Have a grape.' She pushes a plastic bowl towards me. There are green ones and red ones. I take a red one because it's small then she gives me a whole handful to eat.

'I had my breakfast.' I stare at the mound.

'Have some more,' she says. 'Eat your five-a-day fruit in the morning to put wholesome food in your tummy.'

Ben leans over and grabs a few of my grapes. I gobble up the rest in a race to finish first.

'Off you go, boys,' says Paula. 'You can watch TV while I sort out Juno.'

We fight over the remote control, then Ben shoots me with it and I die. Lying flat on the carpet, the woolly bits tickle my nose but I'm not moving. Once you're dead, you have to stay still. I'm good at this until Ben tries rest-us-station and brings me back to life by hammering on my chest. It hurts a bit so I get him back by rolling on top of him. Snatching the remote, I pow-pow-pow the machine gun. It's Ben's turn to die and he lands on the sofa. He's got his slippers on and it doesn't matter if his feet are on the cushions. I'm not allowed to wear my shoes at Ben's house in case they make marks.

I think wrestling is more fun so we stop playing with the remote. Ben stands on the sofa ready to do a Spider-Man jump. Dashing out of the way, I topple over and thump down.

'What's happening?' Paula comes in with her hair hanging about her shoulders like a lion's mane. 'I thought you were watching TV.'

'It's boring,' I say. 'We're playing battles.'

'Not again! I've told you fighting's the worst.'

Ben dashes onto the sofa and pretends he never moved.

'Huxley, go next to Ben. I won't be long then we can leave for the leisure centre to see Bobby Banjo.'

'Who's he?' I ask.

'He plays music for little kids like Juno,' says Ben.

'Today he's giving a special holiday session for six and seven-year-olds. It's lucky I got places for you both.'

'I'm seven and you're only six.' I point my finger and wave it the way Mrs Ward does when there's singing practice at school. I remember my manners just in time, 'Thank you, Paula.'

Juno starts crying upstairs and the noise gets louder and louder. 'Give me ten minutes.' Paula races away.

The cartoons have finished by the time Juno and Paula are ready. It's a big rush to leave the house. Juno doesn't want to go in the buggy but Paula straps her in while Ben sings *Twinkle Twinkle*. I wish I could join in, but Ben hogs his sister. It's not fair on me.

•   •   •   •   •

Bobby Banjo wears cowboy boots with studs on and he has a guitar. All the boys and girls sit in a circle on the floor and we shuffle up to make room for him. The grown-ups have gone off to the café and will come to collect us after an hour. Bobby Banjo is in charge until then.

We sing a song and take turns telling everyone our names. Then we do it again and have to say something that describes us using a word that has the same sound as our name. It is a bit camp-lick-ated until I have an idea: Huxley is happy. Good job I think of it in time but Ben is stuck, that's because he's six. A girl shouts *Ben is beautiful* but Ben doesn't like that and Bobby tells us to come up with a different idea. I'm busy thinking about Ben liking football so I put up my hand and say *Ben is a ball*. Bobby says the sound is right but ball isn't a describing word and he gives us a clue by making himself sit up really tall. At last we agree *Ben is big* and Ben starts clapping to show he's pleased. After everyone's had a turn, we find out it was only a practice and we do it all over again, only quicker.

At the end of the session, Bobby plays his guitar and sings a song about aeroplanes. We fly around the room with our arms out but we're not allowed to crash against each other. The words of the song tell us when to land our planes and we stretch out on the floor as if we're at an airport. He asks us to be ever so quiet in sitting up, then he swings the door open and the grown-ups are waiting for us.

We walk back along the main street and Paula stops to look in shop windows. I know what Paula's got in her bag because I saw her new camera before. She starts using her fingers to make picture frames a bit like taking pretend photos. It's boring hanging around. I have a think about Tim the barber. He never did take a photo of me and Dad. I'm not sure I like my new haircut because my ears get cold. I remember what Leonard said so I zip my jacket and button up. All of a sudden, Paula whips out her camera and tells me and Ben to stand together straight as sticks. I lean against the bus shelter as I'm tired from running around with Bobby Banjo. I want to say hex-or-stead but I'm not sure Paula's interested in one of my jokes.

'Stay still,' she says, 'or I'll miss the perfect shot.'

I give my best smile. 'Don't you want Juno in the photo?'

'She's asleep in the buggy.' Paula holds the camera so I can't see her face and she turns the zoom until it sticks out like a telescope. 'Are you ready?'

I let a smile stretch my face while the clicking noise keeps going. She is taking lots of photos and I don't understand why … we're not wearing our best clothes or anything.

'Just a few more,' she says.

Stiff as a statue I am and I have to concentrate otherwise I wobble. Ben is a jellyfish but Paula doesn't seem to care. We start a game of bumpety-bump when we can't stay put any longer.

'Right.' Paula makes the camera go back into the shape of a brick.

'Did you take some good ones of us?' I ask. 'Can I look?'

Paula's not in the mood for answering. She returns the camera to its case. I have a look around the street to see if anything interesting is going on. I spot Leonard on the other side of the road. He's parked outside the Asian shop. This is where you can buy big sacks of rice and choose fruit from piles of different things. There's a heap of pumpkins that give off a bright glow. I wonder what Leonard is going to buy for Halloween. The only trouble is, chocolate's not for sale in the Asian shop.

I want to shout hello and give Leonard a wave because he's on his own. I know what it's like to be a lonely-only at school and it's not fun. I'm not allowed to be friends with Leonard. There are lots of nice children my own age and grown-ups can only be friends with children if their parents say so. I am full of sadness. Leonard stretches from his scooter to reach a paper bag. He picks up an orange, throws and catches it, then drops it into the bag. I bet Leonard can juggle balls and I want to learn. Right then, a group of boys bundle along the road. They're wearing jackets but these boys are in the same blue colour and that means they belong to secondary school. What a row they're making! Even Paula stands beside me and Ben to watch what's happening. The boys crowd around Leonard and I can't see him. I don't think the big boys are being kind. The one with curly hair snatches oranges from the pile and starts chucking them at Leonard. Poor Leonard! He holds his arms up to make his head safe. I hope his glasses don't get smashed. I can't believe what they are doing. Oranges bounce off Leonard and roll in the gutter. I turn to Paula and she's still staring. I want to go over there and tell the boys to stop but Paula has her hand on my shoulder.

'They're being mean to Leonard,' I say.

'Waste of oranges,' says Paula.

I don't understand. I want to go and help Leonard but Paula holds me back. The shopkeeper comes out and yells at the boys so they run off. Phew! Leonard is slumped on his scooter and takes a handkerchief from his pocket. He sits there wiping his glasses. Oranges are all over the pavement.

'Shall I go and pick up the oranges?' I ask.

'The shopkeeper has a broom to do the job.' Paula turns the buggy and starts walking so fast me and Ben have to run to keep up.

15

Paula tells my mum she's on her knees. This isn't actually true because she's standing like the rest of us. Mum has come to collect me. It's good we don't have to rush off as she's knackered and needs a cup of tea. She dumps the two plastic carrying bags onto the floor and there's a loud clonk. Bet they're heavy! Mum follows Paula into the kitchen. Me and Ben have a sneaky look at what Mum's bought. He goes to one bag and I reach for the other. I pull the handles to make the bag open and Ben copies. We do this quietly but soon as we see what's inside, Ben gives a cheer and I do a little dance.

'Leave those pumpkins alone,' Mum shouts from the kitchen. 'I've got eyes in the back of my head.'

Ben shrugs and goes off to watch TV. I tuck into the corner by the kitchen door where I can have a proper listen to find out what's going on.

'I was hoping to dip out of Halloween,' says Paula. 'I thought Ben would forget about it over the holidays.'

I want to scream *no chance*. Slapping my hand across my mouth, stops words jumping out.

'With adverts on the TV and posters in shops, you've got to be joking,' says Mum.

'After the number I did on Ben when he ate Leonard's chocolate, I can't help thinking Halloween gives mixed messages. I mean, we're going to let them knock on houses and accept sweets. It doesn't sit right with me. I'm not comfortable.'

My knees go bendy with sadness.

'We're going to be with them, that's the difference. If we only call at houses of people we know, I don't think it's confusing for the kids,' says Mum.

Now my legs are steady as tree stumps.

'Although I'm strict about sweets, I want Ben to enjoy everything just like other children. I'm so torn I don't know what to do.'

It's bad when my tree trunks go saggy.

'To be honest, I'm not that keen. But now I've bought the pumpkins, we can't be spoilsports just yet.'

Tree trunks are springy with hope.

'In that case, let's make the best of it,' says Paula. 'I hope there'll be no mention of going to Leonard's home. Anyway, he isn't in a fit state to receive visitors after what happened today.'

'That's news to me … do tell.'

Paula shares with Mum all about Leonard and the gang of boys throwing oranges. Sinking down, I sit on the carpet because the story is sad making. I stop listening for a bit. The Velcro on my trainer is flying free and I need to stick it back down. Bits of fluff are caught in the hooks and when I've picked them out, the strap works. My ears get ready again when Mum says the word *Halloween*.

'Let's carve the pumpkins now and tomorrow we can go for a short walk around the neighbours we know. Or at least the friendly ones.'

I turn my hands into fists and punch the air. But the happy-making talk turns to stuff about work and the boring things Mum has to do in the office. On the bottom of my trainers, the plastic has broken lines to stop me skidding. Stuck between two bits is a little stone. I'm sad the stone is on its own. Picking it out, I put it on the ledge that's called skirting board. Funny name or what?

'It must be tricky with Tony being senior,' says Paula.

'Don't rub it in,' says Mum. 'Anyway, I'll look after the kids tomorrow as I've booked a day off. Bring Ben and Juno round whenever you want. That'll give you a few hours to prepare for Ben's party.'

I let out a little squeak because Ben and Juno are coming to my house.

'You'd like that, Huxley, wouldn't you?' Mum's voice is loud. 'I know you're listening, Mister Big Ears.'

●　　●　　●　　●　　●

Paula covers the table with newspaper then Mum is hot and bothered because making a hole in the top of the pumpkin is hard going. She wants the saw from our shed but Paula tells her to give over and instead she has a turn. Paula is strong and flips the top off. The innards of a pumpkin are orange seaweed and Mum dumps handfuls onto a plate. Me and Ben take turns dipping our fingers into the slime.

'It's yucky,' I say.

'It's yucky-yucky,' says Ben.

'Watch it doesn't go all over the place,' says Mum. 'We'll wrap it up and chuck it out.'

'No, we won't,' says Paula. 'Let's pick out the seeds. They're a tasty snack when they're dry.'

My fingers are pasted as I snatch the flat white bits. I accidentally flick Ben and there's a goldfish hanging from his hair. Paula wipes it off with a cloth before he has a chance to get me back, but the damp patch on his head shows where the fish has been. I can't help laughing.

'Have a felt pen,' Paula tosses one at me. 'Time to make a face on your pumpkin.'

Mine has square eyes and lots of square teeth. Ben's one has a triangle for a nose. We leave Mum and Paula to do the work of cutting out while me and Ben look after Juno in the front room. We lay out a blanket and put toy plates and cups on top so Juno can have a teddy bears' picnic. This is a good game and my bear growls until he's eaten all the biscuits and then there is a fight with Ben's bear. Juno doesn't mind because she's happy giving her bear a cup of tea. After this, we check to see how the mums are getting on and they've finished the job. I don't think my pumpkin is right. The eyes are round not square and I'm sure I did more teeth but the felt pen lines are washed off.

'It'll look great with a candle inside,' says Mum.

I shake my head. 'It's not how I wanted.'

'Don't look so sad, Huxley. I did my best.'

I lug the pumpkin some of the way home and when it's too heavy Mum takes over. She tries tucking it under her arm but carrying wears her out. I want to help by hooking her handbag over my shoulder. Mum says no. We reach the end of the road before Mum needs another rest. The street lamps are on and this helps to keep the dark away. Mum's a little bit grumpy, to tell the truth, so I try to dream up something to make her feel better. It's hard to do and in the end, I just say what I'm thinking.

'Let's knock at lots of houses and shout out trick or treat.'

'I'd rather you didn't!'

'You have to shout or you don't get any chocolate.'

'There's no need for that. People can give you a treat for dressing up but they don't have to. You know Paula disapproves of sweets. Too many aren't good for you. Please don't go getting ideas.'

What is Mum talking about? Getting ideas is a good thing in school. I don't understand why I can't shout trick or treat. I think she's in a bad mood. 'What if I only *say* the words trick or treat?'

'Okay, that's agreed. When I was your age Gran didn't let me out on the night of Halloween. She said it was imported from America and we should celebrate our own traditions. I don't mind us joining in but we'll only call on people we know.'

'And not strangers.'

'No. Definitely not strangers! Only the friendly people that live around here.'

'Our neighbours?'

Mum nods. Oh dear! We're not going to have many treats because our neighbours are old and don't get new things. Mrs Vartan lives at number six and she calls me sweetheart even though I'm a boy. Mum pops over to water her plants when she visits her sister in a place called Sofia. That's a girl's name. Crazy! One time I was helping Mum do watering and I needed the loo. I couldn't wait until we got home as the number two was on its way. Mrs Vartan's toilet pusher-thing is very strange but I made it work. Mum thought I was messing but I told her you can't leave a poo floating in the water, it's not polite.

Mrs Vartan gives walnuts away as presents. The shell is hard and looks like a brain but inside your head, brain is soft as tissue. I want to go to Leonard's home instead. He lives in a flat at the top of town where there's a sweet shop. I bet he has lots of chocolate in his cupboards.

'Can we call on Leonard?'

'Of course not! You know Leonard is out of bounds.'

'He lives near a sweet shop.'

'It's not a sweet shop, it's a newsagent. Anyway, I'm not going to talk about Leonard.'

'It isn't fair. Leonard is the only person who gets my jokes.'

'As if I need reminding,' Mum mutters. 'We're not having anything to do with Leonard from now on.'

'I want to be sure he's okay. Some big boys did picking-on him.'

'I know,' says Mum. 'Paula told me he was blocking the pavement and it served him right.'

'I feel sorry about it.'

'Forget Leonard. He uses his disability so that people feel bad. It's part of his act.'

Mum is actually cross. I can't say anything else although it doesn't stop me from thinking. When I see Leonard again, I will try talking to him. I know what it's like if children at school do picking-on. It's not fair and it's not nice and I can't understand why Mum is being mean. I will be friendly to Leonard. I just have to make sure nobody sees.

16

Today is Halloween and it won't be long until it's dark. When this happens, Mum says my pumpkin can go on the porch with a lit candle inside. Juno looks pretty in her Halloween colours – she wears black leggings and a bright orange jumper. Mum's bought cupcakes iced with spooky spiders' webs for tea but we have to eat something healthy first. It's one of my favourites, mac and cheese. Mum thinks Paula won't moan because she's made everything fresh.

Juno has a cloth that she carries everywhere. It's mucky as a dishrag but it keeps her happy. Mum worries she'll trip over Juno when she follows her about the kitchen. To keep Juno busy, Mum gets out a big saucepan and a little one so Juno can bang them with a wooden spoon. What a horrid noise! Mum comes over to me and Ben but she can't sit still as she's always got to have one eye on Juno.

We sit at the table for tea. The top of the mac and cheese reminds me of the moon. It's crinkled and a bit burnt where there are craters. I wonder what it's like to walk on the moon and how astronauts do a wee in their spacesuits. This makes me think of something funny and there are bubbles of laughter in my chest. Mum breaks the crunchy top of the mac and cheese and serves up dollops. My plate of food is steaming so I blow on it. Ben copies me but Juno can't do it without spitting.

'Have a piece of bread while your food cools.' Mum tears off a chunk from the end of a French stick and passes it to me. This is just the right time to share my joke and my throat is furry with excitement. I can't help kicking the chair because this is going to be so good.

'I don't want the crusty piss,' I say.

'Piss-piss-piss,' says Ben. He knows we're being rude and he thinks it's funny. We crash our feet against the chair legs and make out we're drummers.

'Stop the banging! You're worse than Juno,' says Mum. 'And don't say that.'

One or two more thumps on the chair and then we stop. It's Juno's turn to join in and bits spray from her mouth as she tries to say *piss*. It comes out as *iss-iss-iss*.

'You're setting a bad example.' Mum sounds cross but her face isn't. I think she's almost smiling. 'Time to eat up.'

We forget about the bread. I aim my fork at the cheesy-crunchy top and a bit breaks off. Ben spoons the macaroni and Juno uses her fingers. Mum drops cherry tomatoes on each of our plates and we count them, one-two-three as they land. When we've nearly finished, Ben and me race to eat the last wodge of mac and cheese. He starts coughing and that means I'm the winner. I throw my arms in the air and say, 'Champion, champion'.

Paula's rule about brushing teeth after every meal has to be followed even though I don't normally bother. Mum gives Ben a new brush and we barge into the little room. We dig our elbows at each other and spit in the sink. Juno has to have her teeth brushed by Mum as she's not clever enough to do it herself. There's knocking at the front door, so we leave the sink splattered with toothpaste. I know it's Paula as she always gives one loud bang then two quiet ones.

'Are you ready?' Paula steps inside.

'In a minute,' says Mum.

We have to get sorted. Juno is strapped into her buggy and Paula plonks a pumpkin sticker on Juno's forehead. She peels it off to take a look then returns it to her cheek. My wizard cloak is loose and goes over my jacket. I stay nice and warm with my zip up. Ben wears his Batman mask and says I'm Robin. I don't bother answering.

'Let's be off,' says Mum.

Me and Ben follow the mums down the path and onto the pavement. They're chatting away so they don't notice our game of bumpety-bump until Ben crashes into a fence.

'Walk sensibly,' snaps Mum.

'Are you okay, Sweet Pea?' Paula brushes Ben off but there's no damage. 'You boys had better hold the buggy.' We walk on, all bunched up.

'Who shall we call on first?' asks Mum.

'Your neighbours are lying low.' Paula nods at the houses where the windows are dark although our porch shines bright with the pumpkin lantern. 'Why not try my road first and then you can call on the others on your way back.'

'Good idea,' says Mum.

When we reach Paula's road, there's another group calling at houses. We hang back because we don't want to follow. The big children wear glow bands which are see-in-the-dark and very cool. I wish I had one of them but I try not to feel sad. Paula and Mum say we can go up the path of the house on the corner. That's where the lady has a goldfish pond in her garden. It's not worth trying to see any fish in the dark. The gate makes a proper Halloween creak and Ben bangs his knees together like he's really scared. There isn't a knocker on the door, but I press the bell once and a whole tune comes out. Next thing, the lady's there and we shout trick or treat loud-loud-loud. She pretends to faint and we get very jolly. It's my turn to pretend to faint when she shows us her basket full of sweets. I'm busy doing my act and then I see Ben turning over the chocolate bars. He'll take the biggest one if I don't stop him.

Mum is watching. 'Just choose one!'

I have to decide quickly but it's not easy. I think the black paper means toffee. Ben grabs the purple bar that is Cadbury chocolate. I hope he might do a swap but he stuffs it into his pocket. We say *thank you* and run back along the path before some girls with glitter on their faces make their way in. They're wearing sticking out wings. Being an angel isn't scary – they should have dressed up as goblins. That's what I think, so there.

At the next house, the sweets are very small. I take a handful and the lady tuts. I drop a few of them back onto the plate. Walking along the path, I eat a sweet. I remember to put the wrapper in my pocket and not throw litter. The chew is fizzy and goes pop in my mouth. I want to tell Mum what's happening.

'You can't talk and eat at the same time,' she says.

'As soon as we're home, Ben, you're going to have a good brush.'

Paula is going on about teeth again. I've got the toffee bar to eat later and Paula can't stop me munching that. I think she dizzy-proves of sweets.

'Let's try another house,' says Mum.

'Just one more,' says Paula.

I think she dizzy-proves of Halloween as well.

At the last stop, Ben chooses a chocolate football and I pick another chew. We say goodbye at Ben's house. He has chocolate around his mouth and it looks like he's wearing lipstick. He says I've got a blue tongue so I stick it out to show everyone, but Mum tells me to put it away.

We're nearly back at our house when Mum says I can call on Mrs Vartan. She lives along a bit and on the other side of the road. Her house looks the same as ours with sash windows that go up and down. Mum holds my hand as we cross to the other pavement but I'm not hopeful of a special treat. A group of big boys are charging out of her gate. They're hooting and laughing as they run off. I look at Mum and she looks at me. There are loads of questions in my head but we don't say anything. We let our eyes do the work because Mrs Vartan is standing with her door wide open and she's covered in white powder. There's even a splattering on her slippers. She looks sad as a ghost with her red lips going down at the ends.

'Are you alright?' Mum shouts and now we rush up Mrs Vartan's path.

'Oh no,' she folds over and patches of white flake from her face.

Mum holds out her hand and Mrs Vartan takes it. 'That's a terrible thing to happen. Come onto the grass and I'll brush you off.'

I put my hand over my mouth to whisper to Mum. (It would be rude if I ask my question out loud.) 'What's that all over Mrs Vartan?'

'It's flour,' says Mum. 'Those hoodlums!'

'Flour?'

'You bake cakes with it.'

Oh yes, flour. And you use it for playdough. Although I don't think anyone is interested in knowing about Lucy's playdough at the moment.

'Horrible lot,' says Mrs Vartan. 'I don't believe in this trick or treat business at Halloween. Look at my walnuts scattered on the porch.'

'Huxley, please pick them up.' Mum turns towards Mrs Vartan. 'Let's get the worst of the flour off you, Mrs Vartan, then you can go inside.'

I find a bag with long handles and scramble to pick up the nuts that have rolled around the place. I am sad because Mrs Vartan is covered in flour and this has something to do with Halloween. Mum's breath makes puffs in the night air as she tidies Mrs Vartan.

'Shall I tell the police?' asks Mrs Vartan.

'Or report it to the school.'

'I'm not sure.'

Mrs Vartan is ready to go inside and I give her the bag. 'Now, sweetheart, you're not going to trick me, are you?'

My mouth drops open as I start to understand. 'Trick or treat actually means playing tricks? Like throwing flour?'

'Not usually,' says Mum. 'I've never heard of anyone being floured before. Those boys were behaving very badly.'

'I'd have given them a walnut.'

'Perhaps it's best not to answer the door in future.'

'I don't want to be a prisoner in my own house.'

'It's only one night of the year,' says Mum. 'Would you like me to come in and make you a cup of tea?'

'No, it's alright, dear. You go home.'

When I'm tucked up in bed, I think about how Mrs Vartan got covered in flour. It was unkind. Then, I think about Leonard and how some boys threw oranges at him. It's not very safe in our town for old people. I better be friendly with every old person to make up for it.

17

I'm eating cereal when Mum answers the door. I know Lucy is here because her voice is jolly. Mum is chatting so I guess they've made up. Giving my Krispies a stir, I stop them sticking to the edge of my bowl. It's not fair for some of the little Krispies to be on their own. Being an only is a shame. Last time Mum and Lucy were together, there were sad feelings. These got right inside my skin and jumbled me up. It's bad when that happens although jumbling can also be good. Like when you are giddy at the park. If you ask me, friendship is the same as going on a roundabout. You can jump on and off for a ride. In between time, there's getting along and hanging out. I stretch my neck by spinning my head. This is excellent exit-size. For a moment I think my face is a Catherine wheel but I can't move that fast. It's Bonfire Night soon and there will be fireworks. I will go *ooh* and *aah* as colours splash across the black sky. We've done Diwali at school – this is about celebrating light – it's an important Hindu festival. Mrs Ward says Christians celebrate light as well but fireworks for Bonfire Night have nothing to do with it. I can't remember everything she blah-blah-blahs. It's all on Google anyway.

Lucy comes into the kitchen. 'Are you looking forward to Ben's party?'

'A bit.' Another spoonful of Krispies goes in my mouth. These are the soggy ones from the bottom of the bowl and when I chew, milk spurts.

'I thought you'd be keen,' says Lucy. 'It's great that everyone's helping out.'

'Is it?' I'm trying not to be a noisy eater. It's my spoon scraping against the bowl.

'I've made Ben's birthday cake and it's a football.'

'Cool.' I don't really mean it. I'm fed up with hearing about his cake. 'Are you friends with Mum again?'

Before Lucy has a chance to answer, Mum whooshes over holding a mug of tea in each hand. One's for Lucy, the other is for her. 'Me and Lucy are good friends.'

My beaker has a puddle of orange juice at the bottom. I press it against my lips and turn the beaker upside down to slurp the last drop.

'Waste not want not,' says Lucy.

'I want quite a few things but I have to wait until Christmas.'

'I meant you didn't waste a drop of your juice,' says Lucy.

'It's time to put your bowl and beaker in the sink,' says Mum.

She'll let me put things straight in the dishwasher one day. For now, they go splish-splash in the sink water. Mum gives a smile to show she's pleased with me. I decide to give myself a pat on the back for being good. I stretch my arm but I can't reach that far. It's not right that my arm isn't long enough. Pointing it straight in front of me, I let the bones stretch then I bend it over again. Mum and Lucy are chatting away. I think they're making a plan but I don't know what it's about. I find it takes a lot of skill to pat my back and listen at the same time. Mum says *hurry-trap*. This is interesting. 'What's a hurry-trap?'

Mum's laughter splutters. 'Honey not hurry. But, it's got nothing to do with you, Mister Big Ears.'

'Krispies taste of honey.'

'Yes, but breakfast is over. Find something to play with.' Mum turns me around and gives me a little push. I am a soldier marching to where my toys are stacked. Searching through the box of books, I find the one about a train ride. The picture shows an engine with steam coming out of it same as Thomas, although this is not a Thomas the Tank Engine story. This train goes around the countryside and collects children from different stations. I'm looking at the pictures and I can read the words in my head. Some children in my class have to do sounding out but not me! When I take a break from reading, Mum and Lucy's voices reach me all the way from the table. I think I am right – they're planning something. I turn my head sideways to make my good listening ear pick up their talk.

'Paula will have a camera at the party,' says Mum. 'She can take a snap and then there'll be evidence to show what his silly infatuation looks like. You'll be the honey in the trap and Jed will finally understand how annoying it is for me.'

'There must be an easier way,' says Lucy. 'I could talk to Jed.'

'It's too late for that – he'll have palpitations! Believe me, this idea is best. I only mentioned it to give you the heads-up.'

Right as my ears are hearing really well, Mum coughs and I spin my eyes to look straight at her. Her head is leaning to one side, the same way as mine. She's copying me! She's found me out! I scramble to think of something funny to say. I've done my in-fat-your-station joke so that's no use. I squeeze out another idea. Phew! Now I need to think up a way of using this word but then I have a brainwave. It happens all at once when I'm being super speedy! I don't want to lose this idea. I move close to the table to talk in a proper way.

'Now you've made up, it's a wreck-on-silly-station.'

Lucy's face squishes up and Mum stares into space while she's working it out.

'Reconciliation,' says Mum.

'That's a big word,' says Lucy.

'Do I get a bonus for using it?' I ask.

'I get the bonus for understanding you,' says Mum.

Lucy chuckles, 'And I get a bonus for finding it funny.'

'We've all got a bonus!'

'Perfect,' says Lucy, 'that adds to my good news.'

'Now don't go sharing,' says Mum. 'Someone around here likes spilling beans.'

'I don't spill beans – I gobble them up.'

'Very true, Huxley,' says Mum. 'Now off you go. Find another book to read.'

I wander over but my brain is busy. Lucy has good news. What can it be? She prays for stuff at Light Club and Junior Church and at school, so maybe Jesus has done something special for her. To do praying, I have to keep my hands pressed together and not clap them. Someone always sees if I open my eyes, but they shouldn't be looking either. I walk in a circle and before I know it, I'm back beside Lucy. 'Did Jesus do something for you?'

Mum picks up the mugs because the drinks have been swallowed. Her eyes go extra wide but no words come from her lips.

'Absolutely,' says Lucy.

'If you ask me, it's because you're the right person. Don't sell yourself short. And, watch what you say to you-know-who.'

'I don't mind Huxley hearing,' says Lucy. 'It's all around the staff room and they'll announce my adoption leave soon.'

I'm trying to work out what Lucy's talking about. Thinking so hard makes me giddy. I fall over and land in Lucy's lap. She helps me stand up again and I'm close enough to whisper in her ear. 'What's going on?'

Lucy smiles. 'I'm going to be a mummy.'

I stare at Lucy's tummy. It's not big enough for a baby to be in there.

'I'm not actually having a baby!' Lucy laughs.

I slap my forehead when I remember. 'I know. You're doing add-hop-shine!'

'That's right. My little girl is already born but she needs a new mummy.'

'Why?'

'Her real mummy can't look after her very well, so I'm going to take over.'

'We have to say congratulations.' Mum reaches for my hand and swings my arm. 'Lucy will be a great mum.'

'I know.' I don't want to hold hands any more. Breaking free, I go over to grab a teddy from the toy box. 'You can put this under your jumper to be fat then everyone will know a baby is on the way.'

'There's no need for that,' says Mum.

'Or you could use a football,' I say.

'Football!' Lucy springs up. 'I've got to finish icing Ben's cake. Sorry, Kirsty. I must be off.'

'Don't forget about the haitch tee,' says Mum.

Lucy frowns then Mum mouths some words without any sound coming out. Lucy gives a nod, 'Oh, I get you. I'll be ready.'

•   •   •   •   •

Dad sits on the armchair in the lounge. He's reading a newspaper with the pages out wide so I can only see the top of his head. He's had a busy morning buying paint to fix the ceiling and now he needs a good rest. There's the photo of a footballer scoring a goal on one page and BREXIT in big letters on the other. Not football again! Not Brexit again! A story book is much better, even if you've read it one hundred times. I let my book slip off my lap but it doesn't fall far when I'm scrunched against the radiator. There is a paper-turning noise. I look over to see Dad folding the pages and I think they're ready for the recycling bin. I don't have any luck as he carries on reading. I take a big gulp of air and blow out my breath. There are a few biscuit crumbs on the carpet. I lick my finger and vacuum them up. Yum! They're still crunchy. I wonder if there's more vacuuming needed. There's usually something worth finding between the cushions on the sofa. One time, I dug out a pound coin. Finders keepers rules in our house, so I stuck it in my piggy bank. I push my hand down the back of the sofa and prod about. Nothing much is there, just a pencil. When I lost the railway turntable, Mum was a genius at getting it out from inside the sofa. I ram my hand into the crack. It's tight but I can almost press my whole arm in.

'Stop that, Huxley.'

Great! He's talking to me at last. I roll around and make my arm fly free, then I go and stand close to him. The page he's reading has small words. I can't be bothered with them. 'How much longer until we leave for Ben's party?'

Dad looks at his watch but he doesn't let go of the paper. He's glued to the pages. 'Another two hours.'

'Have you ever stuck a football up your shirt?'

'No. Why would I do that?'

'In case you need to show people a baby is coming.'

'Men don't have babies.'

'I know.'

'When am I going to have a baby sister or brother?'

'That's a leading question.'

Dad doesn't say anything else but starts reading again. I pull up my shirt to have a look at my tummy. It sticks out over my shorts. I can make it extra flat by sucking my breath. I do a little dance like the girls in the playground. I can move as good as them. Then I push my tummy out so it's fat-fat-fat.

'What are you doing now?' asks Dad.

'I want my belly button to pop out.'

'It's fine the way it is.'

'Babies get in through their mummy's belly button.'

'Oh dear,' says Dad. 'Perhaps it's time we had a little talk.'

18

The disaster is all to do with Nanny Phil. She's caught a sick bug so can't help at Ben's party. I wonder if she says *bugger* because she's got a bug! It's sad she won't be there to do the dig and poke game. It's one of the best ways to say hello.

Me and Dad are bringing stuff to the park. I have a tower of cones that are taller than my head and Dad holds a net with loads of footballs inside. We both wear football kit but it's not flash like the proper Nevern Town strip Ben and Tony have got on.

Ben rushes up to me, 'Where's my present?'

'Mum has it.'

'Okay.' Ben play punches my arm. 'Why are you wearing a yellow shirt?'

'What this?' I pinch the sleeve and I think of something to change the talk. 'Where's your cake?'

'In the pavilion.' He means the house in the middle of the park that has a large porch. No one lives in it, though.

'Can I have a look?'

'Let's go see.' Ben puts his arm across my shoulder and I think this makes us special friends.

I've never been inside the pavilion before. There's one big room with some doors to the toilets. Behind a counter, there's Paula banging kitchen cupboards and Mum's piling up plates. I walk over to say hello to Juno in her buggy. She reaches her arms to give me a hug and then she falls back because she can't get out. I tickle her under the chin and she laugh-laugh-laughs. Mum's shopping bag is dumped on the floor and Ben's present is poking out. It's a rectangle shape and the wrapping paper has footballs but it's not a great big package.

'This is for you!' I wave it in the air for Ben to see. Juno flaps about but it's not her birthday.

Dashing over, Ben grabs the parcel. 'What is it?' He gives it a shake but it doesn't make a noise. Book-shaped presents never do.

'Can you guess?'

'Is it a tin for pencils?' Ben's nose is the same as a pig's snout. I don't think he wants one of them.

'No. Mum bought it over the internet.'

Ben lifts a flap of wrapping paper.

'You're not allowed to open it yet!'

'Why not?' Ben tears a little piece of the paper away.

'I'll give you a clue. There are many different types of these.'

Ben rolls his eyeballs around like there's no guesses in him.

'Save it for later,' Mum calls over.

I mustn't tell Ben what's inside because it's a secret. Words try bursting out of my mouth and I have to keep my lips stuck together. I think Ben will enjoy the book. It's about a boy who plays so much football he actually lives in the goal.

Mum's busy putting tables in a long line and Paula helps by laying paper over the top to make them look nice. Ben drops the present back into the bag and rushes to the door. He wants everyone to arrive right now. Joining him for a look, I see there's no one around. Swinging the door, I nip inside and lean against it to stop him getting back in. He bangs and barges until there's a gap, then he squeezes through. Next second, I'm outside and doing the same. It takes all the push in me and lots of shouting until he gives in. Mum says we're making too much noise and sends us both away. She's got things to do in the pavilion and she can't be minding us as well. Dad and Tony have to look after us but they're in a competition of keepy-uppy. Tony catches the ball on his foot and bounces it on his toe caps for ages. Dad isn't as good and has to admit Tony is the winner.

'You're a good sport, Dad,' I tell him.

'Thank you, Huxley. Why don't you and Ben have a go?'

'Me first,' says Ben.

I'm not interested so I walk onto the grass. A little way off I see the purple flash of chocolate wrapping. At first, I think the chocolate hasn't been opened, but reaching down I find only the paper is there. Two paces away there's another wrapper. I will have better luck this time. Again, the paper is empty. Someone's been scoffing mini bars! By the time I hear boys from our class pelting along the path, I've collected TEN chocolate papers and one with the chocolate still inside! I push the unopened mini bar into my pocket for later. I have to leave my finding mission now the party's going to start. Before I do, I take a careful look over the field. My brain tick-tocks into action when I see more crumpled purple packaging. There's a secret trail and this one isn't like Hansel's breadcrumbs. None will get eaten by birds. Using my detective skills, I watch the line going over to the far gate where the road leads to the top of town. I have it! I know who's leaving clues.

Walking over the grass, I step carefully as I don't want to drop any of the wrappers.

'Come on, Huxley!' Dad's standing by the rubbish bin and is waving his arms madly in the air.

I break into a trot and I'm next to him in seconds.

'There's a good boy.' He slides his fingers through my hair. 'Very thoughtful of you to do a litter collection. Look! There's someone copying your very fine example.'

A woman follows the line of purple from the gate and uses a proper litter picker so she doesn't have to bend over. Maybe she'll be lucky like me and find one with chocolate still inside. I let go of the wrappers I found, and watch them float to the bottom of the bin.

'I blame Halloween revellers for being inconsiderate. Fancy leaving their rubbish!'

I don't say anything because I know different to Dad. It's a secret message from Leonard inviting me to his place. A whistle blows and it's time to follow Tony.

'Let's get this party started!' says Dad.

We race over to join the others. There are three girls at Ben's party and one of them wears football kit, another is in shorts and then I see Samira running towards us. She's got her jogging bottoms on and it's easy to spot Samira's mum as she wears a black scarf that goes right over her head and covers everything. Just her feet in shiny shoes stick out.

'Over here you lot.' All of us children stand in front of Tony. He's next to the cones which are lined up in a row. 'We need to warm-up.'

Tony starts doing star jumps and we copy. He's on a go-slow then he speeds up until we're hot and out of breath. 'If you're wearing Nevern Town kit go and wait in front of Jed.' Ben leads the line while the rest of us straggle. 'Let's even the numbers.' Tony mixes us into multicoloured teams. 'First task is to dribble the ball around the cones.' He shows us how to keep the ball under control by doing little taps with his foot. 'When everyone's had a go and there are two straight lines, that's the end of the game.'

'There are treats for the winners.' Dad pulls a bag of gummy bears from his pocket.

Tony blows his whistle and the leader is off. Dad and his team are being very shouty but Tony stays calm and says *good man* and *come on, mate* even if he's talking to girls. I go quickly around the cones but our team drags behind. Ben is shouting his head off then suddenly it goes much quieter. I turn around soon as I hear a spurting sound. Ben's kneeling and there's a pink mess on the grass. It's got lumps and strings in it. I look at Ben and his face is white as a skull with his lips bright red. He spits bits and dribbles then wipes his mouth with the back of his hand. One long blast on Tony's whistle stops the game and we make a circle around Ben. He's wobbly as a leaf in the wind.

'Is he okay?' asks Dad.

Ben flops against Tony. 'Clearly not.'

'What shall we do now?' asks Dad.

'You hold the fort.' Tony lifts Ben in his arms. 'Better take my poor sickly lad home.'

'What about his cake?' I ask.

'You get on and enjoy yourselves. The party isn't over until the parents return.' Tony breaks through the circle and we shout goodbye and happy birthday to Ben, but he's not listening. His eyes are closed and there are bubbles coming from his lips.

'Ask Kirsty to come over and help,' Dad shouts at Tony's back.

Tony gives a wave and heads for the pavilion.

'What next?' I ask.

'Stay in your teams,' says Dad. 'We'll start the dribbling again.'

There's loads of cheating going on because Dad isn't watching properly. Zac didn't go round the last cone and raced back so that his team finished first. I don't like it when the rules are broken. Then Mum arrives with a tray of cut oranges at half time. This is good and we fall out of our lines to have a munch. Some of the boys ask for a proper drink and Mum takes them on a trip to the water fountain. I wait with Dad and the others.

'It's not much fun without the birthday boy, is it?' says Dad.

'Poor Ben.' Samira shakes her head and the clips holding her hair blink in the light. 'What shall we do?'

'Let's have a think.'

As Mum comes back with the thirsty children, she slips and mud splatters her trousers. 'Oh no!'

'Don't worry about that, Kirsty. Come over and help me.'

'I've got the tea to prepare.'

'Where the hell is Paula?'

'Tony picked up Juno and Paula on the way home with Ben. They don't want to risk Philippa's sickness bug going through the entire birthday party.'

'Marvellous,' says Dad.

Mum stares at the mud on her new boots and tries to scrape some off on a clump of grass. 'You'll have to cope.'

'Cope?'

'Yes.' Mum turns around and heads back to the pavilion.

'Right,' he says. 'A few more star jumps.'

·　　·　　·　　·　　·

Ben's cake is round as a sphere and there's icing criss-crossing to look like a football. We get together and sing happy birthday to Ben but because he isn't around to blow out the candles, we do it for him.

'I'm not going to cut the cake,' says Lucy.

'Why not?' asks Zac.

'We'll leave it for Ben to do when he's feeling better.'

'Boo-hoo.' Zac isn't really crying.

'You can have your party bags instead,' says Lucy. 'That'll keep you busy.'

Lucy passes around the bags. They are brown sandwich ones with football and balloon pictures stuck on to make them good for a party. Zac turns his out searching for sweets but I already think Paula won't put any inside. She dizzy-proves. That's when I take the Cadbury mini bar out of my pocket.

'Where did you get that from?' asks Zac.

'I've got a proper friend and he lives near a sweet shop.' I quickly unwrap the chocolate and stuff the whole thing in my mouth.

'You're greedy!'

I can't answer because my mouth is full.

Zac pulls out his whistle and gives a big blow. Eating a chocolate bar is nicer but the others don't know this so they copy Zac.

'I'll take all the kids outside.' Mum is talking to Lucy but it's hard to hear with the whistles blasting. 'Then you can go through with the plan.'

'It's no use without Paula,' shouts Lucy. 'There'll be no one to take a photo.'

'Never mind. I'll round up some children, and we'll burst through the doors to give Jed the shock of his life.'

'Are you sure?' says Lucy.

'Nothing to lose.'

Mum rubs her throat to warm up her extra loud voice.

'Children,' she shouts. 'Everyone on the veranda to wait for your mums and dads. You can blow your whistles outside.'

We are charging bulls and there's a stampede to get through the doorway. My elbow digs against Zac's tummy. I wish it was a horn.

'Watch out,' he says.

I'm too quick for Zac and dash away. It's funny when Zac's mum comes to collect him. He starts moaning to her about me and my elbow. She ignores him and asks where Paula is. In the end, Zac has to say thank you for everything to Mum and it's like he's saying thank you to me as well. I know he doesn't want to do it. That means I'm the winner and he's not. After they've gone, I stay outside with Mum to be sure none of the children wander off or leave with the wrong person. Bit by bit they go until there's only me and Samira left.

'Can we go inside?' Samira pretends she's shivering in the cold.

'Not yet.' Mum stares through the pavilion window and is not even looking at Samira.

'Can I go to the toilet?' asks Samira.

'Hang on a minute.' Mum's face doesn't budge from the glass then all of the sudden she spins around and crouches. Talking in a whisper, she says, 'Let's make this a game. When I open the door, we'll rush inside and shout *honey trap*. That will give Dad and Lucy a surprise.'

I don't understand why we have to shout *hurry-trap* but that's what happens.

·　　·　　·　　·　　·

I walk home from the party with Mum. She carries the bag of balls and I've got the cones. Dad is going back with the car to pick up everything else. Mum has her smiley face on. Every now and then, she splutters with laughter.

'What's funny?' I ask.

'These balls are awkward to hold.'

'Is that a joke?'

'No,' she says. 'But wasn't it funny the way Dad jumped out of his skin?'

'I don't think so.' Dad said it wasn't fair to play a trick and I'm on his side. 'Laughing at people is picking-on and those games aren't fun.'

'There's no need to be like that, Huxley,' says Mum. 'It means Dad will behave himself in future. When he comes home, I'll brew a lovely pot of tea to make up.'

'Okay.' I give Mum a smile because I'm pleased about that. 'No more hurry-traps.'

'No more HONEY traps,' she says.

19

Nanny Phil brings Ben to school on Monday because Paula is laid up. Mum says the mild November weather has spread germs. We don't do the poke and dig routine at school as I need to be sent-a-ball. Soon as the bell sounds, Mum grabs the neck of my coat and yanks me over for a kiss. After that, I race for the line. Already there are a few children standing up straight. I try to cut in to a gap but one of the football boys trips me. I don't want to be near them, so I head for the back. Children at the end are called stragglers and that's not right. Good job Samira lets me step in beside her. I watch as Ben joins the boys in front who slap his back as if he's a hero. I look over to see Mum but she's already gone. It's always busy at her work.

We're sitting on the carpet and Ben shares his news. Mrs Ward stops him talking about the globs in his pink sick. I wonder how Paula is feeling and I hope Juno won't catch the bug. She wouldn't like being sick even if it was Barbie pink. Mrs Ward reminds everyone we can't come to school when we're ill, and we should be free from sickness for twenty-four hours. That's a whole day of being at home. Perhaps getting a bug isn't bad when there's Nanny Phil to do the looking after. My gran lives in Spain and that means she can't drop her hat to help Mum.

After Mrs Ward has finished talking, we do sums. I have a special book to write the answers in and I'm clever at counting on from the first number in the sum. Everyone on my table does this, but others start their adding with number one. They'll learn how to do it properly with Lucy, I mean, Miss Choi's help. There is only one ruler on our table for when we need to draw a straight line. We have to share and Samira always puts it back in the middle of the table after she's finished but Zac doesn't. He hogs the ruler and only passes it when he has to. Sometimes he makes the girls say *pretty please* first.

The bell rings. I tell everyone it's time to go into the big hall for arse-hem-play. Mrs Ward's face goes sharp to show she's cross and I think that's because she's heard me. I can't help talking in a loud voice if I've got a great joke. It's a pity she's lost her sense of humour. Mrs Ward lets children from the other tables line up at the door but my group has to stay put. Zac's muttering that it's my fault we're last and he'll get me for it. I don't understand what the fuss is about, it's only arse-hem-play, not like real play time.

I have to wait while my class goes into the hall. Mrs Ward leans over me and my neck is stiff as I have to look her in the face.

'You know perfectly well how to say assembly properly,' she says.

Of course! 'Yes, Mrs Ward.'

'So why do you do it?'

Because it's funny! 'That's how the word came out.'

'In future, please say it correctly. In fact, you might as well have a practice straight away.'

I keep my eyes wide open as I work out what she wants.

'Say assembly!'

'Ass-embly.'

'Now you're testing my patience.'

Just as the piano music strikes up, she says, 'We'd better join the others in the hall'.

I jig along the corridor in tune with the music.

My Head Teacher's best advice is to choose your friends wisely. I don't know who's fallen out this time, but it's got nothing to do with me. While others are closing their eyes and praying to Jesus, I think about having friends. It's okay if you like football or playing with girls, then there's always someone to choose. I'm an only at home and a lonely at school. It's different when our class goes on the climbing frame then everyone is a mate. I'm sad it only happens once a week.

116

We spill out into the playground after the bell goes and all the children scatter. I dawdle because Ben's off playing football. From the corner of my eye, I spot Samira and she's smiling at me.

'Come over here, Huxley.' Samira doesn't play with other girls much and ends up on her own at lot. I wander over to where she stands and Samira gives me a flash of biscuit she's keeping in her pocket. It's a plain round biscuit so she's allowed to bring it to school. Breaking it in two, she gives me half.

'I breaks-it.' She does a little dance. 'Do you get it? Like Brexit!'

'Oh yes.' But Samira's not as funny as me. The biscuit is the shape of a half-moon. I take a bite and it becomes a crescent.

'The cow jumps over the moon.' I copy Samira and dance for a bit then I scoff the rest of the biscuit. It's not my favourite – chocolate chip cookies are best. I feel a bit sad because Samira doesn't eat some things that are really nice.

'Why don't you eat gummy bears?'

Samira shook her head when the bag was passed around at Ben's party.

'I don't like sweets.'

'You don't like ANY sweets?'

'Just the chewy ones.'

'You eat chocolate?'

'Yes.'

'That's good.'

I munch the rest of the biscuit quickly and crumbs drop onto my jumper. Samira looks at my tummy.

'You're mucky.' She brushes away the bits.

My mum does that, too. I guess Samira thinks I'm okay. Trouble is I'm not sure why Nanny Phil goes on about her. She calls Samira names like four-in-ear and that has something to do with leaving Samira out. It's another sort of picking-on! I like Nanny Phil when she's kind, but not so much when she isn't.

'What's a four-in-ear?' I ask.

'I don't know.'

'Watch me.' I stick one finger in my ear and do a mad plugging-up routine.

'You're crazy,' she says.

She finishes her bit of biscuit and we hold hands until the bell goes.

In class, Mrs Ward tells us we are going to learn about poetry. We hear a proper poet read from her book on a CD. The words have a sing-song pattern that Mrs Ward calls rhythm. The poem is great but now Mrs Ward wants us to think up a class poem. We are going to write one about our school. It starts *at St Michael's we're the best*. A few children share ideas, although Mrs Ward's favourite is the line she comes up with. It goes, *you can put us to the test*. Everyone is worn out by the time we get to the end of the first verse, then Mrs Ward tells us we have to write the next one on our own to finish the poem. The square table have an adult to help them, but us diamonds work on our own.

Samira sits next to me because we're friends. She begins writing on her paper but I'm stuck. I thump my forehead to help my brain start working. School isn't my favourite thing so I write about going home time. This is when Mrs Ward reads us a story. I like stories with bears and crocodiles. The best ones include trains. There is one book called *Riding on a Train* and the words make the sound of an engine going along the track. After I've done my writing, Mrs Ward says my verse is very clever. I get a house point and a sticker that says *well done*. My tummy grumbles to remind me what's coming next.

There's a lot of barging in the queue so the dinner ladies make us wiggle backwards. We have to put the distance of an arm between us by tapping on the shoulder of the next person in the line. We are a slithering snake until we drop our hands and bunch up again. It's fun sliding my tray along the counter and watching spoonfuls of food land on the plates. There are big dollops of meat and mashed potato. I eat these one after the other. Samira waits for me by the way out. She says she's on door duty but there isn't such a thing. The ideas she has are funny and make me laugh but then Lucy, I mean Miss Choi, comes over. She is in a very happy mood and I know why, she is getting her baby soon. But baby or not, it's her job to shoo us out as we're not allowed to block the doorway.

'You're a daughter and I'm a son,' I tell Samira.

'Do you want to play mums and dads?'

'I want to go on the climbing frame.'

'Too bad it's not our day. Let's go and say hello to my sister in the nursery instead.'

We walk to the fence that keeps the little ones over there. They might be knocked down if they come into the big playground. Nursery children have scooters and ride-on cars and all sorts of things.

'Zahra.' Samira calls to the little girl by the sand tray. She turns around and waves.

'That's my sister.' Me and Samira wave back but Zahra isn't watching us. She's digging in the sand and showering bits over the ground.

'What's it like having a sister?' I ask.

'She always copies me.'

'Do you play together?'

'Sometimes.'

The wind blows the brown leaves around the edge of the playground. I stamp on one, crunching it to bits. Before I know what's happening, we're making up a game. It's called *gotcha* and we shout the word every time a leaf is flattened under our shoes. There are so many that we dash around and laugh and get out of breath.

Mum doesn't want to go to Bonfire Night at the allotments this year. (My dad can't be bothered growing vegetables in a plot down there because he's got enough to do mowing our lawn.) It's his turn to take me to Bonfire Night and it's not easy waiting for him to get back from work when I'm also waiting for my tea. There isn't a sign of any food. I think it's best to say something before I starve to death. Going into the kitchen, Mum's sitting there drinking from a mug with a cow picture on the side.

'What am I going to eat?'

'How about fish fingers?'

'And chips?' I ask.

'You're pushing it, Huxley.'

'I'll eat some peas.'

'Only if they're drowned in ketchup,' says Mum. 'I know you too well.'

'Yippee.' I'm going to have my best tea.

With my tummy nice and full, we set off for the station to meet Dad. Mum makes sure I've got on my hat, scarf and gloves as well as my jacket. I have a feeling she's up to something. On the platform there's a yellow line to keep people from going too close and falling in front of a train. Good job for me, the platform is big at Nevern Town Station so when the train arrives it's okay to play a game. I have to wait for all the passengers to clear out of the way, then I rush over to Dad. Stuffed with surprise, he staggers around. I hold his hand to stop him falling over.

Mum starts a bit of argy-bargy on the steps going down to the road. She wants to hold Dad's briefcase but he's not letting go. In the end, Mum wins and this means she's taking his work stuff home so that me and Dad can go straight to the allotments.

Tony grows vegetables in a plot by the gate but no one does gardening at night. He wears a jacket that shows up in the dark and this means he's an important person. There are bales of straw to sit on and burgers are for sale at a stall. Dad buys me one but I had double helpings of my best tea so I only take one bite and pass it to him. Dad gobbles up the rest. Looking around, there are children from school but only Ben is in my class.

Away from where we're sitting, a massive bonfire warms my back. I turn around to watch golden tongues lick the night sky. It's amazing! I wish Dad would watch with me but he goes off to chuck the burger boxes into a black sack hanging from the stall. As usual, he's gone for ages. When I check to see what he's doing, there he is chatting with Tony. I climb on the bale to watch the bonfire. Everyone standing around is different. Some people are black shadows and others have their faces turned the same colour as the bonfire. Over at the edge of the group, there's Leonard's scooter with the paintwork extra shiny from splashes of firelight. I want to go over and talk to him but I'm not allowed. Next thing, it's like he's read my mind and scoots towards the shed that breaks up the circle of sitting places. I jump to the next bale as if I'm on an assault course. I am a giant standing above Leonard.

'Hello Huxley,' says Leonard. 'You don't mind me coming over, do you?'

I take a sneaky peek around and Dad's not looking my way. 'I'm not a teller-on.'

'What do you mean?' asks Leonard.

'I'm not supposed to talk to strangers.'

'I'm hardly a stranger.'

'I know.'

I wonder if there's anything in Leonard's basket. Leaning over, I have a clear view and it's empty.

'No chocolate today,' he says. 'I've given the last bar to a boy called Faisal.'

I am sad because Leonard's got a new friend.

'I'm teaching him a few words of English every day. The chocolate is a reward for saying the right things.'

I think about the chocolate wrappings left at the park. Was it really a message from Leonard? 'I thought you wanted me to visit.'

'You're welcome anytime, Huxley. Us chaps need to stick together.'

That has me wondering. 'Okay.'

'Anyway, I've got to head off now.'

'Wait for the fireworks!'

Leonard is turning the scooter around. 'There's a much better view from the top of my block. It's possible to see fireworks exploding across London. The lift goes up so fast it makes my stomach wobble. Want to join me?'

I am full of confusion. I can't think what to say.

'You don't seem that keen.'

'I have to ask my dad.'

My eyes spin over the allotments and they land on Dad. He's coming my way.

'Perhaps it's not such a great idea,' says Leonard. 'You can visit any old time. The flats are at the top of town and mine's above the sweet shop.' Leonard gives me a wink, grips the yellow spongey ends of the handlebars and he's away. I watch as he steers to the gate. My heart goes droopy when I can't see him any more.

'Bloody hell, Huxley.' Dad's all puffed out. 'Who were you talking to? I hope it wasn't the bloke from the barber's shop.'

As he gets the last word out, there's a horrible screeching noise that goes right by me. From the corner of my eye, I see a blob of white swipe past. I have to duck! A spurting noise is loud-loud-loud and makes my ear go dead. I can't hear properly. I'm giddy like I've jumped off the roundabout and my eyes start making water but I'm not crying. It's hard to watch what's going on with Dad's stamping around. Some people jump out from the bushes but I only see shadows. A hullabaloo is happening but it's not fun because everyone is angry. Then Dad is right beside me again and tugs me against his chest. I close my eyes tight and let the warmth of his body spread into mine. After a bit, it's too squashy inside his arms so I break free and that's when Tony comes.

'Right bunch of idiots.' Tony's puffing and panting. 'Give me a minute to catch my breath. One thing's for sure, they're well away.'

'That rocket could've taken Huxley's head off! It nearly gave me a heart attack. I mean, what the hell were they doing?'

'I'm so sorry, mate. It was that group of lads from the secondary school. Do you want me to call the police? To be honest, having a rocket misfire scared them as much as it did us. I think they've learnt their lesson.'

'It's scuppered the whole evening,' says Dad. 'We'll be going home as soon as I've recovered from the shock.'

'Don't do that, mate. Arrangements for tonight's display have been followed to the letter. Huxley won't want to miss out.'

The grown-up talk has been going round my head. It's only now I understand Dad wants to go home before the fireworks! 'I love rockets and the Catherine wheels.'

'See what I mean,' says Tony. 'No one's hurt. Let's enjoy the rest of the evening.'

Another man in a bright jacket arrives with a cup of tea for Dad. 'I've put sugar in the brew. It should help settle your nerves.'

Dad has a sip. The man pokes around in his pocket and brings out a can of Cola. Soon as I get my hands on it, I pull the ring and have a big slurp. Bubbles fill my mouth and my nose and I am full of excitement.

'What do you think, Huxley?' asks Dad. 'Do you want to stay?'

I nod my head up and down then take another slurp.

Tony does lots of talking over the loud speaker but I'm not interested in listening until there's the countdown. That's when I spring onto my tiptoes and Dad's behind me. We shout the numbers back from ten and my heart goes bang-bang-bang. The allotment is silent and we have to wait. The first rocket rips from the ground with a great big whoosh. Up, up it flies and I jiggle around waiting to see what will happen. After a crack, the sky is filled with sparks of green and pink and white.

'You just wait until we're home and I tell your mother about Tony's incompetence.'

The next rocket shoots away, bursting into tiny stars that flicker. I can't help being happy when the sky is pretty.

'What were you doing by the shed anyway?'

There's another crack. This time snowflakes fall and then turn to dots.

'Tony can't have done a proper risk assessment.'

Dad goes quiet and I look up at him. I can see the hairs on his chin in the light from the fire. Voices go *ooh* and *aah* and I'm glad I'm at the allotment with Dad.

After the rockets are finished, Tony's voice booms over the loudspeaker. 'Only a minute or two until we have the Catherine wheels.'

I remember these from last year. They are nailed onto posts and spin around and around. I'm ready to hear the screeching that Catherine wheels make. It starts when one, then two, then three are lit up. I like watching bright circles. After that there are the fountains. I stand on a bale to get a better look and Dad moves close to me.

Before we go home, there are sparklers. I stand in the row of children. Dad is beside me. He doesn't want another bloody thing to go wrong. I have to wait for the lighting of the sparkler to come along the line. At the top, children have sparklers that are already lit and the sticks are spitting and fizzing with light. I'm excited as my turn will be soon. Rubbing my hands together, nothing is smooth as the wool on my gloves is knobbly. It's called friction. I learnt this at school but I don't need to think about it now. The man passes me a sparkler and I am careful to hold firm the metal piece. I keep my hand well away from the grey bit that lights up. You have to wear gloves to protect your fingers because a sparkler is a bit like holding a burning stick. I press my sparkler against one that's already lit. It's magic when it catches and begins to snap and spray. I am allowed to wave the sparkler carefully and I draw a dragon that slithers in the air as it hisses white pins. It is over soon as the sparks stop and I drop the glowing end into a bucket of sand.

Dad and me walk home but he's in a rush and I run to stay close. I grab his arm so that he'll go slower. I've got my breath back by the time we're in front of our porch. Dad searches his pockets to find the door key but it's not where he thought it was. This means I am allowed to bang the knocker. I do this really hard to make the sound echo.

'What a racket!' Mum takes off my hat as I walk inside then she holds the tips of my gloves so I can pull my hands free.

'How were the fireworks?'

Before I have time to answer, Dad says, 'One nearly lopped Huxley's head off. Fancy putting Tony in charge ... something had to go wrong.'

'I had a sparkler.' I put my jacket on my special peg.

'Bloody rocket misfired and shot directly at him,' says Dad.

Mum turns to look from me and back to Dad. 'Quite an evening.'

'Tosser,' says Dad. 'I think that bloody Leonard bloke was hanging around.'

My ears go into a good listening shape.

'He packed off when he saw me.'

Mum is staring at Dad and her lips move but no sound comes out. Even with my ears ready I can't hear silent words.

'What are you going on about?' Dad's face is screwed up. He can't work it out either.

'Never mind. Let's get Huxley off to bed.' My mum's arms go all around me like she's an octopus. There's nothing more to say when I'm in a great big hug.

'Candles are for Christmas.' Mrs Ward reaches for the tissues.

'And birthdays,' I say.

'You should have a handkerchief.' I check both my pockets but I've forgotten it. Mrs Ward takes a tissue from the box and puts it into my hand.

'Don't just stand there,' she says.

I get what she wants me to do but quick as a flash I sniff the snot back up.

'Honestly, Huxley,' she says, 'have a good blow instead.'

I press the tissue against my face and shoot breath down my nose. I end up with a sticky face. Yuk. I knew sniffing was a better idea.

'Here's another.' She gives me a new tissue and I do it over again. Three times later and she is happy at last. 'Now go and put that lot in the bin.'

I wander over to the other side of the room but I keep watch on Mrs Ward from the corner of my eye. All the children sit on the carpet although she has a spongey chair. She makes her head go right up to hit the ceiling. Getting back to the group, I sit in an empty place between Ben and Samira. I copy Mrs Ward by making my neck extra long but I'm the last one. Mrs Ward takes a big breath and I can see her chest go in and out. She always does this when there is something important to say. Usually it's a bit of news, like there's indoor play because of rain.

Only the sun is out, so it can't be that. We wait while she turns the pages of her notebook. After she finds the right page, her eyes whizz from side to side. I know she's reading and one day I will be as fast as her.

Mrs Ward writes the word bullying in the middle of the whiteboard. 'Listen, children. We are going to learn about bullying. This is when someone is picked on for being different. They're treated unfairly.'

Putting my hand up, I wait to be chosen.

'What does bullying mean to you?'

Loads of other hands wave in the air. My arm is the stem of a daisy with fingers for petals. She chooses a girl at the front to answer and my flower dies. Mrs Ward carries on talking so I tuck my hand under my other arm to stop it shooting up again. I can tell her about bullying because it's the same as picking-on and I know all about that. Well, not the picking-on bit (I never do that) but when others are picking-on me. Zac's not the only one. Sometimes, I'm in the line ready to come into class and the bigger kids in the next row say nasty words. I can tell what's going on. They look at me, then they look at each other. After that they get in a huddle and start talking in whispers that are loud enough to hear. I'd like to bash their faces or stick each one of them with my very pointy finger. It's a shame school rules don't allow it. Anyway, there are too many of them. I try not to listen and start ignoring but it's not easy. If I tell them to stop it, they say it's a joke. Bullying's not funny and I'm not stupid. It's easy to know when someone's being mean but it's hard knowing what to do.

Mrs Ward says friends can fall out but it's not bullying. I have to say sorry after I do something wrong and things are better for a while. But it doesn't stop Zac from telling everyone I bit him. He thinks it's funny to call me Jaws ... but it only happened once. He's good at prod-o-station and that's not kind. It makes me want to hurt him again but I have self-control and I use it.

Mrs Ward goes on and on and my head is heavy as a cannon ball. I hold it in my hands to stop it rolling onto the floor. At last, there's a bit of quiet and I look up again. She's reading from her notebook. I hope it's time for play.

'Here in St Michael's, we don't tolerate bullying and every child is safe,' says Mrs Ward. 'If you think bullying is happening, you must tell me or Miss Choi straight away.'

That's okay to hear but it's not easy. Mrs Ward doesn't always listen and I never get to tell my side. I've got a rep-you-station and teachers don't give me a chance. I think tall-or-ate is a funny word. When there's bullying, it's a bit like being eaten. Or gobbled up. Mum and Dad say I'm not to worry about it because they love me loads.

'Following an incident yesterday, you must also tell us if bullying happens on your way to school or on your way home.'

I wonder why Mrs Ward is saying this. Picking-on happens in the playground most of the time. Zac is nudging the boy sitting next to him and their heads are going up and down like the lid on the kettle. (The ones that have a hinge.) There are whispered words going from one group to the next group. Everyone knows more than me but I hear the names Piotr and Kuba. They're new boys in the top class and they hang around together. In the playground, they talk in their own language and the words don't make sense to me. Before they came to our school, a display was put in the hall with photos and information on Poland. This is a country in Europe and Wictoria from my class goes back there for a holiday every year. After Brexit is done, Nanny Phil says there won't be new children filling up St Michael's. She says this is a good thing but I'm not sure why.

'Quiet now, children.'

The bubble of voices stops.

'I'm not going to share all the details, but two children walking home from school yesterday were approached by a man who tried to hit them. They got very frightened and we're relieved the children aren't hurt. This kind of behaviour is wrong and against the law.'

Samira's hand goes up.

'I've already said I'm not going in to details. Put your hand down.'

Samira doesn't do as she's told. Her arm is straight as an axe handle and her eyes are staring like she's ready to chop off Mrs Ward's head.

'If you must, Samira. What is it?'

'Are the police coming?'

'That's not for you to worry about. Everything's been dealt with. This is just to remind you about letting us know if anything happens when you're with your responsible adult coming into school or going home. There's a letter being sent to your families this afternoon to explain everything. Let's not spend our time fussing. Come on, sit up straight children.'

Making my back stiff, I fold my arms and my head pops up tall. What Mrs Ward says is very interesting. Picking-on happens to me in school but it goes on in other places and with other children as well. Finding out about bullying is important and I wish I had listened better. I need to know more!

'Let's see who's ready for playtime,' says Mrs Ward. 'The triangle children are looking very smart.'

I slump down because I want to stay in class today. It's my chance to ask questions.

'Okay, triangles and rectangles are first out.'

The children tramp over to the hooks in the corridor to get their coats then they line up at the door.

'Now the squares. Very good for you! After that, it's the diamonds.'

I want to talk to Mrs Ward, so I hang around her desk while the others line up. Mrs Ward opens the door and everyone tears out but not me.

'You're being a slowcoach, Huxley,' she says.

I'm a bit worried because there's picking-on when Nanny Phil says stuff other people don't like. It was sad when she went off without a proper goodbye. Then Mum got cross for having to mind Juno in the office while Paula took photographs of the big houses. It's alright again with Nanny Phil helping out.

'Do grown-ups bully?' I ask.

'Yes. As I was telling you.' Mrs Ward picks up her mug from her desk. 'That's why it's always important to tell someone in school.'

Now it's really hard to think.

'Don't look worried, Huxley. These things don't happen very often in our community because we care for each other. But it's playtime and you have to be outside.' Mrs Ward opens the door for me and I'm standing on my own watching children dash around. I spot Samira and

I think she's waiting for me. I go over to her and she finds my hand. Through the window, we see into the hall where the nursery children practise arse-hem-play. I'm allowed to say the joke in my head (so long as Mrs Ward doesn't read my mind). We can't say hello to Zahra as she's busy.

'Do you know how babies are made?' I ask.

'Of course,' says Samira.

'They don't get in through your belly button.'

'I know.' Samira's eyes spin.

'There's a special hole near where mums wee and the dad plants a seed there. It's what my dad told me,' I say. 'He doesn't lie.'

Samira makes her eyes spin again. 'Everybody lies. We can't help it. My mum calls them silly stories.'

'We're not supposed to lie,' I say.

'No, but silly stories don't matter.'

'Okay.' We don't talk any more because ideas tumble inside my head like clothes in the dryer.

Back in class, I find it hard doing work and I'm all in a muddle for the rest of the day. I'm pleased when school is nearly over and Mrs Ward finds a book in the class library. She starts to read it out loud. It's not my best one about the train but I enjoy the way she changes her voice to read the different bits. Ben bashes into me as we put on our coats. I bash him back as we go outside. Nanny Phil, Paula and Mum are in a huddle around Juno's buggy. They're all friends. Nanny Phil sticks her tongue out when she sees me. I poke mine back at her.

'Enough of that,' says Paula. 'Honestly, Mum, you're as bad as the kids.'

'I'm on my best behaviour, got to keep it zipped.' Nanny Phil presses her lips together to keep her mouth shut.

'You have to eat,' I say.

'It's the talking that gets me in trouble,' she says.

'I know, it's the same for me.'

22

Church happens on Sunday. Sometimes Mum doesn't feel up to it because she works very hard in the office. Today she has energy and doesn't lie in. We arrive early and I can sit at the front. When the song ends, I'm too busy clapping and forget to follow the crocodile line into Junior Church. After I catch up, I turn around to wave at Mum and she waves back. Before the door closes, I have a chance to whizz my eyes around the rows but I know Leonard isn't there. No scooter you see. I wonder if that's why Mum is smiling.

It's a busy morning doing colouring and munching biscuits. I drink a lot of blackcurrant squash and Lucy says I have a moustache. She sends me to the sink to clean up. I see my face in the mirror and quite like the look. I don't want to wipe away the flash of purple but I have to in the end. Lucy hands me a wet paper towel and I give a good rub. After that, she watches me walk to the coffee bar where Mum's waiting. On the table there's a beaker for me and it's got orange inside. Yippee! I jump onto the chair and she puts her arm around my back while she chats to some ladies. You can tell they're old because they wear white helmets – all the colour has gone from their hair!

The sitting area of the coffee bar doesn't have brick walls. Instead, there are big glass windows that go from the ceiling to the floor. This means it's easy to watch what's going on in the high street and also along the side of the church that's called a garden. I don't think this is the right name because there are only paving stones and no flowers. Making my neck into a crane, I swing my head down and up like a hook. I see all sorts of funny things when I'm pretending. My eyes zoom in and out and finally I realise who's sitting on the garden bench. It's Leonard!

I take a sneaky look at Mum. She's talking to the ladies so I slide off the chair and bumble along the windows until I reach the door to the garden. It really is Leonard because his scooter is parked nearby. I know I'm not supposed to talk to him but it must be okay to smile. I wonder if he likes that other boy better than me. The one he told me about who's learning English. How can I find out?

It's sad when you have to be by yourself. Being left out isn't kind and Jesus doesn't want it to happen. If I slip outside, no one will notice. It will take two minutes to check Leonard and me are still friends. I don't even have to speak. Smiling is enough. I can be quick with my speedy smile.

I go into the garden and watch Leonard reading a book. The page has lots of pictures. It's not the Bible. In our church, they're made of blue cardboard with gold letters stamped on top. I take a step closer and he sees me. We give each other a good stare. Leonard smiles and opens his mouth as if he's going to say something. Before the words come, I whip out my finger and press it against my lips. This is the signal to keep quiet but we can have fun without talking! I get an idea and I think Leonard will join in. Soon as he shuts his book, I do the same, except I haven't got a book so I close my hands together. He takes a flask from the basket of his scooter. (We use one of these on family picnics so Mum and Dad can have hot tea.) I pretend I'm holding a flask as well. Leonard takes off the cup and balances it on his knee. I can't put anything on my legs – that's because I'm standing on them! I pretend to unscrew the top same as Leonard. We can't stop smiling at each other because we've made up a game and it's called copying.

I'm having a great time with Leonard and I won't be in trouble because I haven't said a word. The problem is, I really want to talk! I put my hand across my mouth like a gag and this makes Leonard laugh so much the cup tumbles off his knee and there's tea spilling onto his trousers. Quick as a flash, I find my handkerchief and dab it on Leonard's leg to dry up the wet. His hand is on my shoulder. Without me being there and being helpful, I think he might fall off the bench from the shock of it. The trouble is, I have a sneaky feeling I've been out of the coffee bar for too long. Just as I turn to go back, there's Mum standing in the doorway, filling up all the space with her hands on her hips. Ooh-ooh, I'm in for it. I look to see what Leonard's doing and he's getting on his scooter and escaping. Good for him. I look back at Mum and her face is pink. She stands still as a statue and I am ash-aimed because I've been caught. My legs turn to jelly and I wobble along the ramp and up to the door. She doesn't actually say anything until we're back at home. I have to sit on the stairs like when I was little. It's called the naughty step for a reason.

'I didn't talk to Leonard.' The words fall out of my mouth. 'I didn't say one thing. You ask Leonard, if you don't believe me.'

'I'm not going to check with…' Mum takes a big breath and tries to change her face to a happier one. 'You know what I've told you about staying safe. If you go wandering off and I don't know where you are, anything could happen. Imagine if there was an accident!'

'I was in the church garden.'

She gulps a breath and her eyes go stiff. 'You were with Leonard and it isn't safe for you to be around him.'

'But he hasn't got many friends.'

'Exactly,' says Mum. 'Other people know better.'

Mum kneels on the carpet and looks up at me because I'm taller than her from my place further up the stairs. 'I'm not angry with you, Huxley. It's my job to keep you safe and I can't do that if you're with someone we don't trust.'

'Other people trust Leonard.'

Mum screws up her face, 'Who?'

Searching my brain for the best answer, I'm about to say Leonard's friends with another boy. All of a sudden, I get an idea, 'Lucy!'

'Yes, well. Lucy has inside knowledge because she's part of the church management. That doesn't mean we have to agree with everything she says. For once, Dad actually thinks differently to her. I'm going to have to tell him what you did and he's not going to be pleased.'

Oh dear! Dad in a mood. This is not a happy-making time.

'We'll talk some more when Dad's back from the shops.'

I'm told to go into the lounge and Mum puts on a DVD but I'm not interested. My head is full of worries. Mum is in the hall and she's on the phone and I think she's talking to Dad. She says stuff about Leonard. This makes me angry so I push my toys off the shelf and they fall bang-pong-bash in a pile. I am not going to tidy them. I take a pencil from the upside-down basket and drum it against the radiator: pling, plang, plug.

Soon as Dad gets home, he comes to find me. He moves around tidying the place like he's on a special mission. When the carpet is cleared of my things, I have to sit on the sofa. Dad's knees stick out because he's on the tiny stool meant for putting up feet. He brings his face close to mine and I can see the lines that spread from around his eyes. Putting my hands on either side of his face, I stretch the skin to smooth away the folds.

'Stop that, Huxley.' His voice is low and slow.

I cross my arms, not sure what to do with them.

'You're not in any trouble,' he says.

My sock has gone thin where my big toe is. I waggle it to see the nail.

'There are one or two things I need to ask you about this morning at church.'

'Lucy made me wash off my moustache.'

'What?'

'I slurped juice and the colour stayed on me.'

'It's not that.' Dad stares at the carpet then at me. 'It's about Leonard. Tell me what happened.'

This is serious business. I must be honest and helpful, that's the rule. 'He played a game with me.'

'That's not allowed!'

'I didn't talk to him.' The words come out shouty.

'It's okay, Huxley.' Dad holds my hand and my fingers are hidden inside his. I try to turn the gold ring he wears and this uses up brain power. He squeezes my fingers to stop them fidgeting. 'Just tell me everything.'

I gulp to get my memory working. 'Leonard and me did a copying game.'

'Yes.' Dad looks straight at me but I don't want to stare back.

'He poured tea from his flask and it spilt over his trousers.'

'What happened next?'

'I wanted to help so I tried to mop up the wet with my handkerchief.'

Dad holds my chin and I have to look him in the face. 'Now this is important, Huxley. Did he touch you?'

I don't understand what Dad's going on about. 'I was the one with the hanky. It was me trying to dry the spill.'

'Did his hands go anywhere near you?'

I think hard. I don't know what is the right answer. All of a sudden, a tear spills from my eye. I'm sad when Mum and Dad are cross. Dad puts his arms around me and I snuggle under his chin. I wipe my wet face on Dad's T-shirt.

'Or did Leonard make you put your hands on him?'

This is a strange question. 'Like where?'

'On his willy.'

'Don't be silly.' I pull away from Dad because I have to laugh. 'Silly-willy!'

'We're not playing rhyming words.' Dad is cross again. 'Did he touch your willy?'

'No!'

'Or anywhere else?'

It's Dad being silly now. But his face is cross and his eyes are sad.

'Just tell me the truth, Huxley.'

I've got to say something. 'He patted my shoulder.'

'That does it.' Dad pulls away and shakes his fist in the air. 'Can't keep his bloody hands to himself.'

My dad is a jack-in-the-box! He springs off the stool and he's out in the kitchen shouting. I race to follow him. Mum raises her hand – she's a police officer stopping traffic. Everything goes quiet. No more shouting, no more moving, we are frozen.

•   •   •   •   •

Cheese goes runny when it's on toast and heated under the grill. I mustn't touch the oven but I watch through the glass to see what's happening. I see drips falling and tell Mum it's ready. We sit at the table and eat together on Sundays. Dad puts on the radio to hear the news then turns it off again before the man has finished speaking. My first bite is extra hot. That's because Mum hid a slice of tomato under the cheese and it burns. I flap my hand over my mouth to cool my tongue. Although Mum watches me, she doesn't say anything, just reaches over and cuts my bread into smaller bits.

The phone rings and Mum jumps out of her chair to answer it. My plate looks like a jigsaw with all the pieces mucked up. I've eaten one bit, so there's a hole in the puzzle.

'Lucy's coming round in half an hour,' says Mum.

'She's got some explaining to do,' says Dad.

Although I'm sent to play in my bedroom, my bat ears are working. I can hear Lucy's voice and Mum's and Dad's. The way they speak reminds me of walking over stepping stones. This means being careful or you might fall in the river. Their words come one at a time. It's not even interesting stuff! They're going on about meetings and forms being filled in and making sure children are safe. It's much better when there's chatter. Oh dear, oh dear. I try to be a patient boy but really, how much longer will they be?

23

Mum says I can't go to Light Club again because she's fallen out with Lucy. This is not fair on me. I haven't done anything wrong and I'm missing my chance to make true friends. Ben is only a friend half of the time and that isn't true. Samira is a new friend. And Leonard, he's a not-allowed-to-have friend. In my mind, a true friend is someone who is interested in the same things. They laugh at the same jokes. They're friendly even if there are accidents or times you don't think the same.

'There's no point in sulking, Huxley. You'll get used to what we've decided. Go and find something to play with. I need to cook the dinner.'

I stand there in the kitchen not moving. Mum turns her back and does stuff in the sink.

'Go on, scoot!'

She is looking at the wall and I'm surprised she says scoot because Leonard is the only person with a proper scooter. Maybe Mum is watching me with the extra eyes in the back of her head, but she's got too much hair to see me properly. I wish I had a scooter, 'With handlebars made of Neoprene'.

'How's that?' Mum turns and looks at me.

'Leonard's scooter's got Neoprene,' I shout. 'And you told me to scoot.'

'We're not talking about Leonard.' Her face screws up. 'I meant you're to get busy doing something.'

I fold my arms and my head is filled with grumpy thoughts. 'Get busy doing what?'

'You've got homework, haven't you?'

Mum takes our dinner out of the fridge. I know it is a chicken because of the humpy back and the not really white colour. I watch her spread butter over the skin with a paper towel. Yellow goes over all the little bumps where the feathers once stuck out. I'm glad we don't eat feathers. They would tickle.

It takes ages for a roast chicken to cook and I am surprised we're having one as it's not Sunday. Mum didn't have a chance to cook it at the weekend because of all the things she and Lucy and Dad had to say. I don't want to think about it again. Even doing homework takes my mind off that. On the pages in my writing book, there are lines going across. I've got to write words so they sit straight. Some letters have tails that hang down and others have arms that stick up. My letters bounce around the page like they're astronauts on the moon. It's funny because I've got to write about space. The programme we watched at school showed the real live landing but it's not easy to write things down. I wish I could suck the end of my pencil but the ones at home don't taste good. Hmm. Better make a start.

Mum looks over my shoulder as I jab the last full stop onto the page. I'm finished!

'One more sentence,' says Mum.

'Awh.' I can't imagine anything else to write. Instead, I count the words. Sixteen. Everyone wants me to do more. 'It's not fair.'

'Do you wish you were on the moon?'

I wish the chicken was ready. Mum is staring at me and this means she is waiting for an answer. I nod.

'Well, write that and then you're done.'

I'm stuck with my spelling. 'How does chicken go?'

'Let me see.'

'I've got the *ch* but I'm not sure if it's *kicking k*.'

'You're supposed to be writing *I wish I was on the moon*.'

'Oh, I thought you meant *I wish the chicken was ready*.'

'Of course not!'

I try to rub out the wrong words but they stay put. When Mum has a go the mistake disappears and then she watches me while I finish writing. I throw down the pencil and it rolls off the table. Diving underneath to rescue it, I pretend I'm picking up a coin from the bottom of the swimming pool. Soon as I come to the surface, Mum's packed everything away.

•   •   •   •   •

We eat leftovers for two days in a row until I am sick of looking at bones on the chicken car-crash. The last of it goes in Dad's sandwiches. I have school dinners and Mum doesn't have time to eat at the office. It's Mum's turn to take me to school and our bikes are ready to cycle. The path through the forest is slippy and Mum says I have to stay beside her. I'm not allowed to talk to anyone unless she says something to them first. This includes the man we see most days with his dog. I remember to wait for Mum to speak before I can say *hello* to him. It isn't fair to me. I like speaking more than listening.

My bike goes under the shelter and I leave my helmet swinging from the handlebar. Mum leans hers against the railings because she has to turn it around and go to the office. She ducks to say hello to Juno in her buggy and afterwards chats with Paula. Looking around the playground, I decide to join the game of chase. It's fun being part of the group but it's better to be there at the beginning. When the bell goes, I grab my book bag from the basket at the front of Mum's bike. She plonks a kiss on the top of my head then I run for the line. Samira lets me squeeze in with her. We're not at the front and we're not at the back. It's okay being in the middle.

Mrs Ward asks us to sit on the carpet for the register then she starts talking in her extra loud voice. She says the same things again and again. I know how letters build words and words join in a send-tense. There's always a capital letter at the beginning and a full stop at the end. I hold my face between my hands because I'm so bored my head might drop off my neck.

On our table is a pile of special writing books. I topple the lot and look for mine. It's got my name on the front and that helps me to find it. Inside, the first few pages are filled with work and I need to find a clean one. Writing the date at the top comes next. Today, we have to make up a story about transport. I did stuff about space for homework and now there's more writing to do. The blank page is so white it shines like a torch. I can't think of any words. My brain spins around to warm up my head. Chewing the end of the pencil helps and I magic an idea. It's about flying through the air on a frisbee. It's very hard to get going but after I put a few words down, the writing spreads to fill the page. There's no stopping me!

My teacher wanders around the classroom but we're not allowed to. I want my pencil to work better and need to go over to the sharpener. If I stick in the writing end, it gets whizzed to a point. When Mrs Ward stops moving around, I take a chance. My pencil is sharp in a second, then I am a fox roaming back to my place. I have a look to see what's happening on the square table. They can do their drawings first. It's not fair! Diamonds have to wait until after the writing is finished.

'Back to work.' Lucy wears her Miss Choi serious face because she's teaching. 'I'm going to find you at playtime.'

'What for?'

'Nothing to worry about,' she whispers.

It is wet play again. I can't stand it when we're trapped inside. There's no room to move and the board games in school are rubbish. We're allowed to go in the reading tent two at a time but Samira's already looking at animal books with another boy. I'm not interested in playing shops with the girls so I walk outside to the toilets and check for my coat. It's hanging where I left it. While I'm there, I see Lucy coming along the corridor. I can't be bothered to think of her as Miss Choi. Although it's a lot of work, I must try.

'As you're out here, Huxley, you can help tidy up.'

She bends to pick up coats that have fallen off the pegs. There are hats and scarves that need to find a home and we match them up.

'Perfect job, Huxley.' The floor is clear of stuff and one of the dinner ladies brings Miss Choi a cup of tea.

'I want a strawberry milkshake.'

'Askers don't get!' The dinner lady is cross and goes back to the kitchen.

'There's water in your bottle,' says Miss Choi.

'It's not the same.'

'Have a drink and you won't be thirsty.'

'Is your baby coming soon?'

'I hope so.'

'I want a baby.'

Miss Choi laughs. 'Would you like a brother or a sister?'

I have a little think. Ben and Samira have sisters. Zac's got a brother. 'A sister.'

'You'll need to talk to your mum and dad about it.'

I do that all the time. 'Can you ask for me?'

'It's difficult at the moment.'

'I know.'

~~Lucy~~ Miss Choi looks at her watch.

'Is playtime nearly over?'

'We've got a few minutes. I just want to chat about you and your friends.'

'I'm not allowed to talk to Leonard.'

'I mean your friends in school.'

'Oh.' I put on my thinking face and feel my skin stretch across my forehead. 'Skin is a funny thing. You get it on custard and on bananas.'

'Yes, you do,' says Miss Choi. 'How are you and Samira getting on? You've been friendly with her lately.'

I remember the biscuit we shared and that gives me an idea. 'Paula counts fig rolls as part of my five-a-day.'

'I see. Did you bring one into school?'

'No,' I say. 'Not long ago, Samira gave me half her biscuit.'

'That's being friendly. All the adults in school want you to have friends. Happy children learn better. You can always tell Mrs Ward if you're feeling lonely or need a bit of help. Teachers are good at listening to children's worries.'

What is she going on about? 'I'm not worried.'

'I mean, if you get worried … or you feel you need some help staying friends or making friends.'

Her face is screwed up like she's saying the most important thing in the world. I think she's wrong – my teacher's always too busy to listen.

'I'll miss you when you go.'

'And I'll miss you, too.' ~~Lucy~~ Miss Choi puts her arm around my shoulders and gives me a little shake. I rock my head from side to side as if she's made me giddy. It's while I try to get Miss Choi laughing that the bell goes. This means I must go back in the classroom. I have to be there before Mrs Ward or I might be in trouble.

'I'm going to find someone to come into school and help everybody be more friendly.'

'Cool,' I say. 'Will they help you and Mum make up as well?'

She shakes her head. 'Sorry, Huxley.'

24

We're sitting on the carpet at home time and for some reason, Mrs Ward says Mum won't be picking me up today. I'm to go home with Ben instead. I'm pleased Mum is friends with Paula and I'm sorry she's fallen out with Lucy. Then I start thinking about Mrs Vartan and her flaky white face covered in flour. Lots of things in the world go wrong but we have to cope. Mrs Ward sees my sad face and tells me to cheer up. I give her a smile. She looks away before I'm ready and my smile is wasted. I see Paula through the window but I have to wait for Mrs Ward to call me and Ben. After she says our names, Zac is in a mood because I'm going home with Ben and he's not. He bashes the carpet with his fist then shakes his fingers out like they're hurt. He's really stupid sometimes and I wonder why Ben plays with him.

At Ben's house, Paula has put photographs of us on the dining room table. It's fun looking at pictures of me and Ben and Juno. Then Paula tells us we can cut out our faces and stick them onto the back of a wooden spoon to make a puppet. This is a mad idea! We get busy with the scissors and glue. We're going to do a special puppet show for Juno as she's not clever enough to help us with the making.

'You're Spider-Man here.' I pass the photo to Ben. He's dressed up in a special spider suit but he can't bounce to the top of tall buildings.

'Here's another with my birthday cake.' It never got cut up at Ben's party because he was sick. Instead, he had a slice of it in his lunchbox every day until it was eaten.

'Mega-cake,' I say. 'I bet it tasted great.'

'Yeah. I'll have another one like that next year.'

'Cool.' I guess I'll be able to eat a bit then.

There's a photo of me and Ben with our heads pressed together. It's too small to go on a spoon. I find one of me in the garden from back in the summer and it's good because I have a big smile. We are busy choosing, Juno is asleep in the buggy and Paula works on the computer in the corner. There is a room upstairs in my house called a study and it's where our computer and special things are kept. Paula has her camera in the drawer under her desk. It's hidden away so that Juno can't break it. I'm excellent at being careful with equipment but Paula still doesn't let me have a go.

Ben has cut out lots of faces and spends time choosing which one to stick onto his wooden spoon. There's some wool we can put on as well to make crazy hair. Ben is using the glue and it's boring watching him work out how to do it. I sneak up behind Paula to see what she's up to on the computer. There's a photo of Leonard on her screen! He sits on his scooter outside the fruit shop where those boys threw oranges. I'm not pleased when I remember this. Paula's page is like the ones pinned to tree trunks and fences to let everyone know a cat or a dog is missing. At the top there are large words that say PARENTS BEWARE and there's small writing underneath. I screw up my eyes getting ready to read. Soon as I do, the page disappears. Dad's always making this happen when he doesn't want me to see what's on the screen.

'Is your puppet finished?' Paula grabs a pile of paper ready to fill the printer.

'Not yet. Ben's using the glue.'

'He won't be long.' She puts the paper into the slot.

'Why is Leonard on your computer?'

'I've just been playing around.' She straightens the pages.

This isn't right. Leonard's my not-allowed-to-have friend but I can still ask questions. 'Where are the photos you took of me and Ben that day?'

'They were blurry. I couldn't hold the camera still.'

'The one of Leonard is okay. It looks like a poster.'

'You're not wrong.' Now she's searching in a drawer.

'Has Leonard got lost?'

'If only.' Paula mutters then she stops what she's doing to look at me. Her teeth show when she gives a big smile. 'I'll get you some juice and a special snack. You'd like that, wouldn't you?'

Mum comes to collect me and there's time to put on our puppet show before we leave. She sits on the sofa next to Paula and Juno is between the two mums. Me and Ben scrunch up behind a stool so that no one can see our bodies and we poke the sticks above our heads. We make up a little rhyme about Ben and Huxley then we start wrestling with our puppets. Paula says it's not a proper story and we have to do it again.

The second time goes better but then our puppets get bored and have an argument.

'Enough is enough, Huxley.' Mum takes the spoons from us and that means the show is over. 'Put your shoes on.'

I am quick at doing as I'm asked and I'm ready in a flash. Now, it's my turn to wait. Mum and Paula are at the computer and their heads are pressed together.

'It's rude to whisper,' I say.

'Thank you for reminding me,' says Mum. Then she turns away and she's talking to Paula again. 'Why are you so worried all of a sudden?'

'I never trusted him. That's why I took the photo in the first place. I always had this in mind if he tried anything new. All I want to do is put a few notices around town.'

'He's weird,' Mum shakes her head. 'But Lucy's convinced me and Jed there's nothing untoward.'

'Just because he goes to church isn't a guarantee. Think of all the priests who go messing around with young children.'

'Lucy's doing a police check so he can volunteer at Light Club.'

'You never can tell. He could turn any day. How would you feel if he abducted a neighbour's kid?'

'It wouldn't exactly be a rapid getaway on his mobility scooter!'

I really do think they are talking about Leonard. I must listen and watch extra hard. Paula is trying to hand over a bunch of papers and Mum won't take them. I wonder if they are the lost posters with photos of Leonard. Oh dear! I hope nothing's happened to him.

'It's important to warn other parents,' says Paula.

'You could be had up for libel!'

Mum hides her hands so she can't hold any of the pages. If I don't get to understand what's going on soon, I'll burst into one hundred pieces. That's when I come up with a brilliant question, 'What's a lie-bell?'

'Nothing.' Mum and Paula reply at the same time.

'Snap!' I say but the mums don't want to play the game.

'You can't go pinning them around town,' says Mum.

'Oh God, I suppose you're right. Now I've wasted all this paper. Not to mention the ink. I'll dump them in the recycling.'

'You can't! Someone might dig them out and you'd end up in trouble.'

'I was only trying to do the right thing.'

'I'll take a few and put them through the shredder at work.' Mum shoves the loose pages into her bag. 'You can do the rest next time you're in the office.'

I guess that's all right then. Leonard can't be lost after all.

25

Dad takes me to school as Mum's looking at one of the big houses near the park. If Mum sells it, she gets bonus money. More presents at Christmas. Yippee. We walk because Dad hasn't got a bike and it's no fun riding on my own. I don't like pedalling slow as a snail.

When I'm grown up, I will have long legs same as Dad. His arms are stretched from carrying his briefcase. There are heavy papers inside and other important stuff like his packed lunch. I caught a whiff while he was cutting bread so I think he's got egg sandwiches today. School dinners are better. The lady in the cap gives me extra chips for saying *please* and *thank you*.

Under the busy road is the best bit of going to school and because we're walking there's plenty of time. I can hear our footsteps clonking through the tunnel and the cars roar above our heads.

'Why are the walls covered in bathroom tiles?'

'Some council boffin thought it was a good idea.'

'And how come there are puddles?'

'Keep away.' Dad pulls my jacket so I don't get my shoes wet. 'They're not made from rainwater.'

'Funny place for a picture!' I stand in front of the black lines that shoot up the wall. There's a rocket with two balls of flames coming from the engines ready to jet off.

'It's called graffiti,' says Dad. 'It'll take hours for someone to scrub that off.'

'Gruff-eat-tea.' I smile at Dad as I say the word.

He looks into the distance and shakes his head. 'Come on or you'll be late for school.'

There's a ramp up to the road and then we're in front of some houses. I know the way without any bother. Along the little path is next and today there is a group of boys coming towards us. They've got jackets that mean they belong to secondary school. The one at the front isn't wearing his tie but slashes it around like a sword. The others laugh.

'Stand to the side and let them get past,' says Dad.

I have a proper stare at the boy in front and I think he's the same one that threw oranges at Leonard. I turn my fingers into binoculars for a better look and it's really him.

'Dad, he's the one...'

'Hang on a minute, Huxley. My mobile's ringing.'

Dad is talking on his phone. He's got his hand over the ear that's not listening and he's sort of folded over. The boys are coming closer and closer but I'm not scared. I stand in the middle of the path with my elbows sticking out. I've something to say and they won't go by me until they know I'm very angry about what they did to Leonard. I swallow a big breath to make my voice loud.

'YOU THREW ORANGES AT MY FRIEND.'

The boys stop walking and stand still as icicles. Dad now has his briefcase open on the ground and he's crouching so he's shorter than me.

'What's that?' The boy with the tie is holding it in a straight line between his hands.

'Stop blocking the way, Huxley,' says Dad.

'I'm not budging.'

Dad doesn't hear because he's searching in his case and he's talking into his mobile at the same time.

'What's up with you, sprout?' asks the boy.

'You were unkind to Leonard.'

The one with the brown hair yawns and doesn't cover his mouth.

'You need to learn good manners,' I say.

'Calm down, sprout!'

'Come over here, Huxley.' Dad shouts and waves his arm. Next minute, he's speaking on the phone again. I don't budge.

'You must say sorry to Leonard.'

'Who?' asks the leader.

'He means the pervert on the mobility scooter,' says the brown hair.

'As if,' says the leader.

'Don't hurt my friend,' I say. 'He is a kind man.'

'Kind? What's he done that's kind?'

Lots of ideas rush through my head. I want to say he gave me a ride on his scooter but I know that'll get me in to trouble. I think about telling them he's kind to share his chocolate. Then I come up with the best thing that is genius. 'He makes sure I'm zipped in and buttoned up when it's cold outside.'

'Zip in and button up?' The leader says my words over again. The boys fall against each other, laughing and snorting. I don't understand what's so funny. The leader turns his head like a dog that's been in the river and is trying to shake dry. 'I reckon the bloke's a paedo. What else has he been doing?'

I know he's not really interested. 'None of your business.'

Now the leader is very close and staring right in my face. 'Has he been fiddling with you?'

I want him to get out of my way so I yell, 'It's nothing to do with you!'

This time Dad turns around, stops talking and presses the mobile against his jacket. He sticks his other arm in the air and waves it at the boys. 'Clear off you lot! On your way!'

The boys give a yell and bundle along to the other end of the path like it's a big joke. The leader turns as he reaches the main road. 'You better watch out, mate … there's fiddling going on … and we're going to sort it out.'

'You are, are you?' says Dad.

I watch the boys dodge between cars and race to the other side of the road. That's very dangerous! Why aren't they using the tunnel? It's not worth asking Dad because he's busy packing away his papers. He makes the briefcase click shut and then he stands up straight. 'Fiddling indeed. My accounts are in perfect order. Best in the office I'm told.'

'I'm happy they're gone,' I say. 'They were the boys who threw oranges at Leonard.'

'Is that right? They can't be all bad. But, let's not think about it any longer. You need to be in school and I've got work.'

I can't say anything else to Dad when he starts walking extra fast. All I can do is run, skip and jump to keep up.

26

It's friendship week at my school and a special visitor called Tilly has come into our classroom. She has caterpillar cocoons growing out of her head! I'm not going to say anything because that would be rude, but it doesn't stop Ben from nudging me and pointing.

'Listen up, everyone,' says Mrs Ward.

The classroom goes quiet and I sit up extra straight.

'I'd like to introduce you to Tilly who is going to do special work with you today. She is a visitor to our school and I hope you are all going to be on your best behaviour and show respect. What do you say?'

'Yes, Mrs Ward.' We're supposed to say her name together with one voice. Mrs Ward is staring at me. It's not my fault if my lips work fast all by themselves.

'That includes you, Ben.'

Phew! She's not said anything to me. Ben's eyes go all surprised. No one likes being caught out.

It's very hard listening to Tilly because I want to think about caterpillars and that her hair might hatch butterflies. It would be funny if they flew out all at once! But that's not how it works. In *The Very Hungry Caterpillar*, there are holes in the pages to show what's been eaten. I want a caterpillar to munch up the pages of my writing book. It's not going to happen. The only holes I get are after I've done too much rubbing out.

My ears prick up when Tilly starts going on about being friends in school and putting an end to bullying. Zac's an expert bully but he hasn't tried anything since I bit him. Before me and Samira were proper friends, I watched Zac walk straight into Samira and then bash her bag. I know he does stuff like that on purpose but Mrs Ward never sees. If he tried that now I'd make him stop. Samira is my friend and friends stick together. Spying from the corner of my eye, I spot Zac and he's not listening to Tilly. He's playing with the Velcro straps on his shoes and trying to rip them open without making a noise. Him messing around makes me mad. There are loads of words I want to shout at him but I have to swallow them with my spit.

We go to our tables after Tilly finishes speaking. There are some special papers in a pile. It's Samira's turn to do handing out and she's very careful. I remind everyone to say thank you and I'm happy when they do! At the top of the page are the words *stop bullying* and a box where we're to write. My first thought is to get rid of Zac only I know this will land me in trouble. Instead, I write boring stuff like *tell the teacher*. Zac does bad things and he's never found out. I don't want to keep thinking about him, so I let different ideas swim around my head. Leaving people out is another kind of bullying. It doesn't matter about not being invited to someone's party but if there's a game and the same person is never included – that's bullying. Or even if someone is left out when there's talking in a group. Bullying is all around me. I imagine a shark circling under the surface of the sea, and thoughts come into my mind. I shoot my hand in the air as my question is very important.

'What's the problem?' asks Tilly.

'Can secondary boys do bullying?' I ask.

'Yes, but we're doing work on how to stop bullying in this school.'

'Some grown-ups do picking-on other people, don't they?'

'It can happen,' says Tilly. 'Although there are laws to protect people from bullying at work. There are also rules in school to protect children.'

I'm now thinking of Leonard and the way he got oranges thrown at him. 'And when you're going into town?'

'Enough of that talk about walking and town.' Mrs Ward is marching over to my table. It's amazing how she hears everything.

'We're not going discuss the ins and outs of the incident with Kuba and Piotr.'

'It was them!' I say.

Mrs Ward has a pen in her hand and she's tapping her fingers with it. 'You need to concentrate on what you've been asked to do. Think of ways we can be friends and stop bullying at St Michael's.'

'In and around school,' says Tilly.

'Yes. School in general.' Mrs Ward slides the pen into her pocket. 'You must get on and fill up the whole page.'

Tilly comes back a bit later and leans over me to look at my writing. 'That's a good start. Now, write some ideas that come straight from your own head.' She puts a green tick against my words, the bit about telling the teacher, then walks over to another table. Green stands for growing in my school. It means you have to do more thinking and writing. I want to lick the paper and try to rub out the green tick but I'm not going to do that. I squeeze out clever thoughts and write them down instead.

Mrs Ward sorts our papers and we wait on the carpet for the dinner bell to ring.

'If I call your name, you're going to be with Tilly in the corridor space this afternoon. The idea is you'll learn about being yourself and being with others. I'm sure you'll have lots of fun, too.' She finds a list and reads names from it. Me and Samira are in the group. Hurray!

· · · · ·

We didn't ride our bikes this morning, so me and Mum have to walk home. I can hold her hand and this is happy making. I tell her about Tilly and folding paper into a special small book. It has a tuck-in tab to keep it closed so I can write private things. We had to think very hard and decide what makes a good friend. I tell Mum that being friends is knowing the person will be your friend whatever happens. It's a good idea to give someone a chance to be friends.

'Is it okay to not always agree with your friend?' she asks.

I turn my head to look up at the sky. There are big loopy clouds same as curly hair. 'Are you talking about Nanny Phil?'

'I wasn't. No.'

'Nanny Phil says words Paula doesn't like.'

'Paula and Nanny Phil are in the same family. That doesn't count.'

Now my tummy's rumbling and I can't stop the noise from coming. It's only me that knows because my jacket stops sound getting out. I want to eat something to fill the empty hole. I hope there's a chocolate snack left in the tin. Then I remember Samira's joke when she shared her biscuit. 'It's enough to breaks-it friends. Do you get my joke? Brexit breaks up friends.'

'I'd have to laugh if it wasn't true,' says Mum.

'Well, it's not true about Ben. He's only a half-friend.'

Mum's face is pinched, 'Why do you say that?'

'He only plays with me outside school.'

'You're good friends at home. Look at the way you build towers and mountains.'

'At playtimes he's always with the football boys.'

'And you're not keen on football, are you?'

'No.'

'That's a shame.' Mum doesn't say any more but gives my hand a squeeze. We walk on and Mum is staring at the pavement. I try not to step on the cracks.

'You must have another friend,' she says.

'There's Samira.'

Mum gives me a smile and another hand squeeze. 'Samira is a nice girl. Why don't you invite her round for tea?'

Samira's not keen on playing with trains. 'I want to go to her house, instead. She's got a little sister.'

'Of course,' says Mum. 'Let me know what you decide.'

Really, I'm wanting Leonard to visit. Thing is, I know Leonard better than Mum. He is funny and he gets my jokes and we're both the same because we put up with picking-on. After what I've learnt in school today, I can say it's bullying. I stretch my arms out wide-wide-wide. 'I know Leonard this much.'

'Let's not discuss Leonard again,' she says.

'You haven't given him a chance.'

'Yes, I have,' says Mum.

The next day comes and as I look around the playground, I'm still thinking about what Tilly said. Me and Mum stand near the gate while other children taggle inside. A few girls hook their arms together, some boys have arms on shoulders. No one much does that to me. Then I have a reminder. Samira is my friend and we hold hands. When we were with Tilly, we shared our feelings and what to do with sadness. Talking to Mum or Dad at bedtime is a good idea. We also have to think about how other people are feeling.

Nanny Phil is over near the line for the start of school. When Mum begins to chat with Zac's mum, I don't want to hang around. I walk towards Nanny Phil but don't get too close because I'm not ready for going into class. I call over to say hello and she beckons. I mustn't go near in case she tries the dig and poke routine – that might get me in trouble! Instead, I have something important to say.

'Samira is my friend!' I talk in an extra loud voice to make sure she hears.

'Come over and tell me,' she says.

I'm not budging. Nanny Phil looks at the buggy and back at me. She can't be bothered to move.

'You'll have to shout,' booms Nanny Phil.

'Samira's my friend because she doesn't take sides and she plays fun games.'

'You'll never be given a ham sandwich for tea at her house,' Nanny Phil shouts.

The mums standing close go quiet and are looking our way. Not far off, a few girls play a clapping game but around us it is still and things feel strange. I wonder what to say to Nanny Phil. She knows I'm not keen on cold meat.

'I don't like ham.'

'Well bacon then.' Nanny Phil blasts her words.

That's when the door to our classroom shoots open and Mrs Ward is there. 'We need a little chat.'

Oh bother, I'm in trouble again! I've no idea what it's about. I swing around to see if Mum is watching and she is looking but not at me. Turning back, I see Mrs Ward walk over to Nanny Phil. She's doing finger pointing and shaking her head. This is not good news for Nanny Phil. I try to make my bat ears work but they're talking in quiet, slow voices. In the end, I hear Nanny Phil say sorry and she promises to keep her ideas to herself.

Soon as the bell rings, Mum comes over to say goodbye. Afterwards, she makes for the gate but she's way behind Nanny Phil who's already disappearing. It's a shame for Samira that her mum never waits around in the playground because she has to drop Zahra off in the nursery. But then having a sister is a bonus, so I'm not that sorry for Samira. I wait in the line with my head in a muddle. Mrs Ward calls Samira to the front, so she has to stop playing with Wiktoria's hair and go. I don't think she minds too much. It's great being first. All the other classes have gone inside and we're still stuck on the line while Samira and Mrs Ward chat. I guess Nanny Phil got told off from Mrs Ward for talking about Samira. It will be okay because Samira knows silly stories don't matter.

27

Mum says November isn't one of the longest months but it feels like it goes on forever. This is because we have to wait until December for Christmas. I rub my hands together until they're hot and I can't stop a smile pinging my cheeks. Christmas means presents! Mum says she can't think about it until next month and she wishes the shops wouldn't play Christmas songs already. I calm down my excitement by patting my chest then I check the calendar on the wall where Mum writes what happens each day. Some squares for November have got scribble in and lots are crossed out because the days have gone. Take yesterday – Friday – big cross. I flick the page up and there's a few things written in the boxes for December. Letting the November page flap back, it covers everything. The word November is in big print. I count the letters and there are eight. That's a lot for just one word. I whisper the months to check I can remember them in the right order. It's great when the names fall out of my mouth and I don't need to stretch my brain. I do it again but time doesn't go any quicker. I have been waiting ages for Dad to be ready. He's promised to take me for a swim and I have my trunks in my bag and my shaggy towel although Dad's still trying to find his stuff. Mum told him to look in the airing cupboard.

'Ah-ha,' Dad shouts. Then there are his footsteps drumming on the stairs. This is a sign for me to put on my jacket.

The doors to the leisure centre slide open and it's steamy inside. In the café area, there's a crowd of mums blocking the space with their baby buggies. The coffee machine burps and there's a long queue to buy hot drinks. Dad has to pay for our swim at the desk. I go to the window where you can sit and look right over the pool. I am sad to see The Giant In-flat-a-ball is flabby and folded. We're not going to be able to have fun on it today. This means me and Dad will have to make up our own games, so it's not too bad.

Dad flaps the tickets around my head and this is the signal to go into the changing rooms. He takes the one-way track but I reach the way in first by climbing the metal rails. I'm the quickest at changing and there's no beating me today. Swimming is fun! I race Dad doing widths and I finish quicker when he doesn't kick his legs. Sometimes, he throws me up in the air and I land with a huge splash. We call this chucking out the rubbish. I am very good at being chucked and I don't even cry if water makes my eyes sting.

We always get out of the swimming pool before I'm ready but we must obey the voice from the loudspeaker. Dad doesn't bother drying hair and my head is extra cold outside. My ears hurt because of the wind and I keep my head down hoping it will blow right over the top of me. A few of the paving stones are cracked and in the broken bits there are puddles. My foot will fit in the gap.

'Look what you're doing.' Dad drags me close to him. 'This isn't the time for getting stuck in the mud.'

'I won't.'

He grabs my hand and squeezes my fingers so I don't mind leaving the puddle for another time. We pretend we're giants. Two of my big strides are the same as one of Dad's. Then Dad stops joining in and I look around to check what's happening. He drops my hand. 'What's he doing?'

Leonard is driving his scooter. He has to find where the pavement dips to cross the road and he goes in a big loop around us. We watch him heading towards the leisure centre. I want to dash closer and say hello, but Dad holds me back.

Dad shouts, 'Hang on a minute. You're not going in there.'

Leonard keeps his head straight like he hasn't heard and continues towards the ramp. I want Leonard to say hello to me, but I think he doesn't because of Dad. I am in a muddle. All I can do is watch.

'Stay on the bench, Huxley. Wait for me. Don't move.'

True friends always talk to each other. It's sad Leonard and me are not allowed. I will be in trouble from Dad if I don't do what he says. There's a rumble in my tummy, so I sit on the bench and give it a pat. The noise is a sign I need something to eat. To get a snack, I have to behave properly.

The bench is damp from the rain. It's not a very good idea to sit here but I have to stay still. Dad goes to Leonard and stands in the way so he can't drive up the special ramp for buggies, prams and scooters. At first, Leonard smiles like it's a game and he's being friendly. Even bent over, my dad makes Leonard seem small and squashed. I watch Dad jabbing a finger close to Leonard's face. I wish he wasn't doing that. My heart goes boing-boing-boing while I watch. I need to wriggle because the bench is wet and I want to burst out of this place. It's hard sitting still and I can't understand why Dad is so cross.

Leonard flaps his hands about and Dad keeps his pointing finger in the air. He is growling like a dog and Leonard yelps. It's not nice when Dad shouts at me so I'm not surprised to see Leonard with his mouth hanging open. I'm feeling a bit scared, too. My bat ears aren't working that well in the wind and I can't hear what Dad is saying. He's prodding his finger at Leonard again and Dad's still not moving out of the way. Leonard steers his scooter backwards beep-beep-beep and then turns around to go along the path where he came from. I am really sad as I watch him go but then I can't see him any more when the parked cars and trees hide him.

I know about being a lonely-only and this makes my heart heavy. On top of that, my bottom is sore from sitting on the bench. I'm scrunched up from twisting around and trying to listen and hoping everything will turn out okay. I don't know what to do with the thoughts flying around my head so I stand up straight and spring my arms high. Perhaps, I can touch the sky. I have a little laugh because it's a fun idea and the words high and sky make an excellent rhyme. At times like this, you've got to try and stay happy. When Dad comes back to where I'm waiting, he's in a bad mood. I can tell from the way he snatches our swimming bags from the bench and chucks the straps over his shoulder. If he did a stretch, he might feel better.

Dad walks very fast and I have to rush to keep up. I remember my rumbling tummy and that I'm hungry enough to eat a lion. But, we don't stop to buy a snack although I've tried to be good. All we do is walk-walk-walk until we're back at our house. Soon as we're inside, Dad slings our swimming bags on the floor and marches into the kitchen where Mum is ironing. She does this on my school uniform to have it ready for Monday. Wearing crinkly clothes is not allowed!

I don't feel like hanging around in the kitchen. Dad's angry feelings are a volcano that might blow up. If Mum's face changes with the wind it will turn into a question mark. Sitting on the beanbag gets me snuggly and gives me time to think. I hope Leonard's okay but I can't say anything because Dad is cross. It's best to stay out of the way.

'You'll never believe who was heading for the leisure centre,' says Dad.

'I guess from the tone of your voice, it was Leonard.' Mum shakes her head and puts the iron upright. I stare at the base where steam hisses out. Don't put a hand near it and be hurt. I've never had a burn but Mum gets them if she's not being careful.

'I gave him a thorough bollocking and told him to clear off,' says Dad.

'He goes to the right places,' says Mum. 'It's full of kids at weekends.'

'Children in swimming costumes and toddlers under the showers. I ask you!'

I'm not sure what they're going on about and I don't like the way they're talking. Leonard is my friend not theirs. And he can go for a swim if he wants. I know this because I've seen Leonard get help from one of the ladies at the pool. He can have a splash and a swim same as everyone. I decide to tell Mum and Dad. 'There's a disabled chair at the pool to help Leonard into the water.'

'Stop shouting, Huxley,' says Dad.

'He uses the special chair to have a swim.'

'Leonard isn't interested in exercise.'

'You don't understand.'

'Look, Huxley. He isn't a good person. I don't want Leonard going in the leisure centre and gawping at the little kids. It's not right.'

'Shush, Jed. Be careful what you say. And I can't believe Lucy continues to insist he's no harm.'

'I'm not having this.' Dad zips up his jacket again. 'I'm going round to speak to Tony. We have to sort this out once and for all.'

•　　•　　•　　•　　•

We can't eat our dinner until Dad comes home. To stop me from starving, Mum lets me have a cheese sandwich. Dad is gone for ages and the snack I ate was so long ago, I'm hungry again. Soon as Dad's back, we sit at the table. Mum tells Dad to *keep shtum*. This means he's not allowed to talk and even if I ask a question no one answers. On my plate are potatoes and carrots and broccoli and beef. My meat is brown because I have the end bit. I think Mum finds it very difficult to concentrate when Dad is flying off the handle. We eat our dinner without saying much and this means you can hear noises. Dad's teeth go crunch-crunch-crunch and in between he hums to show he's enjoying his dinner. Mum licks her lips. I like gnashing and gobbling although that's not good manners. Soon as it goes quiet again, I kick the table. It's strange that tables have legs but they haven't got knees for bending in the middle.

'Please stop the banging, Huxley,' says Mum. 'You're giving me a headache.'

I make my feet stay still. When Mum has a headache, she goes to bed early and it's boring without her around. I wonder what Ben is doing and this reminds me of a question.

'What kind of words did you say to Tony?'

Dad's fork stops on the journey to his mouth. It's loaded with food and he's almost ready to land it.

'It's a private matter.' Mum gets in before Dad has a chance to speak.

'Absolutely right,' says Dad.

'You're making a plan and I'm not included.'

'Too right we have a plan,' says Dad. 'Sometimes there are things only adults can deal with.'

That puts an end to the talk. I sit there with my feet still, and I eat what's left of my dinner. Silence is back again but I am clever in dreaming up something to say.

'Is there any pudding?' I ask.

28

It's dark outside and Mum is on the phone again. The first call was from Dad and she kept saying stuff like *I can't believe it* and *oh no* and *everything's okay*. I ask her what's going on and she says I have to wait until Dad comes home. It's a good job I've got patience. Now, she's talking to Paula. I know this because Mum nods while she's speaking. I want to say a thing or two but Mum points towards the table where I'm meant to be doing my homework. I turn on the spot and slide my feet across the floor.

Having a slip-slop means I'm a skater. This is great practice for when the ice rink is set up again. Last winter, I was able to go right round the edge by hanging onto the fence. I am very daring on ice. Sometimes I shoot right across the middle and if I'm about to fall, I grab the hand of the nearest person to save me. Nobody minds helping. Mum is hopeless. All she does is stand by the side and watch and laugh at me. She buys hot chocolate after it's over so I don't mind.

A sock comes off my foot as I sit on the floor near to where Mum is chatting on the phone. The balled-up sock is a gerbil. This one is a spotty gerbil and you don't find them in real life. Zac has one that lives in a cage in his bedroom. I know this because I went to his house a long time ago (before the biting happened). He didn't want me there but we had to do something as my mum and his mum were busy with school stuff. Zac's mum runs the PTA (the letters stand for parents, teachers and something or other). This means she's always getting other mums and dads to help her. So, Mum and Zac's mum were chatting and he took me into his bedroom. The only nice thing that happened was being allowed to hold his gerbil. Its little feet tickled my hands and its fur was soft. Gerbils have whiskers just like cats.

Barley is a friendly cat. He purrs and turns around my legs if he wants something. The man we see walking through the forest on the way to school says dogs are good company but Mum reckons she's got enough to do looking after me. I'm an only and I don't have a pet. It's just not fair.

'I want a baby.'

'Get on with your work, Huxley.' Mum has the phone against her neck while she talks to me.

'I want your help.'

'I can't at the moment. Have a try on your own and I'll come over as soon as I've finished.'

'Finished what?'

'Speaking to Paula.'

Ah-ha, I was right! But being right doesn't mean I can stop doing my work. There's no more slip-sliding into the kitchen. I pull out the chair. My book is open on the table and there's a pencil. I can't be bothered. Mum spends hours on the telephone. I only use it when Gran rings from Spain although Skype is best because it's easier talking if you have a face to look at. On the phone, I need to spend time thinking before I speak. Mum is always beside me trying to help answer Gran's questions. I listen to my breathing with the phone at my ear. I don't always want to tell her about school. It's boring and the stuff we do in class never changes.

Mrs Ward asks everyone to keep a diary of the things we eat. Monday was the day for starting but I didn't get round to it. It's Saturday night now and I must make up the work for a whole week. Breakfast is easy because I eat Krispies and I can write the same word in each box. This is what I mean about school being boring. You have to do the same thing again and again.

At last, Mum comes over to see how I'm getting on. 'You had Krispies every morning last week?'

'Yes.' That's because there's a great big container of them and I've got to finish it.

'It's not much variety. Dad makes porridge some days. Why don't you have it for a change?'

'I'm eating all the new cereal so you can go back to buying proper Krispies in a box.'

'I'm trying to reduce waste. It's easy to buy more from the Zero Waste shop in town. Much better for the planet, too.'

'It's not better for me. The boxes of Krispies have toys inside. I need them for my collection.'

'I thought you were fed up with Sillybones. You never play with them.'

'It's a nice surprise opening the box.'

'Not always,' says Mum. 'Not when you get the same old Sillybones time after time.'

This is true but I don't care. I'm not giving up. 'You promised to buy boxes again.'

'I did, although I was hoping you'd change your mind.'

'Well, I haven't.'

The word Krispies fills up all the breakfast squares, so now Mum points to where I must write about school dinners. She can't help me because she doesn't know what I eat at school.

'Why do I need to fill this in? Mrs Ward can ask the serving ladies.'

'Let's concentrate on what you've eaten at home this week instead.'

I turn my pencil around my fingers. 'My memory isn't working.'

'We had pasta on Monday.'

'And crumpets on Tuesday.'

'I'm not sure it's a good idea to say you ate all the crumpets.'

'But I did eat them! It was a challenge to myself.'

'Four buttered crumpets don't form part of a nutritional diet.'

'I love them!'

'Could you write sandwiches instead? I mean, if you put one crumpet on top of another, it's a sandwich of sorts.'

'It isn't the truth.'

'Leave that one for the minute and fill in the other sections.'

'But I can't remember what I ate at school.'

'Was it jacket potato?'

'Yuk.'

'Or stew?'

'No.'

'Well, you'll just have to make it up.' Mum finishes loading plates and bowls and glasses into the dishwasher. When she turns it on, the sound of water splatters then churns, swishes and hums like an underwater creature. I write really quickly before the ideas vanish.

'I've finished.'

Mum reads my sheet. 'I'm not sure Mrs Ward will believe you ate squid, octopus and shark for school dinners.'

'She probably won't believe I had four crumpets for tea, either.'

'At least the rest of the week is reasonably healthy.'

My homework is done so I pack it away in my book bag. There's still the reading but I can do it in bed. 'Will Dad come back before I go to sleep?'

'I'm not sure.'

'Why's he taking such a long time?'

'Listen, Huxley.' Mum sits down and scoops me onto her lap. 'I'd better tell you the news before it gets around town. It's about Leonard.'

29

On Monday, I'm bursting to get to school. I rush-rush-rush into the playground, leaving Mum way behind. I'm on a search for Ben. I know he's here because I spot Nanny Phil. My heart goes pang-pang-pang – I can hear the noise in my ears – it sounds the same as Juno bashing saucepans with a spoon. A tennis ball shoots past me but the goal isn't set up so the game hasn't started. My eyes whizz around. Children are midgets against the stripe of field beyond the fence and the huge grey sky that drops from heaven like a roller blind. Where can he be?

I rush to the end of the building to see if he's mucking around there. Turning my head from side to side, I still can't find him. One second later, he's tripping on his own feet while he tucks in his shirt. I can't believe he's been in the toilet! My running legs get good exit-size. When I screech to a stop in front of him, I'm almost ready to pop.

'My dad and your dad are heroes!'

'Yeah.' He's jumping like a kangaroo.

'Yeah-yeah-yeah!' I have to copy him.

To celebrate some more, I want to give him a high five. The problem is, I can't put my hand in the right place while we bounce. In the end, we knock our foreheads together! The bump doesn't hurt so now we're laughing and falling about the place. Next minute, Ben gets me with an arm around my neck and I get him back. We're champions because our dads did a brave thing.

In the main playground, the football boys are in a circle with me and Ben in the middle. Their faces are raisins – squished up from surprise. I'm so puffed from having pride, I think the buttons will burst off my shirt. It's like a whistle's gone at the start of a running race but their voices scramble not their feet. I don't know how to answer all the questions. This is amazing! I'm at the centre of the crowd, Ben's my mate, and everyone wants to find out what happened.

'My dad saved Leonard from a fire!' I shout.

'And my dad was there!' shouts Ben.

'My dad saw smoke coming from Leonard's letter box.' I'm smiling so much my cheeks stretch as if they're made of elastic.

'And my dad chased the gang away.' Ben shakes his fist in the air and I shake mine as well. We're both winners.

Before we have a chance to say any more, the bell rings, but it doesn't stop questions flying. *Who started the fire? Was anyone hurt? Were the police there?* Mrs Ward comes along to break up the circle. She doesn't tell us off because I think she's heard, too. She promises we can share our news at carpet time. I am itchy with ideas but I have to wait for the boring register to end. When Mrs Ward's finished, we spring to our feet and tell the class what happened. I talk about my dad and Tony going to Leonard's flat. They went because they didn't think Leonard should be at the leisure centre. This idea was wrong but they had to find out. As they got close, Tony was pushed out of the way by a gang charging off. They stood beside Leonard's door and there was a smell of burning. Dad flicked open Leonard's letter box and saw flames! He shouted and managed to bash the door in to rescue Leonard. My dad said he wouldn't have been burnt alive because of the smoke alarm ringing. He's still a hero for saving Leonard and I'm proud of him. Dad says the police are looking in to it. He and Tony had to answer questions and Leonard went to hospital. It's a good job he got the all clear. Now, the police are going to find the gang. Funny thing is, it turns out the dads didn't need to have a word with Leonard in the first place. The police say there are no black marks on him and he can help out at Light Club and go to the leisure centre soon as he's better. I'm happy they got there in time, otherwise Leonard's flat might be toasted.

With our story over, it's back to Mrs Ward talking. Nothing much changes in our class.

'Thank you very much, Huxley and Ben, for sharing your news.' She flaps her arm up and down in the air. This means we have to sit on the carpet. 'Although there is a happy ending, it's a timely reminder to be careful of fires and to check smoke alarms regularly.'

I don't want to sit because I've got lots to say. Mum and Dad are going to be kind to Leonard. I hope they mean me and him can be friends but they didn't answer yes straight away. They didn't say yes at all but I can hope. Anyway, I'm sat back on the carpet with my legs crossed and I'm ready to listen.

Mrs Ward goes, 'First thing concerns reading your books at home. Most of you do it every evening and I'm very pleased with you, although there are one or two who forget.'

This is boring after my exciting news. That's school for you. Mrs Ward's eyes dart and I wonder who is going to get a stare. I turn and try to see who she's looking at. It's not me because I do my reading every time so I can't be in trouble.

'Face front, children.'

My eyeballs go where they're supposed to.

'I'll be writing a reminder in your home books. Please don't let's have any more silly excuses. It's very important you practise reading at home.' Mrs Ward's eyes go bounce-bounce-bounce. 'I have another thing to tell you. Today, you can have an extra turn on the climbing frame as no one's using it.'

There's a chirrup of voices going *hurray,* and *cool.* I look at Samira and she's smiling. We whisper *yeah-yeah-yeah* and nod our heads like we're doing a sit-down dance together.

'Yes, it's great to have this extra opportunity.'

Zac throws both his arms in the air. He's trying to start a Mexican wave but no one joins in. I think it's funny because he's not popular in class today. Me and Ben have the top spot. I give out the maths books and Ben goes round with the pencils. It's a pity that sharing news is finished and we have to start our work.

We copy sums from the whiteboard in our group and then we use our brains to fill in the answers. Sometimes the empty square is after the

= sometimes it's not. Copying sums is okay but copying answers is not. My arm is a castle wall around my book so that nobody can peek over to steal my work. I'm clever at numbers and that means I don't even need to check them. I'm sure they're right.

Mrs Ward tells us to put our books in a pile – this is the sign that we're ready for play. We can't all get through the door at the same time as that makes argy-bargy.

'Quiet now,' says Mrs Ward. 'All the children with white socks can go and collect their coats.'

I never have the right colour on. Samira gives my back a rub before she leaves the table. She has a nice way of making me feel.

By the time I am allowed to go out of the classroom, there are already loads of children on the scramble net and others queuing up for a go on the slide. My favourite thing is the monkey bars and that's good because not many of the others go on them. Zac is there before me and he's back to being Mister Popular so he goes first. Some of my class stand watching as he springs then grabs a monkey bar. He makes a big deal out of everything but I don't think he'll be able to swing himself right across to the other side. I hold my breath and hope he doesn't. I want him to crash to the ground. When this thought pops into my head, he swings his body to reach the next monkey bar. Blast it! He's there and as he goes for the last one, his hand slaps about. He can't stretch far enough! Zac is a conker dropped from its case. He plonks onto the ground.

I collect conkers but they're all gone now. The tree in front of our house doesn't have them but there's a whole row of conker trees in the park. If they're ready, the conkers drop straight down and bounce on the path. You need to be careful walking underneath or one might land on your head! Conkers are actually seeds but Zac isn't a tree growing. He spreads his arms and legs like a spider then stands up. I have to swallow hard to stop a laugh coming out and the noise turns into a burp.

'Better out than in.' Samira gives my back a slap.

I smile. 'That is very true.'

Zac picks himself up and rubs his hands together. Bits of bark fall back to the ground where it's safe for landing. From the corner of my eye, I see Ben on the edge of the playground where they've made a football goal out of jumpers. I think he's waiting for Zac so they can start a game. It should be called tennis ball not football as they're only allowed to kick small balls. The rule is there to keep the little children safe from being ball-bashed. Ben and Zac moan but in my book, Mrs Ward is right for once.

I have the monkey bars to myself now Zac has gone. Samira and some of the other girls are in a line beside the wall. They never have a go and so I think they're here to see me. There's a special word for people who watch sport and because I am funny, I turn the word into a joke. This will have them laughing.

'Are you speck-stay-toes?' I ask.

Samira smiles and covers her face with her hand. The other girls do the same. I practise how I'm going to jump up by testing the bounce in my knees.

'Hurry up, Huxley, if you want us to speck-take you.'

It's my turn to chuckle at Samira.

I'm fast as a squirrel. Catching hold of the bar, I hook one arm over. I could hang there forever but my job is to move along to the end. By swinging my legs from side to side, I get energy. Next, it's time for the very tricky bit of getting my hands moving across to hold the next bar. Swapping hands, I am speedy at going across. My legs are dangling and swaying. Before I know it, I'm at the other side! I plop down and the girls are clapping. I wonder what to do. I have an idea and bow as if I'm an actor on a stage. That's when the girls start jigging in a dance and they shout *wa-hoo*. This is fun! I shake my hands and I think they might fly into space, but it's just to stop them aching. I'm a champion of the monkey bars! This is better than being a champion because of Dad. Samira and her friends are making so much noise that Zac comes back to see what's going on.

'Did you go all the way over the monkey bars?' he asks.

Before I have a chance to answer, Samira and the other girls are jumping and shouting, 'Yes-he-did, yes-he-did!'

Zac turns to me and crinkles his nose. 'Bet you can't do it again.'

'Go on, Huxley,' says Samira. 'Show Zac.'

Now the challenge is on and I start again. Samira claps once I've made my giant leap and a whole big crowd gathers to watch my swinging and grabbing action. I'm into my pace and go easy all the way. I try to make it look simple but my breath is noisy. I triumph to the other side and there's Mrs Ward smiling. I can't help feeling proud. This is a very special day.

I get back to Samira and she holds my arm in the air. She won't let it go. There's wind blowing up my shirt but I don't care. Everyone is happy with me for a change.

Ben walks up and slaps my shoulder, 'You did it!'

Zac follows Ben and stands beside me. I don't really want Zac here when I'm being popular. Then he does a strange thing. He holds out his hand for me to shake. The last time this happened, I had to put my hand out first to say sorry for biting. I grab Zac's hand and our arms go up and down.

'Well done,' says Zac. He's not trying to shake me to pieces – he must mean it.

Mrs Ward watches to check for hard feelings but there aren't any. 'It's excellent having such good sports in my class. That was quite an achievement, Huxley.'

I don't want the bell to ring because I could stay in the playground like this forever.

30

I'm having a splash in the bath. Mum lets the water go deep although it's not like swimming. There are small buckets and boats to play with but I still prefer my trains. I don't want them to drown so I never bring them into the bathroom. One time I slept over at Ben's house and the two of us got in the bath with Juno. It was a bit squashy and Juno cried soon as she got water in her eyes.

'It's time you were out,' Mum shouts from her bedroom.

'Not yet!' I know when I've been in too long because my toes turn to shrimps.

Next minute, Mum comes in and pulls the towel off the heated rail. She stands there with it held out. 'Let's be having you.'

'Okay.' I climb from the bath and get wrapped up. I can't help jiggling when she gives me a rub-a-dub-dub. My pyjamas are warm and they stick to me where there are patches of wet. I'll dry out so I don't mind.

'You're done,' says Mum. 'Remember our deal? Straight off to bed for you.'

Mum read extra chapters before tea so that she wouldn't have to do it after my bath. 'Where's Dad? You said he'd be home by bedtime. I want to tell him about my excellent day.'

'I'm sure he's keen to hear everything. But you have bed. Everything will keep until the morning.'

'What if I'm still awake?'

'He always comes up to kiss you goodnight.' Mum takes my hand and leads me into my room. The duvet is lumpy – I jump on top to flatten it. I could be a flying duck landing on a pond. Turning my arms, I pretend I'm drowning but Mum doesn't seem to care. I'm slithering so much, I fall off the bed. On the carpet, I pretend I'm dead but it's no fun because Mum isn't fooled. I might as well sit up. 'If I'm awake, I can tell him what's happened?'

'If you're awake.' Mum pulls back the cover and this is a signal for me to dive into bed. She tucks me in and plonks a kiss on my forehead.

I listen for Mum's footsteps as she goes downstairs and then there are voices from the radio. A giant yawn sends my lips flat and open. I don't bother putting my hand over my mouth because there's no one to see. I think about Mrs Ward and her tut-tut-tutting at anyone doing this in class. I'm going to try to keep Mrs Ward happy with me. And I'm going to stay awake until Dad is back. He'll want to hear about me being a popular boy. And how I beat Zac on the monkey bars and that I'm a good sport because I shook hands. My brain's telling me to go to sleep so I keep blinking to stay awake. One more big blink but my head goes fuzzy.

•   •   •   •   •

I don't know why my eyes spring open when it's still dark. Morning hasn't come because street lights are shining into my room through a crack in the curtains. The windows thump and bang. It's probably the wind but it could be Spider-Man climbing my house. I hop out of bed and press my nose against the glass. It's not easy to see although I'm sure Spider-Man's not around. He only lives in films. I send my eyes straight and I see right into Mrs Vartan's front room. She doesn't use her curtains to block out the night and the light inside her room is bright and then dark. I think she is watching TV and she is sitting very still. It happens to me as well. The fidgets vanish if I'm interested in something.

In our house, pipes give a swishing sound after the toilet in the little room's been used. This is a sign that Dad is home and all of a sudden, I remember my excellent news. Dad hasn't come up to see me, so now I have to go downstairs and surprise him. I creep-creep-creep out of my room and my toes find the carpet tickly as I jump from one step to the next. It's hard to do this quietly but I'm an expert. The only trouble is I want to take the last two stairs in a big leap and this makes a bang.

'Huxley!' Mum comes out. 'What are you doing?'

'I woke up and Dad didn't come to see me.'

'He's only just got home.'

Then Dad's in the doorway and he's drinking from his dad-size mug. He takes a swallow of tea and his face disappears. I wait for him to talk.

'Finished!' he says. 'Five seconds for you to get in bed and I'll be there.'

This turns into a race. Dad's feet clomp but I'm in front. By the time he's in my room, I'm a lump under the duvet. My breath is steamy and I'm hot and smiley. I hear Dad moving about with his puff-puff-puffing and then there's a bottom landed and I'm trapped. I have a scramble around then I find an exit and my head pops up into the air. My face is cool and fresh.

'Congratulations.' Dad's shaking hand is pointing at me. 'Mum told me about your day.'

'I wanted to say everything over again.'

'I know,' says Dad. 'It's just that good news travels fast. Come on, shake.'

His hand is way bigger than mine and my fingers are covered up. A proper shake is good practice because I'm going to be a dad one day.

'There's stuff I need to tell you, too,' says Dad.

'Oh yes.' This sounds interesting.

'It seems I should have listened to you, Huxley.'

'Oh yes.' This is news to me.

'You always said Leonard was okay.'

'Oh yes.' This is true.

'It's our job, mine and Mum's, to love you and keep you safe. We didn't want other parents or children being afraid of Leonard. It turns out we were wrong to be suspicious. Leonard's okay.'

'Oh yes.' This I know.

'Now it's time to return to normal and you can start at Light Club again.'

'Oh yes!' This is excellent.

'Although Mum has to make up with Lucy first,' says Dad. 'That might be a challenge.'

'Not for Mum!'

'Let's wait and see,' says Dad.

31

My eyelids don't ping open this morning because I'm fuzzy with sleep. At night your body is charged same as a phone that's plugged in. It would be funny if we went green like the bar on a mobile. I wriggle to go further under the duvet and this makes Thomas the Tank topple on my shoulder. The engines are supposed to be lined up but they don't always stay where I put them. I shunt Thomas back to his place.

There are voices coming from Mum and Dad's room. My ears aren't tuned in to hear what they're saying. My power supply is low. I didn't get much sleep. I was too busy with dreams. Dad rushed into Leonard's flat to save him. My dad is a hero. That wasn't part of the dream. It really happened! I fill my chest with breath so it sticks out because I am proud. Then one more breath and my body is flat again. Poor Leonard. It's a good job Dad stopped a disaster. The whole block of flats up in smoke! I saw what was left of a burned down tower block on the TV. Not pretty. At Leonard's flat, the fire started because someone posted burning rags through the letter box. It wasn't the postman – there was a gang. In school, Zac and his mates are a gang when they do bullying but he won't try it again now I'm champion of the monkey bars. There are also those boys in a gang from the secondary school. They were nasty, throwing oranges at Leonard. I did my best to tell them off. I start imagining. I see the leader and the brown-haired boy and I remember they were in my dream. I watched them race from Leonard's flat. Tony ran after them but he wasn't quick enough and they got away! In my dream, there were other boys waiting. They went head over heels along the road, tumbling over and over. It's silly how they turned like wheels and were rolling. That's what happens in dreams. They're a bit real and a bit made up.

Mum helps me put my clothes on because I am slow and floppy today. My bones are sore and heavy, but I can still land my legs into my trousers. It's my shirt next, straight over my head and Mum does the buttons up. Then there's my jumper and that's it. I will put my shoes on when we're ready to go.

'Time for breakfast,' says Mum. 'How about Chocopops for extra energy?'

'Chocopops! Woo-hoo!' These are usually a treat so I race to the kitchen as I don't want Mum to change her mind. She goes on tiptoes and stretches her arm to reach into the cupboard above the cooker. I've found her hiding place!

Chocopops turn the milk in my bowl to slushy chocolate and I gobble up the pops so I can slosh the milky chocolate back in big slurps. I'm not supposed to drink straight from the bowl but Mum doesn't mind today. I'm having an excellent day and I've only been awake five minutes. I'm a runner at the starting blocks, so I slip off my chair and charge around the room. Then, I'm an aeroplane that swoops onto the runway. There are obstacles in my path and I turn to dive bomb them.

'Go into the lounge.' Mum shouts because my engines are noisy.

'Eeeek.' I turn on the brakes to stop me charging straight into Dad.

'What have you been feeding him?' asks Dad.

'Chocopops to get him going this morning.' Mum packs the cereal away.

'That's too much chocolate.'

'Not for me!' I shout. Now I know where Mum keeps the box, I might have Chocopops all the time!

'Hold up, young man.' Dad takes a handkerchief from out of his pocket and he rubs it over my chin. 'If that muck on your face was blood, you'd be Dracula.'

I have another idea and start gnashing my teeth like I'm going to eat Dad up. Grabbing his leg, I try giving it a nibble. 'If I wanted a puppy, I'd choose one from the dog's home.'

Dad shakes his leg and I have a job holding on.

'Away with you.' Mum chases me into the lounge and then shuts the door.

I'm by myself so I dive onto the sofa and take up all the cushions. Rolling on one side, I stare up at the ceiling, then I go back the other way. I make a game of tossing and turning to become giddy. The world is a giant blur and there are stars whizzing around inside my head. I have to stop in case my brain becomes muddled. There I am stretched out, but it isn't fun being on my own. I dive on the carpet, crawl over to find one of my books, and I carry it to the kitchen. If I was a dog, I'd grip the book between my teeth but I better not try that today. I got into trouble for biting and I don't want Mum to think I've gone back to old habits. I hope Mum or Dad will read to me.

'Good to see you've calmed down, Huxley,' says Dad.

I flop against him and the book slips out of my hand. It lands on the floor and the cover does the splits. Samira tries this in the playground but I'm not interested in stretching my legs until I crack into pieces. Mum picks up the book because she likes to be tidy and I let my fingers go walkies across Dad's shoulder.

'I love you too, mate,' he says.

I press my head against Dad's and hug him tight. 'I had foggy dreams.'

'Did you?' Dad spreads butter on his toast.

'I know who was in it.'

'Oh yes.' He unscrews the jar of marmalade. 'Are you going to spill?'

Dad's being funny! He's the one spilling big chunks and runny juice on his toast. Ha-ha-ha. 'I dreamed about those boys. The ones that tried to set fire to Leonard.'

'They go to the secondary school.' He takes a huge bite and half his toast vanishes.

'We passed them on the way to school last week.'

Dad swallows, 'Did we?'

'They were the ones that threw oranges at Leonard so I told them off.'

'You did?' The skin on Dad's forehead turns into waves.

'You were on your mobile.'

'Oh yes.' Dad rubs his chin. 'What exactly did you say to them?'

'I told them to stop bullying Leonard.'

'Yes ... and they seemed to suggest I was out of order. Fiddling the books indeed.' Dad swigs the last of his tea from the mug.

'Zip in and button up,' I say.

Dad can't have shut his lips properly because tea spurts from his mouth like a fountain. I'm quick and move before I'm splattered, but there are drops over the table.

'Are you okay?' Mum slaps Dad on the back.

'Did you hear what Huxley just said?' Now he's using his handkerchief again but this time he dries his own lips. 'No wonder those lads started shouting about fiddling. Oh, hell! They weren't referring to my accounts!'

Mum and Dad stare at each other and I think they need reminding. 'Zip in and button up!'

'Why did you say that?' Mum's eyelids stretch wide open and show more white than actual eyeball. She's silly sometimes.

'You have to do this when you put your jacket on. Leonard told me. It means you won't get cold even if the wind goes right round your neck and freezes your ears. It's what I told those boys. To prove Leonard is kind and helpful.'

'When did Leonard say this to you?' asks Mum.

I have a think. 'When we were at the park.'

'That's down to you.' Dad nods at Mum.

'And when we were in the barber's shop.'

'That's down to you.' Mum nods at Dad.

My mum and dad think nodding is a lot of fun so I have a practice. I look at my toes wiggling in my socks then I shoot my eyes up to the ceiling. It gives my neck a good stretch. I send my eyes straight again and I see Mum and Dad saying silent words to each other. I can't work them out. 'Tell me what's happening!'

'It's nothing for you to worry about, Huxley.' Dad plonks his hand on my head and runs it over my hair. 'Mum will take you to school today.'

'I will?' she says.

'Yes. I have to share this new information at the station … with the police.'

'You'd better be off!' Mum snaps.

'It's funny trains and police have stations.'

'Don't forget there are buses and bus stations,' says Mum.

'Talk about change the subject,' mutters Dad. 'Fire stations and electricity stations, too.'

'Cool,' I say but I don't really know what they're going on about.

'I'm leaving,' says Dad. 'The sooner I get there, the sooner this whole misunderstanding can be sorted out.'

'Too right, Jed. You sort it out,' says Mum.

Phew! It makes a change when my mum and dad think the same.

32

Juno has to stay at home with Paula because Nanny Phil is taking me and Ben to McDonald's for a treat. I don't need to stand there for hours looking at the display as I already know what I want. It's chicken nuggets! Me and Ben go off to find a table and we can choose wherever we want to sit because there's only three of us. I check to see if there are balloons on the rack but nobody's blown up any today.

Me and Ben fold our arms and push them across the table so that we ram into each other. It's time for argy-bargy! We're only bashing about for two minutes before Nanny Phil comes over carrying a tray. We need to put our arms away to make room for happy meals. The top of the box springs open. This means I can reach for the bag of chicken nuggets quickly. While I'm counting them, Ben gets hold of his toy – it's a robot. I hope I've got one the same so I dash my hand in the box. Yippee! Mine's got a gold helmet and his is black.

'Do a swap.' Ben swings his robot by one of its arms.

I admire my robot and wipe it against my jumper to give extra shine.

'Eat up,' says Nanny Phil.

I'm not letting go of my robot in case Ben snatches it. I keep it in one hand and the other is busy diving a chip into the pot of ketchup. After it's covered in red, I send the chip straight in my mouth.

Ben takes a bite from his burger and I check to see what Nanny Phil is having. She's gone for a fillet of fish. I've never tried one because nuggets are best. I've had a burger before and they are okay, but chicken nuggets are better as you get a few of them. 'I like coming to McDonald's.'

'You're right, Huxley. It's not often I have the company of two young men.'

'Woo-hoo! Young men!' says Ben. 'Only we're not like the ones who set the fire.'

'Of course not,' says Nanny Phil. 'They're young vandals or worse. Anyway, Leonard is okay, thank goodness. I could tell he was just a disabled chap in need of friends. He is a bit clumsy and awkward at times. You know, he says the wrong things a bit like me.'

'Wait a minute.' My brain box starts working and I remember what Dad told me. 'It's called foot-in-mouth syndrome.'

'You're not wrong there,' says Nanny Phil. 'It's not surprising when you live on your own. Look at me! I've turned into a complete one off. There are lots of people who go barking up the wrong tree.'

'What about trees?' asks Ben.

'Trees?' says Nanny Phil.

'You said barking up a tree,' says Ben.

'Oh that,' says Nanny Phil. 'It's just a way of talking. It's when you jump to the wrong conclusion. If there's...'

'I know, I know.' I spring my bottom up from the chair.

'Calm down and tell me sensibly.'

It's hard sitting still if you've got something to say. 'It's when there's a...' I think I can be funny but this word does it all on its own, 'miss-under-standing'.

'Correct,' says Nanny Phil.

'Blah-blah-blah.' Ben lets his robot boing into the air like it's an astronaut and then he crash-lands the robot on its head. 'Boring.'

'Finish your burger, Ben.'

Nanny Phil doesn't have to remind me because I've scoffed the nuggets and I'm halfway through my fries. (They're called this in McDonald's but they're the same as chips, only thin.) I pick out a burnt one and show it to Nanny Phil.

'If my dad hadn't got there in time, Leonard would be the same.'

'You're telling me! What might have happened is terrible. Let's try to stay positive. Leonard is okay, the police are investigating everything and there's certainly no paedophile in our midst.'

'Pea-doh-file?'

'Yes. Well. I probably shouldn't have said that. Forget about it. I'm just pleased this silly episode is over.' Nanny Phil picks up the rubbish from our table and screws it into a ball. 'It's not looking good for those lads. You can't set fire to stuff and expect to get away with it. Apparently, they were responsible for flouring Mrs Vartan and the mishap on Bonfire Night. I feel sorry for the parents. I mean, you bring a child into this world and you try to do your best. It only takes some stupid action and then things escalate. You never know what's going to happen next.'

I can't help yawning.

'Hand over your mouth,' she says.

I do as I'm asked. The trouble is, I can't eat the last chip with my hand in the way.

'Ha-ha-ha.' Ben copies me and tries to stuff his burger with his hand in front of his mouth. It's a drawbridge that's shut! He's getting ketchup everywhere.

Nanny Phil tosses a napkin at Ben. 'Give yourself a clean-up.'

Ben can't stop laughing then I join in and Nanny Phil starts. She goes ho-ho-ho because she doesn't want to be left out. It's great having fun and being happy.

33

Dad says tonight is the right time for taking me round to Leonard's flat. I'm glad because I can make sure Leonard's okay. Dad's also going to set him straight on a couple of things. This doesn't mean ironing his bent body. Impossible!

We walk along the high street and don't go through the park where I saw the chocolate wrapper trail. That's because the park gates are locked soon as it's dark. I like being out when the Christmas lights are on and there's the face of Father Christmas hanging from every lamppost. I can see Leonard's block poking up – it's a magic wand in the sky! I know we are close when we get to the sweet shop. There are stairs going up and this is good exit-size. For babies in buggies and disabled people, there's a lift. We go along an outdoor strip where a line of mobility scooters is parked. I think the end one covered in a clear plastic coat is Leonard's but I don't bother going over to check. We find his flat with the bright red door. Dad gives a tap-tiddly-tap-tap on the glass bit. There's a shadow moving inside.

Finally, the door opens and I see Leonard leaning on one stick. 'Welcome!'

'Hello Leonard!' I'm happy so the words come out extra loud.

'Evening.' Dad holds out his hand for Leonard.

'We meet under favourable circumstances, Jed.'

They have a proper shake but I'm bored with standing on the doorstep. Leonard shuffles to the side so we can move indoors. 'Careful as you come in. The housing people haven't fixed the damage yet. There's a new mat with the old burnt one underneath.'

This sounds interesting. 'Can I see?'

'Let me close the door first,' says Leonard.

Dad and Leonard stand against the wall in the passage while I'm on my hands and knees for a proper look. The burn hole goes right through the carpet to the stone underneath.

'I had a lucky escape thanks to your dad and Tony,' says Leonard. 'I owe a huge debt of gratitude.'

'The smoke alarm would have brought help if I hadn't been there.'

'I needed human contact. It's something I'll always appreciate. No matter the reason for your calling.'

'Least said soonest mended.'

'Agreed,' says Leonard.

I run my finger over the wall. It's not smooth like the ones in my house. The knobbly bits are black from the fire.

'I'm going to have everything painted to cover up the damage. Wallpaper is a bit old fashioned these days,' says Leonard.

'It'll be lighter and brighter with a lick of paint,' says Dad.

'Come on through. The rest of the place is completely untouched.' Leonard uses his stick and leads the way. 'How about becoming my other walking stick, Huxley?' He puts his hand on my shoulder and we shuffle along.

'Is that absolutely necessary?' says Dad. 'I mean, putting your hands on a young boy was one reason for this fiasco.'

'Of course. You're absolutely right.' Leonard stops moving.

'Take my elbow if you need to,' says Dad.

'Very kind of you, Jed. I'm sure I'll be able to manage. The next time I answer the door, I'll make sure I've got both my sticks.'

We go into the front room and I can't decide where to sit. There's an armchair but it's got all Leonard's stuff on a table next to it. Packets of pills, a half empty glass of water, a magazine and much more. I spot a little footstool made from string tied tight across the top and a bench for two people. On the bookcase, there's a shelf full of DVDs, another's crammed with books, and there are a few photos. I go up to take a look at the one in a silver frame. Leonard's dressed up in a suit and the lady beside him is wearing a hat. There are gravestones in the background, so I think they're at church. I am such an excellent detective!

Leonard goes in slow motion to reach his chair.

'Your knees don't bend very well,' I say.

'Huxley,' says Dad.

Leonard sits. 'Muriel's in that photo. She passed away several years ago. By the time we got together, it was too late to think about children. We had ten wonderful years. Unfortunately, her going was the start of my downfall. I never kept to a good diet or did any exercise. The diabetes kicked in and I lost my market stall. It's all history.'

'I'm sorry to hear that.' Dad moves over to the bench.

'What did you do at the market?' I ask.

'Sold vegetables. And do you know what? I never knowingly let one pass my lips! Of course, Muriel had her ways of getting me to eat sensibly. It's a sorry story. Once I'd lost the business, I couldn't pay the rent and found myself homeless. All my furniture had to go when I moved into one tiny room in a hostel. I'm delighted to have my own place again. I will be making a special effort to live healthily.'

Turning away from the photo, I jump from one foot to the other. 'Good for you!'

'Steady on young man. Why don't you have a rest on the stool?'

I plonk down and it's quiet in the room. No one's talking. Somehow the idea of chocolate springs to my mind. 'Have you got any Cadbury?'

'Huxley!' says Dad.

'I think there's a mini bar in the basket on my scooter. But it's outside and covered up for the night.'

'What's it doing there?' asks Dad.

'For the children, of course!'

'You can't go around giving chocolate to children!' says Dad.

'They enjoy it,' says Leonard. 'They're always asking for more.'

'I'm not surprised. Don't you realise it's giving totally the wrong messages?'

Leonard looks like he's trying to find the right answer. 'I suppose you could be right. To be honest, it's only the children who want to talk to me.'

'After this incident, now's the time for a fresh start,' says Dad. 'I'm sure there must be a pensioners' club where there'll be people of your own age.'

'I'm not actually that old, although I take your point about mixing with adults. The police mentioned it. I've had a high old time these last few days. Community officers, my doctor, people from the council calling on me. Haven't had so much company in years.' Leonard whips a hanky out of his pocket and sniffs into it. When the cloud of cloth disappears, Leonard's smiling. 'Who's ready for a nice cup of ginger tea? I make it myself with root ginger from the shop.'

'Sounds ... interesting,' says Dad.

'Or there's regular tea if you want.'

'You stay there,' says Dad. 'I'll get three glasses of water. That'll do us just fine.'

While Dad's in the kitchen. I take another look at the photo of Leonard and Muriel. She is a neat and tidy lady. Suddenly, I have a thought. Mrs Vartan is the same as Leonard. Those boys floured her at Halloween and this made her sad and lonely. I have a feeling Mrs Vartan and Leonard might be the same in other ways. There's a jigsaw box on Leonard's shelf with ONE THOUSAND pieces. I've got it – they both like jigsaws! I've seen Mrs Vartan's table laid with one that she never finished. The picture has too many holes. It must need more than one brain to put all the bits together. Putting my thinking cap on, I need a good idea to help Leonard and Mrs Vartan get together.

There's tinkling coming from the glasses Dad holds. He's got three of them in a triangle between his fingers. That's a clever carrying trick – I'll have to try it one day. I take a slurp of water. It's a pity though, ginger tea sounds nice.

34

It's the first of December and the big brown envelope wants to be opened. On the front of the package is my name. It's come from Spain – I can tell from the stamps. I'm thinking there's an advent call-end-aah inside. Gran sent me one last year. Call-end-aah. Ha-ha-ah. Advent means you count the days until Christmas. At school, it also means we have to learn our Christmas songs double quick and I'm going to be a sheep. (It's not the best part but Samira stands near me. That makes it okay.) Mum slices off the end of the package with a pair of scissors and I feel inside. There is tissue paper that rips as I pull the box out. It's not very heavy, I'm just acting! I tear away the rest of the paper and there's a picture of Thomas the Tank Engine. He doesn't really have antlers growing out like ears, it's done just for Christmas. There's lots of snow on the ground and it will be difficult for Thomas to go around the tracks. Me and Ben have fun sending my engines up mountains and then they slosh back down again. I don't want this box to crash – there is chocolate inside. It says so on the box but it's hard to read the rest of the words. I try sounding out 'ad-vi-en-to'.

'Calendario de adviento con chocolate,' says Mum. 'Advent calendar with chocolate in English.'

'I know about the chocolate. I can read!'

'Open the number one if you want. It's the first of December today.'

'I know!' I poke my finger and turn the flap. A tiny chocolate Christmas tree falls out. Quick as a flash, I pop it in my mouth.

'There's no stopping you,' says Mum.

'I didn't want it to melt.'

'You could have shown it to me before you gobbled it up.'

'I'll get out the next one.'

'No, you don't. That's for tomorrow.'

Eating chocolate at the start of the day is happy making. It's also something I can talk about at school. Mum says she's got lots to do because Christmas will be here before we know it. I'm not so sure. It takes ages for Christmas to come. Nearer the time, there are going to be lots of parties. We have a party at school and at Junior Church and I bet they have one at Light Club.

'Can I go to Light Club again?'

'Hmm. I've got to apologise to Lucy first. It's a pity I didn't believe her when she said Leonard was a responsible person.'

'And me! I was right as well. I told you he was my friend.'

'You did.' Mum holds her hands up as if she is surrendering and I'm not even pointing a pretend gun at her. 'We've reached an understanding.'

'Why didn't you believe me and Lucy?'

'Leonard was someone we knew nothing about. Suspicion got the better of me. There's really no excuse.'

'To think bad of Leonard?'

'That as well. Fortunately, everything's fine now. Your visit to Leonard's was a good idea.'

I nod. I liked seeing him, even though Dad told Leonard to stop giving chocolate away. The only day that's allowed is Halloween. It's a reward for dresser-uppers. Leonard's going to remember that from now on. It doesn't matter to me because I've got the chocolate from Gran's advent calendar. That reminds me, I have to put the calendar somewhere safe.

'There's no need to climb on the chairs, Huxley.'

Mum takes the calendar and stands it on the counter. 'No more until tomorrow. That's the rule.'

'I'm fed up with rules.' Ideas in my head take turns in coming to the front. 'Is there a rule about making up with Lucy?'

Mum stacks the dirty dishes from breakfast. Each time she piles one plate onto another there's a clonk. When Gran's on Skype and hears her doing this she says it's amazing our plates survive. Mum never laughs but I think it's funny. You know, because plates can't breathe – that means they're not alive.

'Why don't you talk to Lucy after you drop me at school?'

Carrying the lot, Mum goes to the dishwasher. She slots the knives and forks into the basket then finds places for the plates. Mum is an expert at loading the dishwasher, so Dad leaves the job to her.

'Lucy's usually at school in the morning,' I say.

Mum picks up a teaspoon that dropped to the floor. If I balance on tiptoes, I can see the top of her head. She's got a parting just like me. One second later, she's standing up again.

'I'm not ready to face Lucy yet. It's too embarrassing. I keep thinking about her and wondering. What on earth is going to happen next?'

'She's going to get a baby,' I say. 'I want a baby sister or brother.'

'I know, Huxley. We'll just have to wait and see.'

'Wait and see what?'

'Come on. We'd better leave for school now or we'll be late!'

Guess what? The next thing is we're rush-rush-rushing.

35

It's the end of another week at school. We are sitting on the carpet with our coats on ready to go home. Mrs Ward gives everyone a letter.

'Make sure your mums and dads read this. It has important information regarding Miss Choi. She isn't able to help us in class any longer.'

I'm an owl and turn my head all the way round, but Miss Choi isn't at the back of the classroom.

'Face the front children. I don't want you bothering Miss Choi with lots of questions. The newsletter explains everything. Ask your parents and they will help you to understand. It's very good news for Miss Choi and she'll come back to school when she can.'

Mrs Ward puts her hands together like she's going to start praying. Instead, she gives them a rub and then lets them fly free. She forgets the no finger pointing rule and pokes the air. 'Right. I can see Zac's mum and Samira's mum. You two come to the front.'

It's a shame I'm not going to be first out of class today. I let my head pop up and I see Mum in the queue of parents waiting. She isn't last in line, so that's something. We collect my bike from the cycle rack and even though I wear my helmet, it's not worth riding until we cross the road. As we walk, I count the number of cars parked on the yellow lines. Cars shouldn't be left there but some parents are in a rush to collect their children. The counting keeps me busy while Mum looks at the letter. She is pushing her bike as well as reading. Doing two things at the same time is clever.

'What does the letter say?'

'Lucy's taking adoption leave. Arrangements are moving very fast. It'll be exciting when she has her baby. All in time for Christmas.'

'She's getting a baby for Christmas?'

'Don't be silly.'

'Can I have roller skates? I've seen some on TV and smoke comes out the back because the wheels turn very fast.'

'It's just advertising, Huxley. Roller skates only go as fast as you work them.'

'They're the same colour blue as Thomas the Tank Engine. That makes them special.'

'You'll just have to wait and see what Christmas brings. It won't be a surprise otherwise.'

'If you don't get them for me, I think Father Christmas will.'

'As long as you're good.'

In a flash, I remember Zac's hand and the big bruise I made with my teeth. I hope Father Christmas wasn't watching. Breath comes out of my mouth in a big puff. It was a one-time thing, and anyway since the monkey bars, we've made up. 'I am a good boy.'

Mum gives me a smile. 'Yes, you are.'

We stop talking and wait by the side of the road. I hold tight to my bicycle because it wants to keep going. I have to stop it rolling into the road but I let the front wheel wiggle. It goes to the edge of the pavement. Mum's hand is on my shoulder. She doesn't want me to step off the kerb until the cars have stopped.

'Over we go,' she says.

That's the signal and I'm off. I like making my bike bump up the other side although Mum rolls her wheel over the pavement where it's dropped down. She doesn't make a fuss because I am quick. I ride around in a circle waiting for Mum to catch up. Next, we're heading straight for the tunnel and before I know it, we're making our way out. This means getting off our bikes again and going zigzag around the barrier.

'I wonder what Lucy will call her little girl,' says Mum.

'Lucy number two.'

'You're being silly. She has to find a special name for the baby.'

Sad feelings start coming. No Lucy at school means there won't be any quiet chats. Also, how are the square table going to do their work without Miss Choi to help? It's good having her around. 'Lucy is one of my adult friends. I want her to stay in class.'

'She'll go back to school when her little girl is ready.'

'Waiting for Lucy to come back will be hard.'

'I know … but you've got other friends.'

I let go of my bike and it falls onto the ground. There's a big clonk that makes Mum stop moving.

'What are you doing?'

I fold my arms to have a think. Samira is one of my favourite people but that doesn't mean I won't miss Lucy. All of a sudden, another idea comes. 'Lucy's baby is an only as well.'

'All first-born children are on their own to start.'

'Why can't I have a brother or a sister?'

Mum stands her bike up. It's got a proper bit of metal that touches the ground after it's kicked. She comes to pick up my bike and rests it against a fence. 'Let's not go into that again.'

She isn't being fair to me. 'Ben has Juno, Samira has Zahra. I want to be the same as them.'

'It's not that simple and this isn't the best place to talk. Let's cycle home. When Dad comes back from work, me and him can have a talk. What do you say?'

'Sounds boring.' I show Mum my back and watch the cars go by. They're going to London from here – it's called an A road. Mum moves beside me and takes out her mobile. She's reading stuff so she isn't thinking about what I've told her. Then, there's a tiger in my tummy that's beginning to growl. 'Can I choose a snack the second we're home?'

'Course you can,' Mum smiles and slips her mobile into her pocket. 'There's maybe even a chocolate biscuit just for you.'

This idea makes me speedy. I'm back on my bike and pushing off before Mum swings her leg over. Beating her home will be no problem today. I use my energy to pedal fast. I swoop around the puddles on the muddy bit of path. When we're back on the pavement there's no stopping me.

36

Me and Mum go to the family advent service in church where special candles are lit. If you ask me, my chocolate advent calendar is better. More yummy! I can tell Leonard's in church as his mobility scooter is parked at the entrance. I spin my head around when we get through the doors and he's sitting on a row nearby. I can't think properly because Mum's in a rush but I want to say hello to Leonard. He sees me and gives a little wave by waggling his fingers. I waggle back.

'Come along,' Mum's prodding my shoulder and it's not very comfortable. I don't like being hurried and I make up my mind. I will talk to my friend. One step and I'm next to him.

'Hello, Leonard.' I'm in the middle of the way in, and people are squeezing by. We have to budge over.

'Good morning, Huxley,' says Leonard. 'Morning to you as well, Kirsty.'

'Morning, Leonard.' Mum's voice is crispy.

I look up to check whether she's smiling ... and she is. She's also looking around the church.

'There are a couple of places near the front,' she says.

Before I have time to say anything else, Mum takes my hand and walks me towards the empty chairs. Plonking down, I don't sit still but squiggle about to check if I can see Leonard's face. The church has filled up and I'm looking for one bubble in a squirt of foam. Impossible! I pull my arms out of my jacket. Mum unwinds the scarf that goes round and round her neck. We're ready for the music to start and when it comes, I know the tune. There is always a bit of talking afterwards and today the man tells a story about trifle. This is a pudding we eat on Boxing Day after we try to finish the turkey left over from our Christmas dinner. I'm not keen on cold meat but I have to do my bit to eat up the food. The sponge cake in trifle is old and dried but no one knows this because the layers of jelly and fruit and custard and cream make the cake good to eat again. The man says trifle gives cake a new lease of life same as being a Christian. Paula always says it's important to eat fruit and vegetables to stay healthy. It's good news that eating pudding is good for me as well.

The organ starts and this time it means us children leave after the singing's over. Junior Church is not like school. We don't stand on lines and wait for bells. There are rules but the grown-ups never go on about them. If you speak out loud to answer a question or say something important, you still have to put your hand up. Lucy is in charge today even though she's not working at school. She doesn't have a baby with her and that means more waiting. There is another lady who helps and she has a smiley face. She sits with her legs crossed one over the other and she's wearing a dress that's brown. If she had green hair, her head would be a pea balanced on top of a potato. This makes me chuckle and I put my hand over my mouth as it's rude to laugh at anyone talking about Jesus. Christmas happens because it's his birthday. He is very good at mending people and his hair is long. I suppose with a name like Jesus, he likes eating cheese. Cheese-us! So long as the cheese isn't orange – it just doesn't look right melted on toast.

We don't have snack time at Junior Church as there are cakes for sale after the service. If you want a drink, there's juice. Swallow it and then you drop the beaker into the washing-up bowl. We have a story about Jesus and then we pray with our eyes closed. This is what it must be like for a blind person. You can hear everything that's going on but you can't be sure who's speaking. There's a girl who can't see very well at my school and she wears extra thick glasses. She spends playtime indoors and there's a rota for children to keep her company. When we say *amen* that's the signal to ping my eyes open. I'm the fastest at doing this.

I don't need to go to the toilet, so I follow the leader wearing the brown dress through the church and into the coffee bar. Everyone waits there before heading home. There's a line at the counter to buy drinks and another for the cake stall. Mum gave me a fifty-pence piece before we left home and I've kept it safe in my pocket. At the right time, I whap it onto the table and grab a cake covered in yellow icing. I start eating it as I walk over to where Mum sits. Lemons are funny things. In real life you can't eat one without dying from the horrible taste but lemon icing is yummy. It's nicer than the rest of the cake. I've eaten it all by the time I get to Mum's table. There, I sit and listen to the grown-ups talking. It's boring! I try to hook my feet around the wooden legs of the table. When I turn my head, I can see Leonard and I wonder what to do. My legs are stuck in place, but it gives me time to think.

'Can I say hello to Leonard?'

Mum looks over and watches Leonard drive his scooter to the tables where the chairs are scattered and empty because people have left to go home. He puts the dirty cups and saucers into the basket on the handlebar of his scooter.

'I want to help Leonard clear up.'

Mum does an extra long blink. 'Only if there's no riding on his scooter.'

'I'll be good.'

'I'll be watching.' Mum shifts in her chair. 'Remember, I've got eyes in the back of my head.'

I'm not sure I believe Mum. 'That means you've got four eyes.'

'Cheeky!' says Mum.

I go the long way around the counter to give Leonard a surprise. No bits have fallen off his head and onto the back of his jumper today and Leonard is wearing strap-on shoes so that he's smart.

'There you are, Huxley. Have you come to give me a hand?'

I nod my head and look inside one of the cups on the table. 'Someone's left half their tea.'

'Careful passing it over. I don't want to spill anything on my trousers again. Remember how much trouble that caused.'

'I'm a good carrier.' I hold the cup extra steady and give it to Leonard. He lands it in the basket no problem.

'Well done,' says Leonard.

I collect an empty dirty cup and think about balancing. At school, I hold my arms out wide to walk the plank. It's not a real one on a pirate ship although it could be. 'If the teachers aren't watching, I walk on the rail that stops people treading on the grass beside the playground.'

'You're a bit crafty.'

'I'm not always good at making stuff. My papier-mâché mask had a big dent in it.'

Leonard's face squishes then the lines disappear. 'When I said crafty, I meant you're clever at not getting caught. Keep at it young man and you'll go far.'

'Right.' I put the cup in the basket and look at the other things that need clearing.

'How about fetching the saucer now?'

'That's easy.' I pretend I'm going to chuck it like a frisbee.

'Steady on.' Leonard crosses his arms in front of his face as if he thinks I might actually throw it.

'Don't worry,' I say. 'It's just a joke.'

'Obviously.' Leonard smiles and we both have a laugh. As I turn to put the saucer on top of the pile in Leonard's basket, I see Mum watching. I hope she is proud of me for being helpful.

'We're doing a great job,' I tell Leonard. 'Your basket is a good cup collector.'

'I couldn't manage without you,' says Leonard.

'We're a team.'

Leonard holds up his hand and I give him a high five. I guess it's called that because we've got five fingers. When they're smacked together that adds up to ten. I think it should be called a high ten instead.

Soon as the basket is piled with dirty things, Leonard drives the scooter to the counter. The cups and saucers go clank-clank-clank. People at the coffee bar help to unload everything and they fill up the dishwasher with dirty cups. There isn't any room behind the counter for me. I go roaming around the empty tables and push the chairs underneath to make everything tidy.

After I've finished, I look for Leonard. This time he's sorting the papers that grown-ups read during the service. He shows me a page from inside.

'The notice says there's a nativity play at school. Are you going to be in it?'

'We practise songs a lot. The popular children get special parts. I'm one of the sheep.'

'Sheep are important – you'll be centre stage,' says Leonard. 'Shall I come along to watch? I'll give you a wave.'

I can't help smiling, 'Yes, please!'

'That's a deal.' Leonard tucks the paper into his pocket and starts up his scooter. 'Time I was going home. Can you hold the door for me?'

It's heavy but I manage to tug the door open. I stand in front with it pushing against my back. I don't mind because it makes getting out of the church easy for Leonard. 'Bye bye.'

'See you soon, Huxley.'

I watch Leonard drive down the ramp and when I turn around, Lucy comes in carrying a stack of beakers. They're the ones we have a quick drink from if we're thirsty in Junior Church. She pops the beakers onto the coffee bar and then goes towards Mum. I want to scamper over but something holds me back. It's the way Lucy stands and how Mum looks up. Lucy slides into the chair where I was sitting. Her back is straight and Mum's back is straight as well. They're the two wooden bits on a peg. It's not how they used to be together. There is making up to do and I feel sorry for Mum and Lucy. It's not easy after there's been a fall out. I should know.

My head is full of worries as I watch Mum and Lucy. It's best to get busy when this happens, so I put one of my trainers in front of the other and take pigeon steps over to the table where they sit. Getting closer, I hear their quiet voices mumbling. All of a sudden, everything is better. Mum and Lucy start laugh-laugh-laughing. I rush over to be with them in their happy place. Stretching out my arms, I fling one around Lucy and the other around Mum.

'Whenever the sea is rough, you have to throw me out as an anchor to keep the boat steady.'

'Goodness,' says Mum. 'You're a bit old for row-row-row the boat.'

'No one's too old for that.' Lucy holds my hand and she holds Mum's. Together we start the song. Next minute, we're laughing and rowing and singing. This is more like it, I think.

37

I'm watching TV after school when there's a tap-bang-bang on the knocker. No one I know makes it sound like that, so I'm not bothered who's at the door. Paula's knock has a different tune and Dad's got his own key. I'm home with Mum so she's not outside and Nanny Phil sings out as she bangs. Anyway, I'm comfy on the beanbag. I've poked my bottom in the right place to be snuggly. The tap-bang-bang comes again. If I get up from a beanbag, it will change shape and then I'll have to do the wriggling over again.

'Huxley.' Mum is calling. 'See who's at the door. I'm washing my hair. I'll be there in a second.'

Getting out of a beanbag takes skill. The best way is to crash forward on your hands and knees then crawl. By the time I'm at the front door, Mrs Vartan is heading back along the path. I know it's Mrs Vartan because of her white hair and the way she drags one of her legs. It must be hard being old. The power of my stare makes Mrs Vartan turn around as she goes out through the gate.

'There you are!' Mrs Vartan unhooks the gate to come back in. She carries a rather large box tied with string. I remember Mrs Vartan's hands are covered in blue veins that are the same as tiny rubber tubes.

'Can you help, sweetheart? This is heavy.'

I run outside even though I only have my socks on, and I put the corner of the box on my shoulder. We stumble along. Next thing, Mum is in the porch. Her wet hair lies likes snakes around her shoulders. She grabs the package, taking it off my back and out of Mrs Vartan's hands in one go. My mum is stronger than I think. She plonks it in the hall.

'Thanks, Mrs Vartan,' says Mum. 'It's very kind of you to drop this off.'

'What is it?' I ask.

'Nosey, nosey,' says Mum.

Noses have nostrils. These are the holes you breathe through. They get blocked if you're snotty and you have to blow very hard for a clear out. I'm not going to think any more about that because I have another question.

'Who's it for?'

'Huxley! Move away and let Mrs Vartan pass you.'

'Okay.' I didn't even think she wanted to come into our house.

'Mrs Vartan is going to have a cup of tea.' Mum swings the door wide open.

Mrs Vartan looks at her watch. 'I have a little time.'

As we walk into the kitchen, I wonder what's in the box.

'Did it come from Spain?' I ask Mrs Vartan.

'It may have. I can't be sure. I didn't look.'

I need to be a detective in this house to find out stuff. Mrs Vartan is too old to work, so she can't follow the clues. It's not her fault. 'Never mind.'

'Never you mind, Huxley,' says Mum.

Mrs Vartan is on my chair at the kitchen table. I don't mind sitting in Dad's place. It gives me elbow space to finish the new map I started at breakfast. It's important as Thomas needs one to go across the cushion mountains.

'Is that your homework?' asks Mrs Vartan.

My chin is pressed against the map to help me do the colouring. I have to keep watch and not go over the lines.

'No, it's one of his games,' says Mum.

'It's not a game.' I let my head shoot up. 'It's a map for Thomas the Tank Engine.'

'Of course!' Mum slaps her forehead like she's surprised.

'What are you doing at school?' asks Mrs Vartan.

Grown-ups always say the same old questions. I can't stop colouring to answer.

'It must be the holidays soon,' says Mrs Vartan. 'You'll have a lovely Christmas.'

Now she's on about Christmas, I know what to say. 'My class is doing a nut-if-eaty play. I'm one of the sheep.'

She looks a bit confused. 'A sheep ... in the nativity?'

I nod. It's easy to tell when grown-ups are trying to understand my jokes. They say what I've just said all over again! This is called repeating but it doesn't mean burping which is another sort of repeating. Nanny Phil told me this. Drinking fast makes burps.

'You're learning a special sheep song, aren't you, Huxley?'

I give a blast of the words. 'Sheep! Sheep! Loving my life as a special sheep.'

'How wonderful,' says Mrs Vartan.

A genius idea is in my mind. 'You can come and watch us.'

'That is kind ... although I'm not sure. What do you think, Kirsty?'

'Fine by me,' says Mum.

'Here's something,' I tell Mrs Vartan. 'My friend Leonard is looking forward to watching the play.'

'Leonard? Is he the man saved from the fire?'

'Correct,' says Mum. 'He goes to our church.'

'That's old news,' I say. 'Why don't you come along? I think you know where my school is.'

Mrs Vartan smiles. 'Of course.'

'You can help Leonard. He rides a mobility scooter.'

'I'll certainly try.' Mrs Vartan nods and smiles.

'Guess what else?'

'What?'

'You can be my pretend gran because my real one lives in Spain. I only see her in the summer.'

'If you can be a sheep, I'm sure I can act as your gran. Just this once. Your real gran won't mind, will she?'

'I'll ask her on Skype.'

'Don't do that, Huxley!' says Mum.

'Well, I'll keep to being Mrs Vartan. It's better.'

'Oh yes, and Leonard will be Leonard. It's only fair for you to come as Ben's got Nanny Phil.'

'Are you sure, Mrs Vartan?' says Mum.

'I'm very happy to join you.'

'And help Leonard?' I think it's true old people need reminding.

'Yes. I'll help Leonard.'

'I'm glad we have it arranged,' says Mum. 'Now, let's enjoy a cup of tea.'

After Mrs Vartan goes home, Mum talks about it again, so it isn't arranged. How am I supposed to know Gran might be upset with me talking about a replacement gran? I know already Mrs Vartan and Leonard are new to each other but they can still become friends. This is what I hope.

38

Lucy is crying. She's sitting in our kitchen and crying. Poor Lucy! Her eyes are slanting, she shows her teeth but not in a smile. I don't know what to do. Mum is there with her arm around Lucy. I can't stop watching them and my ears are sore from listening.

'Fetch the box of tissues from my bedroom, Huxley.'

'Okay.' It's good having a job. Up the stairs I go with my hands patting each of the steps and my feet stomping behind. On the way back, I carry the box under my arm and this leaves one hand free to hold the bannister. When I reach the kitchen, I drop the box of tissues on the table. Lucy grabs a handful and dabs her eyes. If it was me, I'd rub my whole face over like I do with a sponge at bath time.

'Off you go and find something to play with,' says Mum.

Shooting into the lounge, I try to block out the sad feelings that fill my head. They make it hard to get on with stuff and I don't know what to do. When I cry, Mum sometimes calls it blubbing. It's not nice to hear a grown-up making those noises so I press my hands over my ears. That stops me hearing everything, even the TV. I want to watch my programme and I don't want to at the same time. I'm stuck and sinking. One holiday a long time ago, I was playing on the beach. Sand doesn't normally suck your boots and pull you into the centre of the earth. I was caught in quick sand and that's very different. With his thinking hat on, Dad grabbed me under my arms and heaved me to safety. One of my wellingtons came straight off my foot, then Dad had to rescue it. My dad was a hero for saving me. This makes me think about how I can help Lucy.

Going to the kitchen doorway, I peek in the room. Mum's face is pressed against Lucy's and only their heads show. Mum's hair is a wavy line against the straight black cut of Lucy's. I go closer and pat Lucy's shoulder. This makes her jerk. Over her cheeks, there are rivers of tears and her eyes are splashy.

'Take no notice of me.' Lucy blows her nose and dries her eyes. 'A good cry is one way to feel better.'

'A cup of tea also goes down well.' Mum turns away and flicks the switch on the kettle.

I stand still as a lamppost.

'There you are.' Lucy takes a big breath. 'I'm back to normal.'

But things don't feel the same.

'It's stupid for adults to cry.' Lucy crumples the tissues as if doing that uses all her brain power. 'I'm okay now.'

She doesn't look okay to me. 'The skin on your face is puffy.'

'Run along and watch your programme, Huxley,' says Mum. 'I'll bring you a drink and a biscuit.'

'Shall I go, Lucy?' I ask.

'Yes, I'll be fine.'

I give Lucy's shoulder another pat then I move away. I'm not sure if it's the right thing to do. When I get in the lounge, I sit with my back to the radiator and hug my knees. This helps to keep me in one piece.

The glass and the plate clink on the tray as Mum puts them on the table. 'Let's have a hug on the sofa.'

Standing is difficult because everything is strange. Mum helps me up. She hugs me as I fall against her.

'What's wrong with Lucy?' I ask.

'She's very unhappy because she's not going to be a mummy just yet.'

'What's happened to her baby?'

'Important people have decided that the little girl must stay where she is. It's not possible for her to come and live with Lucy at the moment.'

'Oh dear.'

'Lucy is getting used to the news.'

'So am I.' My throat is tied in a knot. I can't speak any more.

Mum reaches for the glass of juice and gives it to me. 'Have a drink.'

I take a few gulps then pass it back to her. 'I'll draw Lucy a rainbow to help her feel better.'

'Great idea,' says Mum.

•   •   •   •   •

On Thursday, Miss Choi is back in school. We're sitting on the carpet and I can see her out in the corridor through the glass bit in the classroom door.

'Are you listening, Huxley?'

I turn and face the front. Mrs Ward gives me one of her looks. I nod my head and try to smile. It's not as if I've done anything very wrong. I know this when she smiles back.

'It's good that Miss Choi is with us again. She's going to help with the nativity.' Mrs Ward's face bobs up and down while she talks. 'We must all be very kind to Miss Choi and not ask lots of questions. She's come back to school because she enjoys being with us and helping everyone.'

I think I know more about what's happened than Mrs Ward. I shoot my hand into the air but before I have a chance to say anything, Mrs Ward tells me to fold my arms like the rest of the class. She watches me until I sink back. On the other side of the carpet, Zac is smiling at me although not in a nasty way.

'Remind me,' says Mrs Ward. 'What do we need to remember about Miss Choi today?'

A forest of arms goes up but not mine. Mrs Ward points to a girl sitting at the front and she says, 'We mustn't bother Miss Choi with silly questions'.

'That's correct. You can talk to her about your work, but you mustn't ask lots of things. We want Miss Choi to feel happy in school, don't we?'

The children in front of me are nodding. If I nod my head really hard, it makes me feel sick. This isn't the time for making myself ill.

'Right,' says Mrs Ward. 'Show me you understand by sitting up straight as me.'

Everyone copies Mrs Ward but I forget that I'm meant to join in. When I look over, her face is screwed up. I get the message.

'That's right, Huxley,' she says. 'You're straight as a soldier now, just like all of us.'

39

We have to practise our play again and again until it's perfect. ~~Lucy~~ Miss Choi says we are real actors. Christmas makes her happy and I don't think she minds about not getting her baby. Today's the day! All the mums and dads are waiting outside the Head Teacher's room until we are in our places on the stage. At last, Mrs Ward opens the doors and lets them in. The grown-ups are filling the hall like a river has burst its banks. They are everywhere and I'm tossing my head around to have a proper look. Mum and Dad find their way in. There's Samira's mum wearing her black scarf and she takes a seat on the same row as Nanny Phil. There are two spaces between them. Perhaps the seats are saved for Paula and Tony but I can't think about that now. I've got bubbles in my tummy from excitement. I hope they don't come out of my bottom!

The word for people watching a show is or-die-ants. This isn't the best time to be thinking of dying ants so I'm going to use the right word: audience. I am at the front of the flock of sheep and we are supposed to be sitting still but I've promised to wave to Leonard. I need to keep looking for him. There isn't much room left in the hall, so I hope he finds somewhere for his scooter. Mum does a show-off wave from near the front and then she sits down next to Dad. My hand shoots up for a quick wave back. Afterwards, I am still and sensible. Sheep do good smiles. My heart starts booming as it's nearly time for the play to start. Mrs Ward walking over to the piano is the signal. That's when I see Mrs

Vartan. Her white hair is easy to spot. There she is, showing the way for Leonard to drive right through to a place at the side of the stage. His scooter is special – he can stay sitting on it and doesn't need a chair! Leonard turns his arm in a semicircle to wave but I've already seen him. He nearly clonks Mrs Vartan on the head as she sits in the seat next to him. I have to laugh although I'm quick to put my hand over my mouth and stop the noise. I wiggle my fingers at Leonard so he knows I've seen him.

The music for the first song ends and I'm getting very hot in the sheep's hat. Samira is one of the angels. She's wearing white and looks cool as ice. This makes me feel better. Not boiling. The angels do a special dance, Mary and Joseph remember to say their words, then it is my turn. I am the leader of the sheep and my job is important. By bending my knees, I bob up and down every time there's the word *sheep* in our special song. Zac and Ben don't always do the actions right but I am perfect. Mrs Ward said this in the practice and I'm doing it brilliantly now. We sit when our part is finished. There are a few more bits and pieces although these don't matter after our song's done. Then it's the end of the nativity and we take a bow. I can touch my toes but I don't bother today as I want to look at all the smiling faces watching us. Bowing is also a sign for the audience to start clapping. They think we're excellent! The clapping is extra loud and there's some whistling. That must be Tony at the back. We do more bowing and the clapping goes on and on. I am in the middle of the long line that is our class and everyone copies me. Clapping is one of my favourite things but bowing is better today.

Our Head Teacher stands on the stage and says lots of stuff. I am too happy to listen. Mum and Dad have shiny faces and I think they're proud of me. I turn my head to see Leonard and Mrs Vartan. They're smiling and nodding to each other like they're special friends. It's a miracle seeing them together. I wonder how it happened.

40

Me and Mum and Dad are walking to town. Some houses have flashing lights dangling from their roofs and where the curtains at the windows are open, you can look right in. There are Christmas trees and cards hanging up. At home, it's the same for us. Everyone is waiting for Christmas Day. It's not long now. I swing Mum's arm and then my dad's. Being in the middle is best.

We go into the café where it's bright and steamy. I spot Lucy on the sofa. She has a bundle of baby in her arms. I bound over and Mum follows. We crowd around to say hello to the little girl but she's sleepy. Her eyelashes make two black semicircles. Mum goes *ooh* and *aah* but there's not much more to see other than a creamy coloured blanket and a baldy head. Then, the baby's eyes spring open and she stretches out a hand. Her fingers spread into a star. She catches hold of my thumb and grips me so tight I don't want her to let go. When she does, it's okay because I race over to Dad. He's waiting to order drinks at the counter.

'Calm down, Huxley, it's only a baby.'

'Only a baby?' I can't believe it! I throw my arms in the air.

'Okay,' says Dad. 'She's a very precious baby.'

That's more like it. 'This is a special day! Can I have an extra large strawberry milkshake?'

'Don't push your luck.'

He carries the tray of drinks and then places them on the table one by one. Mum is having coffee and I have a straw to go in my milkshake.

'Shall I pour your tea, Lucy?' asks Dad.

'It's good to be sharing a pot with you, Jed.'

'Now, now,' says Mum. 'Please don't slide back into old habits.'

'Of course not,' says Lucy.

'Of course not,' says Dad.

The grown-ups sip their drinks and I do my best with an extra loud slurp.

'Jocelyn is gorgeous,' says Mum. 'How long will you be fostering until the adoption is finalised?'

'It's not clear yet. I'm just astonished at how quickly things have turned around.'

'She's beautiful.' Mum stares at the baby like she's in a dream.

'When can I have a baby?' The question pops out all of a sudden.

'That's for us to know and you to find out,' says Dad.

I take another slurp of milkshake while I try to work out what Dad means. The straw goes soggy in my mouth. 'I don't understand what you're talking about.'

'That's the way to keep it,' says Mum.

'Am I right in thinking you might need a Barbie or a rocket celebration cake at some point in the not too distant future?' asks Lucy.

Mum smiles. 'We're working on our own little cupcake.'

'Cupcake!' I nearly jump right off the sofa. 'Can I have a chocolate one?'

Dad nudges me, 'Let's go over to the display. I'll let you choose.'

Acknowledgements

I would like to thank my wonderful husband, David, for his ongoing support throughout the highs and lows of bringing this novel to its readership. To fellow writers Jan and Maria, and my writing friends at Vesta, Vivo and 3-She, thank you so very much. Cheers to the team at Black Rose Writing.

About the Author

Photo: Richard Budd

Gail Aldwin is a novelist, poet and scriptwriter. Her debut coming-of-age novel *The String Games* was a finalist in The People's Book Prize and the DLF Writing Prize 2020. Following a stint as a university lecturer, Gail's children's picture book Pandemonium was published. Gail loves to appear at national and international literary festivals. Following a volunteer placement at a refugee settlement in Uganda, Gail returned to her home overlooking water meadows in Dorset.

https://gailaldwin.com
@gailaldwin

Note from the Author

Word-of-mouth is crucial for any author to succeed. If you enjoyed *This Much Huxley Knows*, please leave a review online—anywhere you are able. Even if it's just a sentence or two. It can make all the difference and would be very much appreciated.

Thanks!
Gail Aldwin

Thank you so much for checking out one
of our **Literary Fiction** novels.
If you enjoy this book, please check out
our recommended title for your next
great read!

*The Five Wishes of Mr. Murray
McBride* by Joe Siple

2018 Maxy Award
"Book of the Year"

"A sweet...tale of human connection...
will feel familiar to fans of Hallmark movies."
-KIRKUS REVIEWS

"An emotional story that will leave readers meditating on the
life-saving magic of kindness." *-IndieReader*

View other Black Rose Writing titles at
www.blackrosewriting.com/books and use promo code
PRINT to receive a **20% discount** when purchasing.

Printed in Great Britain
by Amazon

63738454R00132